UPON A DREAM

FAIRY TALES REIMAGINED BOOK SEVEN

LAURA BURTON

JESSIE CAL

BURTON & BURCHELL

COPYRIGHT

PROLOGUE

TRISTAN

*I*n the cool spring morning, birdsong flooded the skies, and golden beams of sunlight poured in through the evergreen trees of the Chanted Forest.

As the old carriage rocked back and forth over the uneven terrain, Prince Tristan gazed out the window at the thick overgrowth teaming with wildlife. A squirrel scurried up the trunk of an oak tree, passing a woodpecker too busy hammering for bugs to notice he was not alone.

Tristan had heard about the queen of the Chanted Forest. Her name was Snow White, and for such a new queen, her reputation was impressively marvelous. Rumors had it that she was so attuned to wildlife they were drawn to her like a magnet. Some said she even possessed the ability to understand them.

Looking around at the lush green foliage and all manner of creatures roaming in and out of view, Tristan supposed that some of it had to be true. The forest was thriving, and it was a far cry from the days of her predecessors.

Unlike the Evil Queen, Snow White was known to be kind and generous and adored by her people. Tristan wondered if marrying a huntsman had anything to do with how much the people accepted and respected her.

His father would've been proud of her ability to win the hearts of the people. After all, that was the reason he had wanted Tristan to marry Lexa. Tristan understood the advantages their unity would've had for both of their kingdoms. But even though she was indeed a beautiful woman, her eyes didn't sparkle for him. There was no zing between them when they danced, and that was enough for him to know that she wasn't the one.

He wished his father understood. Perhaps if he had respected Tristan's decision to let Lexa go, he wouldn't have gone after her at Neverland. He wouldn't have become entangled in Neri's lies. He would've still been alive. But the man had the prize in his sights and nothing and no one could change his mind.

His father's stubbornness was what cost him his life. Or at least that was what Tristan kept repeating in his mind over and over again for months, trying to stave off becoming consumed with guilt.

His jaw tightened as another memory flashed in his mind's eye. The devastation of the bitter truth hit him in the chest: he killed his own father.

Tristan looked down at his open palms. No matter how often he'd scrubbed them, they still felt dirty. And when he held his father's crown for the first time, the golden metal instantly became stained with blood. Tristan knew it was all in his mind because none of his father's advisors could see it, but that was enough for him to have it put away. He hadn't been able to touch it ever since.

That was months ago.

It was one of the reasons he hadn't yet arranged for his coronation. Although becoming king was inevitable, he couldn't fathom the thought of seeing his father's blood sliding down his crown and onto his royal garment in front of all his subjects, even if it was only inside his own mind.

But he also couldn't prolong the coronation any longer. King Midas from the Golden Kingdom to the north had taken advantage of the Kingdom of the Shores' vulnerability and declared war.

Midas wasted no time moving his troops into the Shores' territory, and the people were already losing their crops as well as their homes. Families had been divided, and lives had been lost. Tristan couldn't stand to watch his kingdom suffer any longer. But he also couldn't rise to power with a haunted mind.

The only way he could become the king his people needed him to be was to cleanse his guilty conscience once and for all. But for that to happen, he needed to find the memory of that night. The night his father died.

He remembered his father throwing the pixie dust at him on the lower deck of the ship. His next memory was finding his father's bleeding body on the upper deck. Between these two moments, there was nothing but a stolen void inside Tristan's mind.

Ella had mentioned something about having found her own memory of that night. Perhaps she could elaborate on how she went about retrieving it because that was what he needed as well.

When the carriage rocked violently again, Tristan cringed in frustration. But not at the old carriage he'd paid for at the marina. Or at the driver. No, his anger rose because had he taken a royal carriage, his identity as a prince would be revealed. And ever since his deal with Rumpelstiltskin, going outside of the palace walls had become too dangerous.

The deal made with Rumple was a document that stated that in the event Tristan died without an offspring, Rumple was to inherit the throne.

But it was a trick.

Rumple had manipulated matters so that Tristan would be put to death that same night.

What Rumple didn't account for, however, was for Ella to have been merciful toward Tristan. Despite everything he'd put her through, she pleaded for mercy and kept Killian from piercing his sword through Tristan's heart. He owed her his life.

But that didn't mean Rumple gave up on his plan.

Even though the document stipulated that Rumple himself could not kill Tristan, it didn't say Rumple couldn't hire low-life men to do his dirty work. And Tristan had experienced many *random* attacks in the past few months which left him no doubt that Rumple was more eager than ever to do away with him.

So, not only did Tristan have to find a way to get his memory of the night his father died, but he also needed to find a wife, sooner rather than later, and produce an offspring to negate Rumple's contract.

Tristan rubbed his throbbing temples for the rest of the way until the carriage finally came to a stop. The driver's voice came from outside. "We have arrived, sir."

Tristan looked out the window to find a home at the top of a hill. A large green field stretched within a wooden fence. Horses and cows grazed the pasture inside it.

Throwing a hood over his head, Tristan stepped out of the carriage. He sucked in a nervous breath. The people he came to see were no doubt going to be surprised at his visit. And at their last encounter, he had almost died.

A woman with golden curls stepped outside, holding a basket of clothes. She began hanging them on a string tied between two trees. But it wasn't until Tristan approached that he noticed her bulging belly.

"Ella?" Tristan called out, his voice careful not to startle her.

She swung around with a smile, clutching her bump, ready to greet the visitor. But upon locking eyes with him, her smile fell.

Tristan immediately lifted his hands.

"I come in peace," he said, keeping his voice soft and unthreatening. He even offered a friendly smile for good measure. "I just want to talk."

She must've sensed his honesty because her features relaxed and her eyes softened at him.

"You have questions about your lost memory," she said. It was more of a statement than a question.

Tristan nodded. "I wasn't sure who else to seek."

"That's all right. Come on in." She motioned toward the door, leaving her clothes basket on the grass outside.

Tristan entered the home, then waited for Ella to guide him as to where to sit.

She gestured toward the sofa.

"Would you like some tea?" she asked.

"I do not wish to bother you," Tristan said, pulling the hood from his head as he took a seat. "I also do not wish to take too much of your time. I simply come seeking answers about that night."

Ella reached for a kettle that seemed to already have been boiled and grabbed it by the handle.

"I believe I already told you everything I know," she said, pouring the steaming liquid into a ceramic mug. "I don't think I left anything out."

"Maybe." Tristan nodded. "But the night you told me everything, I had been drinking. I only remember flashes of information, but not the details."

After sprinkling some mint leaves into the mug, she handed him the drink.

He took it appreciatively. "Thank you." Then his eyes roamed around the place once more. "Where's Killian?"

"Out hunting," Ella said with a pleasant smile. And for a moment, Tristan wondered if she'd meant to paint an image of her assassin husband with a hunting knife.

Tristan swallowed drily at the thought that Killian could walk in at any moment and use that same knife on Tristan.

"So, you want details," Ella said as she took a seat on a rocking chair across from him. When her eyes settled on him, she sighed. "Are you sure about that?"

Tristan nodded as he blew into his cup. "Yes. I need every detail you can remember. No matter how dark. Don't sugarcoat it on my account," he said. "I believe it's the only way I will find closure and be able to move on."

Ella considered it for a moment, resting a soft hand on her belly as she rocked back and forth on the chair. "The tricky thing about memories is that we all have our own. It's about perspective," she explained, looking down as though remembering words spoken by someone else entirely. "When I retrieved my memory, I could only see what my own mind registered from that night. Even though I saw what you—Neri—did, I do not possess the reasons behind it."

Tristan sighed and placed his drink on the coffee table between them, watching as the steam danced above it.

"There must be something I can do," he pressed.

"There is," Ella said, piquing Tristan's interest, and he lifted his eyes to her again. "The fairies told us about the sundrop flower. They prepared it under the moonlight, and when we drank it, we were sent to a dream world where all our memories reside. As well as our deepest fears."

Tristan watched her, enthralled.

"What was it like?" he asked.

"For me…" Ella let out a humorless chuckle. "It was a nightmare involving a Golden Tower, my dead parents, and me barely getting out. If Killian hadn't come for me, I would've gotten stuck in there like Aurora—"

"You wouldn't happen to know where I could find one of these sundrop flowers, would you?" Tristan asked.

"Give me one good reason we should help you." A thunderous voice came from the door, making Tristan jump to his feet.

"Killian." Ella said her husband's name as though

trying to keep a lion at bay. "We've been through this."

Tristan lifted his hands. "I truly am sorry about what I put Ella through. I would never have done it had I known the truth. If there's anything at all that I can offer as compensation…."

Ella smiled kindly. "There's nothing——"

"There is one thing," Killian cut in, pulling out his hunting knife. Tristan stepped back, and an amused grin started to spread across Killian's face. "Relax. I wouldn't kill you in front of my wife."

The menacing look in his eyes gave Tristan the impression that he would not even hesitate to cut his throat had Ella not been there.

"Have a seat," Killian ordered as he stood next to Ella's rocking chair.

Tristan sat back down, hesitantly.

"I have made many enemies through the years because of my line of work," Killian said. "In the event that those enemies come for me, I would like for my family to have a secure place for them to flee."

He placed a large hand over his wife's baby bump, and she rested hers over his. And suddenly, Tristan understood. They were just two parents trying to protect their unborn child.

"Of course." Tristan nodded. "My palace will

always be open for your family." Tristian added, "For you too, Killian," since Killian had asked for a safe place for his wife and child, but not himself. "If you agree to leave the past in the past, I will do the same." Tristan stepped forward and offered his hand to Killian. "From this moment on, your family will not only have protection within my palace walls, but you may choose any property in my kingdom and it will be given to you in the event that you need to leave this one behind."

Killian looked down at Tristan's hand for a long time, then took it in a firm handshake. "Thank you."

Relief washed over Tristan. For a moment, he thought Killian might have been contemplating breaking every bone in his hand.

"Well, I better be on my way," Tristan said, pulling back and securing his cloak. "Thank you for letting me know about the sundrop flower."

As Tristan turned to leave, Killian raised a hand. "Wait. I might have something you can take with you."

Killian walked over to a cabinet in the kitchen and pulled out a jar with a silver liquid inside.

When he returned to her side, Ella's eyes widened. "When did you—?"

"I took it from the fairies before we left," Killian

said, handing it to Tristan. "In case we needed it again. I didn't want to have to go back there."

Tristan took the jar and examined a silver flower floating on the surface of the water inside. "I've never seen a flower this color before," he said.

"The flower is normally yellow," Killian said. "But after they boil it under the moonlight, it turns silver. That's how you know the water is ready to drink."

"Fascinating," Tristan muttered. "Thank you so much for this."

"Be careful in there," Ella said with a frown. "The Dreamworld is a very dark place."

Killian took her hand, and Tristan wondered what had happened to them there.

"I will," Tristan said, shoving the jar inside his bag. "Thank you."

He threw the hood of his cloak over his head and walked out the door. The sun had already begun its descent, but they just needed to make it to the marina. Once back on his boat, he would be among his trusted crew and in much less danger.

As he approached the carriage, he noticed that the driver was sitting in the exact spot he had been when Tristan left.

"To the marina," Tristan said, then climbed into

the carriage. He leaned back on the hard seat and closed his tired eyes as he waited for the carriage to move.

But it never did.

Tristan opened his eyes, the eerie silence prickling his skin as he leaned forward.

"To the marina," he ordered the driver once more, this time a little louder, but the carriage still didn't move.

Tristan peeked out the window to catch the driver finally moving. Except he *wasn't* moving. He was falling.

His limp body collapsed to the ground with a thud, and Tristan jolted back into the carriage. The roof reverberated with a loud thump as heavy boots landed on top of it. Then more footsteps followed, surrounding the carriage.

Tristan reached for his sword, but the space was too tight to free it.

The door flew open, revealing a bearded man with jet-black hair. He flashed a wicked grin at the sight of Tristan. "I've been waiting for you," he said with a growl as he stepped forward.

A wave of painful grunts came from all around the carriage, and the man's grin fell from his face. Then a guttural sound ripped from his throat as his breathing stopped. He fell into the carriage, face down, and Killian came into view, standing at the door with the man's blood dripping from his hunting knife.

"Let me guess," Killian said.

But he didn't have to finish. Tristan nodded. "Rumpelstiltskin."

TRISTAN

*P*rince Tristan leaned out of the window of his castle chambers, overlooking an endless expanse of crashing waves. His mind was filled with sorrow and rage; a tumultuous storm created by the absence of his father's guidance. He felt like he was losing all the wisdom he once gained from his father, and the regret of never being able to receive it again filled him with a deep, burning despair.

As he tried to recall the events of the night his father died, knot after knot of confusion and dread filled his stomach. He could almost hear the creaking of Ryke's ship and see Ella's bloody hands, but every recollection ended in a fog. He wished he could remember more, but each time he felt himself getting closer, a wave of panic would wash it away.

He recalled his visit with Ella and Killian, and the things Ella had told him. But he wanted to remember.

A cough had him swivel around to see one of his guards standing in the doorway. He was a tall man, with broad shoulders and a rough, weather-beaten face. Tristan wondered what bitter memories he held in the darkest corners of his mind, but the guard was giving nothing away. His uniform was exactly how it should be—a blue velvet jacket, white trousers, and a hat with the royal crest pinned to it. There was not even a speck of dirt nor a single crease on his clothing.

"Captain Hook is here, Your Highness," he announced.

"Very good," Tristan said with a nod. He adjusted his fine royal jacket, his fingertips brushing the gold stitching along the edges. Then he strode for the main hall.

As he descended the castle steps, he let out a sigh and threw his concerns aside to welcome his cousin with open arms.

Ryke's shoulders seemed broader than Tristan

remembered. The seas must have been working him hard.

"Are you keeping well, cousin?" Tristan asked as they broke apart and began to stroll around the castle grounds.

"I am," Ryke replied, smiling broadly. And Tristan believed him. Ryke's skin had more color and the worry line between his eyes was less pronounced. He walked with his shoulders rolled back and had a spring in his step. It was like nothing could put him in a foul mood.

Tristan felt a pang of jealousy.

"I am hearing whispers of a royal ball," Ryke said, turning to give Tristan a wry smile. "I am glad to hear you have reignited your desire to dance with pretty ladies."

Tristan clasped his hands behind his back and took in a steadying breath. "It is not just another ball, cousin. This time I must find a wife."

Ryke placed an encouraging hand on Tristan's shoulder. "Finding a queen isn't a decision to rush into, cousin. Take your time."

Tristan's shoulders dropped.

Ryke noticed. "Is something troubling you?" he asked.

Tristan sighed. "I made a terrible mistake." He

then went on to tell Ryke about his contract with Rumple. He admitted to having been blinded by grief and rage at the time, seeking revenge on his father's murderer. But he couldn't bring himself to confide in Ryke the complete truth. He still hadn't figured out how to say the words aloud.

I killed my own father.

"Not to worry," Ryke said cheerfully. "I'll be sticking around for a bit. Lexa has been seasick lately, so staying might do all of us some good."

Tristan's mood lifted a little. "I'm sure Lily will be thrilled to have you around for a while longer."

When they turned the corner and made a full circle around the castle, Tristan caught sight of two guards running toward him.

"There have been new reports, your highness," one of them said breathlessly. "You are needed in the great hall. Your advisors are waiting."

Tristan excused himself, encouraging Ryke to make himself comfortable, then headed inside the castle. He pushed open the doors to the great hall, stepping into a room abuzz with chatter.

His ministers and advisors were in position as Tristan strode to his throne.

"Tell me about the reports," he said, his sharp

eyes narrowing on the gray-haired men surrounding him.

One of them stepped forward. "King Midas has intensified his attacks. We believe he is taking advantage of the fact that our kingdom is vulnerable."

Tristan clenched his jaw. "Vulnerable?"

Tension hung in the air as the advisors exchanged nervous looks. "Yes, Your Grace. Our kingdom is still in mourning."

Tristan's throat tightened as he surveyed the room. Everywhere he looked, memories of his father plagued him like a relentless ghost. An immense weight of sadness pressed on him, threatening to pierce his throbbing heart. He struggled to swallow past the lump in his throat. But then he inwardly shook himself, determined not to show weakness.

Another advisor stepped forward. "Your Highness, there have been too many casualties, countless deaths…we need to recruit strong men from neighboring villages."

Tristan heaved a sigh as he thought on it. "Fine. We shall send out a message. But let it be voluntary. I will not force our allies to risk their lives for us."

The men nodded in agreement, but when no one spoke, Tristan frowned, sensing that there was more.

"Is that all?" he asked.

The first advisor shook his head. "No, Your Majesty. With so many families who have lost loved ones during these attacks, we were hoping to know what will be done to help those who are grieving."

Tristan rubbed the pad of his thumb across his left wrist as his mind returned to his father.

"What would the king have done?" he thought aloud.

Without hesitation, one of the advisors spoke up. "He would ensure that all fallen warriors would have a paid burial."

Tristan hummed, then nodded. "Very well. Send messengers to the homes of all those families in the name of the king."

"You must also set a date for your coronation, sir," another advisor chimed in. This one was tall and thin. "It will boost the morale of the people to see you become king."

Tristan's hands balled into tight fists as guilt ripped through his entire being, threatening to splice him in two. He could not bear to take the crown, knowing that he had murdered his own father in cold blood.

Still, he gave a grim smile to the group of men staring at him. "I shall think on that."

*L*ater that night, Tristan headed to his chambers and stood on the balcony bathed in the milky glow of the moon. He consumed the special flower liquid given to him by Killian as payment for his protection of Ella and her family.

A wave of sleepiness washed over him, muting the agony of his guilt until he became entrenched in heaviness. His limbs were like lead as he dragged his body back to his bed and slumped on the plush blankets, letting his heavy eyelids close.

When he opened them again, he found himself lying on a bunk below deck of Ryke's ship.

The king was conversing with both Ryke and Lexa, but neither of them noticed Tristan's presence. Tristan watched his father, the king, with a heavy heart. His royal clothes hung off of him like an ominous shroud, while the lines on his face were deep and sharp—carved into his skin by years of ruling over his kingdom.

Then he watched as the events from that fateful night began to unfold in real time.

He saw himself, standing immobile in the doorway, listening to the heated conversation between the king and Ryke. The King's nostrils flared as his eyes blazed with anger, but Ryke stood resolute with his jaw jutted out and shoulders squared.

Tristan watched the king pull out a velvet bag and take a fistful of pixie dust. But just before he tossed it over Ryke's head, Tristan leaped in the way, taking the full hit.

Tristan climbed out from the bunk to look at his former self. It was eerie to watch his eyes grow cloudy and a vacant expression took over his face.

Then his stomach churned at the sound of his father's voice. "Kill Ryke."

Tristan watched with rapt attention as his former self lunged for Ryke without a moment's hesitation. They struggled before Ryke broke away and fled the room. Lexa wailed and slashed the air with her nails before Tristan's former self restrained her.

Tristan followed them to the belly of the ship where a line of iron cells stood empty. He saw himself thrusting Lexa into one, and she stumbled over the straw-covered floor with a groan. When the door slammed shut and the lock clicked into place, Lexa's cries came out in violent wails of pain. She begged him not to kill Ryke.

But when Tristan's former self turned around to

hunt Ryke down, Tristan took in his cloudy eyes, the blank expression, and the awkward way he moved. As if he were nothing but a hollow shell, a puppet, carrying out the will of someone else.

With his heart racing, Tristan followed himself up the ladder to the upper deck, then up the steps. He sensed that soon, all would be revealed. He would finally know what happened.

Finally, Tristan stopped when he came face to face with his father, who stood at the helm of the ship.

There was chaos all around. Men battled. Mermaids cried.

But then his father's eyes narrowed at a figure behind Tristan.

"Neri," he barked. "We had a deal! You get the mermaids, I get their medicinal properties for my kingdom."

Tristan turned to find his dream self flashing the king a wicked grin. But when he spoke, it was Neri's voice that came out of his body. "You should know better than to trust mermaids," she sneered.

He then watched as his past self stabbed his father. Each time the silver blade sank with a crunch into his father's flesh, not a single flicker of remorse crossed his face. Neri's face. Instead, he remained blank. Hollow.

As if he was not there at all. Tristan staggered back, clamping a clammy hand over his thumping heart as he watched his dream self turn and charge toward Ryke without so much as glancing back at his dying father.

It all fell into place as Neri's voice echoed in his memory. He didn't kill his father of his own free will. Neri controlled his mind and made him do it.

Tristan stood frozen, his eyes wide and ears ringing as he watched his father slump back with a grunt. Thick blood spilled out like red wine, staining the ship.

He looked up at the sound of hurried footsteps. The air shifted as Ella flew into view and whimpered as she fell to her knees, pressing on the ugly wound in a vain attempt to stop the bleeding.

The scene faded for a moment, and when Tristan's vision cleared, he saw himself kneeling by his father, letting out agonized sobs. His hands trembled with fury and horror, and giant tears rolled down his cheeks.

He looked up to see Ella, her hands soaked in blood and eyes wide like saucers. She shook her head in horror, stepping back while Tristan shouted at her. Calling her a murderer.

Suddenly, the air changed, becoming eerily still and quiet. Tristan could only hear his own heartbeat when his former self turned and his eyes locked on his. For the first time, someone could see him. And a rising sense of fear crept up in Tristan's chest and wrapped around his neck like a pair of strong hands.

He staggered backward while his former self picked up the bloodied knife and headed for him. It was as though he was looking into the eyes of a mortal enemy.

But a sword burst through Tristan's former self's chest, and he slumped out of view with a groan, revealing a hooded figure. Trembling, he shook himself and blinked away the tears in his eyes to see soft, blonde hair flowing in the wind and a pair of eyes glistening like diamonds from underneath the hood. Slowly, the figure pulled the hood back and Tristan stared at a woman, who looked at him with as much intensity as a thousand daggers flying in his face.

"Who are you? You were not there that night," Tristan said, searching his mind for any recollection of the woman.

She moved forward with strength and confidence,

then opened her mouth and spoke with authority. "I'm the guardian of the Dreamworld, and you don't belong here."

At this, she pushed him over to the edge of the ship with both hands, then picked up his legs and tossed him overboard. Tristan could not even yell before his body made contact with the freezing water.

Tristan jerked awake with a gasp, his body drenched in icy sweat and trembling with terror. He remained motionless, his eyes wide open, trying desperately to calm the thundering of his heart as he put the pieces together–the terrifying images that had invaded his dreams now burned in his mind. Finally, he connected everything.

Neri was the one controlling him.

His father was the one who threw the pixie dust at him and then ordered him to kill his cousin. All the while, he was stuck in the middle of his father's twisted deal with Neri.

Still, he was haunted by the image of himself thrusting a dagger into his father's chest. Though they had never seen eye to eye and his father often made ruthless decisions, he knew it had all been done to protect their kingdom.

And above all, he was his own flesh and blood. Now he had no father, and it left an emptiness in his chest that could never be filled. Emotion balled in the bottom of his throat in the form of a hard lump.

But then he found himself remembering the beautiful guardian of the Dreamworld.

Her lush golden locks flying back in the sea breeze. Her plump cheeks like strawberries, and a pair of slender brows knitted together as she looked at him without an ounce of fear.

He was not accustomed to being looked at without fear or concern.

And as he thought about the woman, the pain he felt with the memory of his father was soothed, if only for a moment.

He had never seen a woman so beautiful, and he wondered when, and how, he might see her again.

AURORA

*A*urora's golden hair flew back in the wind like a wild, untamed flame as she spurred on her white stallion, Midnight, to run faster. His hooves pounded fiercely against the ground with increasing speed, every stride growing longer and more powerful.

The scent of pinecones flooded her nostrils and the hostile air bit at her cheeks, but Aurora's sturdy leather garments and thick cloak kept her warm, shielding her body from the frigid air.

As Midnight galloped on, Aurora strained her eyes to see through the darkness, the faint light of the moon casting a ghostly glow on the path before her. Everywhere around her were invisible monsters waiting to strike, each one capable of ending her life in an instant.

The Dreamworld was a treacherous and unpredictable realm. A place of unbridled imagination, where the boundaries of reality were only limited by one's mind. The power of her mind was overwhelming, a curse that could manifest anything she wished —from intoxicating fantasy worlds to gruesome monsters unleashed with a single thought. But once her creations manifested, controlling their actions was near impossible.

The only creature she trusted was Midnight. Even though he was an imaginary stallion that she conjured up with her mind, to her, he was real in every sense that mattered. He was her only companion in that world, and he had been her unwavering partner for as long as she could remember. She trusted him with her life and relied on his keen instincts to guide her through the threats of the Dreamworld.

In times past, she had attempted to create illusions of humans, such as her parents and her maids. She even created the children she used to watch in the square, gleefully playing games in the spring sunshine while Aurora was forbidden from stepping outside.

But it was only a matter of time before they transformed into ugly, vicious killers. Their limbs twisted in all manner of ways and their sharp, beady eyes grew black as they attempted to do away with her. The memory of their claw-like nails grasping the air, hungry to slash her throat, sent shivers down her spine.

As the terrain turned rough and uneven, Aurora whispered to her horse, bidding him to slow to a canter and proceed with caution. Midnight obeyed her command, as if they were somehow in sync. She stroked his mane lovingly, a gesture of appreciation for the unbreakable bond they shared.

"We did it again, my friend. Another person saved," she whispered to him, her voice filled with pride.

Aurora had lost track of how long she had been doing this, but even after all that time, it still felt gratifying every time she aided someone in finding their way back to reality. It wasn't a difficult task; all she had to do was create a jolt strong enough to awaken them. Of course, each case was unique, and it depended on how they had entered the Dreamworld. But, for the most part, a strong enough jolt was sufficient.

Midnight nickered in response, as if he understood her words. Aurora smiled and patted his neck. "I couldn't do it without you, you know? You're the best companion a girl could ask for."

Midnight nuzzled her hand, and Aurora's heart swelled with affection for him. Though he was an illusion, his unwavering loyalty was as real to her as her own beating heart.

Aurora stood at the edge of a cliff and gazed ahead. Before her was a long, wooden bridge only half-built, its planks closely fitted together. She counted the wooden planks carefully, one by one, as she reminisced about each and every person she had ever saved. For every person she had assisted in finding their way back to reality, a wooden plank had materialized on the bridge before her. Like a reward.

Midnight slowly moved closer to the edge of the cliff, and Aurora waited for a new plank to appear. As she gazed into the inky abyss below, her thoughts drifted to the man she had pushed overboard—a desperate and foolish soul who had dared to enter the Dreamworld willingly. Who had consumed the potion brewed by the fairies, a dangerous elixir that brought about both ecstasy and agony to its drinker.

She could still see the look of terror etched on his face as he tumbled backward and splashed into the dark waters. But there was something different about him, something that set him apart from all others she'd encountered.

As he stood on the ship's deck, surveying the chaos around him with a keen eye, Aurora couldn't help but wonder if he had come seeking answers. Perhaps he had been driven to this madness by an insatiable thirst for knowledge.

Clearly, he had no notion of the dangers that lurked in that realm.

The Dreamworld was not a place for the faint of heart. It was a place of nightmares, a realm of darkness and despair, and Aurora seethed with anger at the thought of anyone willingly subjecting themselves to its horrors. How could anyone find pleasure in facing such terrors with reckless abandon?

Aurora had seen countless soldiers pass through the Dreamworld, sent there to hone their skills and test their mettle. But for many, the journey was a one-way ticket to oblivion. If only she had been able to save them all, the bridge would have been completed by now. But so many had been lost to their own inner demons before she even had a chance to reach them.

And as quickly as it had begun, the stream of soldiers stopped. Perhaps their commander realized not many were making their way back and stopped sending the soldiers.

She shook her head, trying to rid herself of the memories. Part of her was relieved that the madness had come to an end, but another part of her knew that without new arrivals, there would be no more planks, and she would never make it to the other side.

To the golden tower.

Its intricate metalwork sparkled silver and gold in the moonbeam, almost as if it was illuminated with power from within. There was a secret within its walls, a mystery waiting to be unraveled if she could only reach it.

She looked back at the bridge, examining it closely, her eyes tracing the wooden planks stretched out before her. No new plank had appeared yet, and her heart tightened with trepidation. The Dream-world was strange and unpredictable, so it wasn't impossible to believe that one day the planks could stop appearing altogether. Regardless of her efforts.

But that wasn't a thought she was ready to entertain. She was so close. The bridge was already halfway done.

Aurora dismounted from Midnight and stepped onto the bridge. The first few planks creaked under her weight, and she clung onto the rope railing for balance as the bridge swayed with the icy chill of the night.

Midnight's warm breath on the back of her neck reminded her that she wasn't alone. She turned to him, a small smile curving her lips. His presence was a comfort, a reminder that she had someone to rely on even in the darkest of moments. No matter what happened, she would always have him by her side. She leaned against him and closed her eyes, feeling the warmth of his body around her.

But before she could get lost in the darkness of her thoughts, she felt a nudge at her shoulder. She opened her eyes to find Midnight staring back at her. He nudged her again, and she understood.

She swung around to find a brand new plank appearing before her eyes. Relief flooded her, and she leaned back against Midnight, the tension in her muscles finally easing. But then a gust of wind blew through the forest, carrying a faint whisper to her ears. Aurora spun around, searching for the source of the sound, but there was no one there.

The ghostly hush of the night was pierced by a deafening bell ringing out from the dark sky, signaling the arrival of someone new into the Dreamworld.

A thick fog rose from the ground, swirling in the air and creating a sphere of mystical energy. Stepping forward, the air charged around her body and the hairs on the back of her neck stood on end.

Aurora knew the portal would take her to the stranger who had arrived in the Dreamworld. With a deep breath, she mounted Midnight, feeling a renewed sense of determination.

With one last glance toward the looming tower with its taunting secrets, Aurora plunged into the swirling mist, disappearing into the fog.

TRISTAN

*T*ristan sat in the council chamber, surrounded by his closest advisors. Yet, he could not keep his thoughts from drifting to the Dreamworld and all the revelations he'd discovered there. He thought of the blonde-haired woman with the face like an angel but who fought like a warrior.

A heavy silence hung in the air, and Tristan burned under the heated stares of the men, all looking at him expectantly.

Tristan cleared his throat and shifted his weight in his seat. The squeak of the creaky floor echoed around the dimly lit chamber.

"Your Majesty, I must inform you that the situation is reaching a critical point. Our neighboring villages have decided to remain neutral and aren't willing to lend their support to our cause. Therefore, no one has volunteered. If we are to fight Midas' army, we need more men. This can mean only one thing."

Tristan inhaled deeply and slowly as a weight pressed down on his chest.

"What are you suggesting?" he asked, already knowing the answer.

The old man leaned forward to give him a steely look and jabbed the table with his index finger. "We send out a declaration that every man of age must sign up and fight."

Tristan scanned the faces around the table as the other advisors murmured and nodded in agreement. The notion went against everything he stood for: free will.

Another advisor raised a hand as he sat back in his seat. "It is what your father would have done."

Tristan's jaw clenched as his stomach knotted at the words. He supposed the man was of the opinion that they were words of comfort. But they were the opposite. They were a painful reminder that his father was not there to guide him anymore.

Midas' army was great in number. Tristan could not roll over and allow his kingdom to perish under his rule.

"I took the liberty of writing the order, you only need to sign it." The advisor on his right handed over a piece of parchment and a quill.

Sighing, Tristan dipped the quill into the inkwell and signed his name on the line. Then he rose to his feet and stormed out of the chamber without another word.

Walking through the bustling halls of the palace, he watched as the courtiers went about to get everything ready for the ball. The one where he would need to find a wife. He wasn't even sure what he needed in a partner. Should she be more beautiful than vain? Kind and gentle, or strong enough to make a good queen?

He hadn't given much thought to those details, for he knew that once true love struck him, he would simply know, without a shadow of a doubt. But that was when he could afford to wait for true love to find him. Now, time was up. He needed to search for it himself, before he was stuck choosing someone for the sake of the kingdom and not his heart. Tristan knew it would be a difficult process of finding the perfect match, but he still had hope. Why couldn't he have both?

The face of the beautiful guardian of the Dream-world surfaced in his mind. Her piercing brown eyes and luscious golden hair haunted him like a fever dream. Though he knew it was dangerous and foolish to go back, his skin burned with an insatiable desire to see her again.

Once in his room, he took what was left of the sundrop flower tonic and gulped it down before his mind could talk him out of it.

With every gulp, a wave of heat overtook him until his body grew heavy. He fell onto his bed, his skin like a smoldering campfire. As he closed his eyes, he plunged into nothingness, consumed by his desire for what felt forbidden: to see the guardian one more time.

When Tristan opened his eyes, he was laying in grass and dirt, surrounded by tall, looming trees. The rays of morning light peeked through their leaves like stars. Birds chirped above his head, and somewhere to the distance, the surf rolled over the shores, reminding him of home. He pushed himself to a seated position, then stood. The salty scent of the ocean filled his lungs as he followed the sound of the waves to a secluded beach.

Tristan squinted through the morning sunlight and made out two figures sitting side by side on the sand. As he moved closer, he realized they were his parents—his mother in her favorite yellow sundress and his father in a white cotton shirt. It had been so long since Tristan had seen his father so relaxed. And the sight of his mother was like a jackhammer to the heart. It had been too long since she passed away.

Two little boys played with their fishing nets at the shore—Tristan and Ryke as kids. His heart swelled to see them so carefree, but then the sound of a dried-up leaf crunched behind him and he turned around.

There stood the blonde guardian of the Dream-world, peeking at him from behind a palm tree where the jungle met the sand.

She stepped out from behind the tree with a puzzled look and approached him, her hand resting on something concealed under her cloak.

"You're back," she muttered, her brows furrowed.

"I am," he said, but his affirmation seemed only to confuse her even more. She gave him an incredulous look.

"Who are you?" she asked.

With a smile, Tristan motioned to one of the boys playing by the water. "I'm the one with lighter hair. And that one with black hair is my cousin. Those are my parents."

She fell into silence, listening to the gleeful laughter of the two boys who were oblivious to them.

Tristan's gaze shifted to his mother again. His

father had his arm wrapped around her waist, and even at a distance, he could hear the gentle humming of his father's voice.

Tristan's eyes prickled. When his mother was alive, his father would sing to her. He had been ruthless and cold for so many years that seeing his tender side made Tristan's throat constrict with emotion. He tore his gaze from them and met the guardian's gentle look. She studied him for a moment, then her eyes lightened with understanding.

"Oh, I see. You've come to reminisce," she said.

Tristan shifted his weight and blinked away the tears flooding his vision. He did not know how, but it seemed as though this mysterious woman could read him like a book. There was no merit to making false pretenses.

His shoulders slumped as a sigh escaped his lips.

"I've lost my father recently," he confessed. "And my mother many years ago."

The woman hummed, as though she had already guessed it.

"I'm sorry for your loss," she said, but her eyes didn't match her condolences. There was no pity in her gaze. Instead, her eyes widened with curiosity as though she had a burning question and could not wait a moment longer before she asked. "How did you hear about this place?"

Tristan was slightly surprised by the question. But he was happy to be off the topic of his dead parents. He rubbed his face with his hand and tried to appear casual.

"Ella and Killian."

The woman's eyes widened with surprise. "Ella?" she asked in a reverent whisper.

Tristan's ears pricked up at the way she spoke. "You know Ella?"

The woman's look of awe faded and she shrugged. "We've had a brief encounter once or twice. She was very friendly."

Tristan surveyed her neutral expression, sensing there was more to tell, but her body language was not giving anything away. He coughed and looked out at the rolling sea.

"Yes, well, she told me about this place, and how to get here. She even gave me the sundrop flower."

The woman was quiet for a moment, then her eyes narrowed as she gave him a curious look.

"What were you thinking about when you drank the sundrop flower?" she asked.

Tristan stiffened and his palms grew clammy as he considered how best to answer the question.

He was thinking about seeing her again, but he had no idea how to say that without coming across ungentlemanly.

He ran a hand over his short, blond hair. "Lately, my life has been filled with burdens I never asked for, and despite them being out of my control, they are still my responsibility to bear. But recently I saw something that, for the first time in a long time, filled me with peace."

It was not a lie. The sight of her face had that effect on him instantly, but he opted to omit that detail from his response. "So, that's what I was thinking about. Peace…and hope."

The woman gave a short incline of her head, then looked up to the sky. There was something tranquil in watching her bask in the golden sunlight, like she had achieved total serenity.

"What's your name?" Tristan asked, breaking her out of her reverie.

"Aurora," she whispered. She knelt down and ran her fingers through the glistening grains of sand. The sun sparkled on its surface like a million tiny diamonds, and she smiled gently as it slipped through her fingers.

Tristan hunched down so their eyes were level, and said with a hint of bewilderment, "For someone who lives in such an incredible place, you seem quite fascinated by sand. How come?"

She whispered back dreamily, without meeting Tristan's gaze, "It's not the sand. It's the warmth."

His expression softened. Her sun-kissed face seemed to glow from within, and her blonde, wavy hair shimmered in the light. She was the most beautiful woman he had ever seen.

"I'm Tristan," he said, keeping his voice soft so as not to interrupt her concentration. He decided not to reveal his royal status just yet. There was something endearing by how fascinated she seemed with something so simple like sand, but he was not yet entirely sure she could be trusted. "What's it like living here?"

The mood changed in an instant. Her calm composure evaporated and her knitted brows deepened as she glared at him. She threw away the grains of sand with a fierce gesture, slapping her hand on her cloak. "Do you even comprehend what this world is?"

He frowned, unable to fathom what caused her sudden change in mood. He gestured to the illusion of his family down the beach.

"A world of dreams, apparently—"

"Absolutely not!" She rose to her feet with a menacing glare. The sky suddenly shifted to an eerie charcoal gray and strong gusts of wind sent a chill down his spine. She took an angry step toward him, and he moved back. She did it again and again until he stepped into the water. "This is a world of never-ending nightmares."

The raging waters rose to his thighs as the sky above them grew blacker than a starless night. The winds whipped around them like an unforgiving tempest.

"No matter how much misery you think you have faced out there," she bellowed over the unrelenting gusts of wind. "It won't even compare to the torment that waits for you here. Now, go! And never come back!"

With a roar of thunder and a blaze of lightning, a bolt of electricity shot from the heavens and struck directly into the water. Tristan's body trembled as thousands of volts of energy coursed through him.

He shot open his eyes to find himself lying on his bed, gasping for air. His heart raced in his chest, the buzz of electricity still lingering.

His heart raced like the pounding hooves of a hundred wild stallions, and he placed a hand over his chest, exhilarated.

After the initial shock wore off, a smile crept onto

his lips. The guardian was quite the force of nature, and it was thrilling to say the least.

Despite her warnings, and out of everything she had said, the only thing that kept looping in his mind was her name.

"Aurora," he whispered, loving the sound of it as it filled his room.

Then he sank back into his bed, a flood of tingles rushing over his body, and whispered, "Until we meet again."

AURORA

*A*urora stood by the water's edge, her eyes fixed on where Tristan had been standing.

"Tristan," she whispered, savoring the sound of his name as if it might preserve the warmth he had brought with him. But the sand clinging to her hand had grown cold, like tiny shards of ice, and she brushed it off against her cloak.

The sky above her was still black, and the icy wind whipped around her.

Aurora shivered and pulled her cloak more tightly around her. She then gazed down the moonlit beach to find that Tristan's illusion of his family had vanished. Her heart squeezed ever so slightly as she recalled the joyful laughter of him and his cousin as children.

She couldn't recall the last time she had heard such carefree, joyful sounds. More often than not, her days were filled with the terrible screams of others or the eerie sounds of scorpions creeping through the darkness.

The reality of her world chilled her to the bone, and Tristan's peaceful illusion now seemed like the cruelest of dreams. Aurora had seen many dark illusions in her time, but Tristan's illusion was by far the most cruel. It made her long for who she once was but could never be again. Worst of all, it reminded her of what it felt like to hope.

Aurora knew better than to believe that her fate would ever change. Time had run out for her, and the lunar eclipse in the sky was a constant reminder of that fact. Unlike the real world, where an eclipse was a rare and wondrous event, in the Dreamworld it was a regular occurrence, resetting every day like a clock. To those who were lost in that realm, it offered a chance for escape. But to Aurora, it was a constant, unrelenting reminder that her case was hopeless.

Still, she found herself shoving her hands inside the warm pockets of her cloak, wishing Tristian's warmth could stay with her longer.

If he never returned, the odds of her ever seeing the sun again were near impossible. Her mind was too dark to brighten the elements in that realm. That was a gift reserved for the rare few, like Tristan.

As much as she wanted to hit him upside the head for keeping his guard down in such a treacherous world, she couldn't deny there was something special about him.

All the more reason he should stay away. The Dreamworld wasn't a realm for the naive or trusting.

Despite her warnings, Aurora couldn't shake the feeling that he would return. She saw it in his eyes—the grief, the longing. She couldn't blame him for wanting to reunite with his parents—however briefly—but grief was a treacherous emotion. One that could lead even the strongest of minds astray. Aurora knew that all too well, having been trapped in that world for far too long. The illusions preyed on emotions, using one's vulnerabilities to lure them in like a moth to a flame.

Keeping the mind sharp and focused was vital in that realm. The slightest instability of emotion could shift the elements and make them attack. Grief blinded logic and sense, making it the Dreamworld's deadliest trap.

Although that was her home, she could never trust it. Perhaps that was why the sun never shone at her will, and the world remained dark and cold around her. She had always thought that was just how it was, but she now realized it reflected the distrust within her. The hopelessness. The emptiness.

A nudge on her shoulder startled her, and Aurora turned to find Midnight nuzzling her hair. A smile played on her lips as she caressed his neck. But then a gust of wind sent an icy chill between them, and Aurora pulled back, knowing exactly what was coming next.

The bell tower rang, resetting the eclipse, and the familiar black fog rose from the ground within the woods. Someone had entered the Dreamworld, and they had until the eclipse reached its apex to escape.

Aurora hurried to mount Midnight. "All right, boy," she said, grabbing onto his mane. "Let's go save a life." With a nudge, she spurred him forward, and they rode into the dense fog. The wind whipped through her blonde braids. It was cold and wet, and it tickled her cheeks.

They emerged from the mist into a desolate clearing, the stench of death lingering in the air. Midnight whimpered, and Aurora knew they were headed in the right direction.

She pushed Midnight to go faster, until they finally reached the end of a dirt road. The sight that greeted them was horrifying. In an abandoned village, a dried-up fountain lay broken in the middle of a square. The small homes surrounding the square were trashed and burnt, and the air was thick with the acrid smell of smoke and death.

As they pushed farther, a man's screams echoed through the ruins of the village. Aurora urged Midnight to hurry, her heart pounding as she searched for the source of the screams.

Aurora found a man on the roof of one of the homes, teetering at the edge.

"Get back!" he shouted, his voice desperate and ragged. He held up his hands to keep whomever was after him at bay, but without a weapon, he would never stand a chance against his attacker.

Aurora drew her bow and arrow, taking aim with practiced precision. A guard with golden armor came into view, and she released the arrow. It flew through the air, finding its mark on the guard's neck with deadly accuracy. He vanished into a cloud of smoke, as did all illusions in that realm.

The man on the roof turned around, his eyes wide with shock and confusion. Clearly, he had no idea those guards were illusions created by his own mind.

"Jump!" Aurora shouted to him, gesturing to Midnight's back.

The man hesitated, but another guard charged at him, and Aurora quickly took aim and fired another arrow. Finally, the man jumped onto the horse's back.

As they made their escape, more guards appeared, multiplying in the blink of an eye. Aurora fired three more arrows, each one vanishing the guards in a puff of smoke.

She gripped the reins tightly, ready to make their getaway, but then the home next to them burst into flames, causing Midnight to rear up on his hind legs. Aurora struggled to hold on as they bolted forward, but the force of the explosion sent her and the man crashing to the ground.

The flames licked at her cloak, threatening to consume her, but she leaped out of the way. Once back on her feet, she spotted two guards roughly grabbing the village man and hoisting him up to his feet.

Aurora drew her bow with a steady hand, her eyes locking onto the guards. "Let him go," she hissed, her voice low and menacing. "Or I'll make you."

The guards laughed, their golden armor gleaming in the pale light of the moon. "You and what army?" one of them sneered.

Aurora didn't answer. She didn't need an army. All she needed was her skill, her courage, and her unwavering determination to protect the man in front of her.

She released two arrows, and they sliced through the air with a deadly whisper. The guards stumbled back, their faces twisted in pain, as they clutched at the arrows piercing their armor.

Aurora strode forward, her sword flashing in the moonlight. The guards tried to rally, but they were no match for her. One by one, they fell to her blade, their bodies vanishing into clouds of smoke.

The village man scrambled to his feet, his eyes wide with amazement. "Who are you?" he asked.

"I will explain everything," she said, unsheathing a second sword, "but we need to stay alive."

The man nodded. "I would very much like that."

Aurora scanned the area for Midnight, and her heart swelled with pride as she saw him wreaking havoc among the guards. But her attention was soon diverted to the army of soldiers closing in on them, their golden armor glinting in the moonlight.

"Take this." She tossed him a sword. The way he almost dropped it made it clear to Aurora that he hadn't been trained in combat. But despite his lack of experience, he turned around and swung the weapon with all his might, causing puffs of smoke to swirl around him as he struck as many guards as he could.

Aurora wielded her sword with precision, making each guard vanish into thin air. The sound of a sword hitting the ground echoed behind her. She turned around to see that two guards had seized the man and were dragging him by both his arms. He screamed at them, not out of fear, but out of sheer fury.

"They're only your illusions!" Aurora yelled at the man. "Fight them!"

Picking up the fallen sword, she charged toward them, her blades swinging fiercely. "Let him go!" she demanded. More guards tried to stop her, but she cut through them with ease, making them disappear.

But then a familiar figure emerged from the crowd of guards, causing Aurora to halt in the middle of the square. It was a king, with a golden robe fluttering in the wind and a crown of gold atop his gray hair.

King Midas.

Aurora froze in shock, her arms heavy with the weight of the swords as memories flooded back to her. Even the illusion of him made her insides twist with nerves.

His eyes glowered at the man caught in the grasp of his guards, and with a swift movement, Midas thrust his golden dagger into the man's chest. Aurora's heart stopped at the sight, and she watched in horror as the man grunted and fell to the ground.

"No!" she screamed, dropping her swords and reaching for her bow and arrow.

The king held up his dagger, the blade slick with fresh blood, and Aurora felt the heat of fury rise within her. She aimed her arrow at his face, ready to avenge the life he'd just taken.

But before she could release the arrow, the king and his guards disappeared, leaving the village man gasping for breath on the ground.

Aurora ran toward him, her heart pounding against her ribcage as she dropped to her knees. The rough dirt and jagged stones cut into her leather pants, but she ignored it.

"I'm…" The man blinked up at her with wide eyes as he struggled to breathe. "I…"

She placed a hand over his bleeding chest, feeling the sticky warmth of his blood seeping through his shirt.

"Don't try to speak," she implored him, "just stay with me. I can still save you. Stay with me."

The man tried to speak again, but only managed to cough up a spray of blood that spattered across Aurora's clothes.

"Don't let him win," Aurora growled, pressing

down on his chest. "If you die, he wins. We cannot let him win."

The man's hand reached out and clasped hers, his grip weakening. "He already did," he gasped out. "He won when he took my daughter twenty years ago."

A pang of anger and sadness stabbed at Aurora's chest, and her eyes filled with tears. Nothing gutted Aurora more than watching a father fight for his daughter.

She took his hand in hers, her grip firm and reassuring. "Your daughter will be free one day," she promised him, her voice trembling. "I give you my word."

The man's eyes closed, and his hand went limp in hers. A profound sense of sorrow stabbed at her chest, but she steeled herself, knowing she could not afford to fall apart.

She rose to her feet, her blood-covered hands balled into fists and her mind consumed with vengeance.

She was going to free every single girl that had ever been taken.

She was going to defeat King Midas.

If it was the last thing she did, she was going to break into that golden tower.

TRISTAN

As Tristan strode along the castle grounds, one of his advisors stopped him. "Your Majesty. We have news from the villages," he rushed out the words. "None of the recruited men are skilled in combat. Without proper training, I fear that Midas' army will surely overtake them."

Tristan closed his hands into fists as he digested the news. He had promised to protect his people, but now it seemed like his promise was nothing but a hollow lie.

"Call a group of our best warriors back from the front lines and have them begin training immediately," Tristan ordered. "They may use the castle courtyards. And tell the cooks to prepare food for them."

He knew it was not a quick fix, but the plan

seemed to reassure his advisor, at least for the moment.

The old man nodded. "Yes, Your Majesty."

Tristan watched him go with a heavy heart. There was no time for training. The war had already begun. And if the new soldiers were unfit for battle, then Tristan was fighting a war he had already lost.

He needed help. And he knew exactly where to get it.

After packing some provisions in a sheepskin bag, he told one of his guards to bring a carriage. It was time to pay an old friend another visit.

On his way out to the carriage, Tristan spied Wendy, one of the maids who had been helping with the preparations for the ball. She wore a simple yellow dress, her rust-colored hair spilling over her shoulders. She looked up from a bouquet of flowers laid out on the table to meet his stare.

"Wendy," he signed, giving her an appreciative smile. "You must be excited as well. It shall be an evening none of us shall forget."

Wendy blushed, a faint pink staining her cheeks. Few people spoke to the maid. Tristan was uncertain if it was because she was deaf and they didn't know how to sign, or if they simply chose not to try. Her twinkling eyes told him she appreciated his attention all the same.

"Yes, my lord," she signed back. "It is an honor to be able to help in any way."

Tristan nodded, then strode closer, glancing at the busy hall filled with staff bustling about their duties.

He turned back to Wendy. "Have you ever heard of a sundrop flower?" he asked.

Wendy nodded. "They grow at the mountain's peak. It's fairly out of reach, but I do have a friend who can easily get there and back quickly if the Prince needs it. His name is Peter."

Tristan set a leather pouch of gold coins on the table in front of her. Her eyes widened at it.

"Tell him to bring me as many as he can find," he signed. "You both shall be compensated upon your return."

Wendy nodded as she took the pouch and hid it in a pocket inside her dress. "Thank you, my lord. We'll be back tonight."

Tristan smiled, looking around the tables of fine china and organza material draped across the high ceilings in waves of blue and red.

"I want sundrop flowers in every room of this castle," he signed to Wendy, then with a small wave, he walked out to his carriage.

Knowing that Rumple had a bounty on his head, Tristan opted to wear a simple old cloak and thrust the hood over his head as he stepped into an older carriage instead of his usual royal one.

A short journey later, he stepped aboard one of his ships and leaned over the railing to look out over the ocean. In the distance, he spotted a bolt of lightning strike the water. The image of the guardian of the Dreamworld surfaced in his mind. Her piercing glare as she stepped toward him. Her harsh words as she rebuked him. Everything about her should have appeared menacing, but instead, to Tristan, she was the most beautiful woman he'd ever seen. The way she closed her eyes and embraced the sun on her porcelain skin. Her strange fascination with the sand. It made him smile. He couldn't even remember the last time he'd felt like smiling.

Once docked at the marina, it wasn't long before he was back in the heart of the Chanted Forest.

The horse-drawn carriage rocked back and forth as the wheels crunched along the dirt path. Tristan had found a moment's peace in the steady rhythm of the hooves and the rolling of the wheels, but as the carriage began to slow to a stop, he sucked in a deep breath, wondering how he would ask a favor from a man who had once tried to kill him.

He stepped down from the carriage, careful to keep his face obscured with his hood, then started up the hill on foot.

At the top of the hill was a small thatched house with a smoke trail curling lazily from its chimney, nestled between two tall trees.

Killian stepped out of the doorway, his body tense and brow furrowed. He rested his hand on something hidden inside his jacket, which Tristan knew to be his blue glass knife.

Tristan pulled the hood from his face and raised his empty hands. "It's me. No need for alarm."

Killian's massive shoulders dropped, along with his suspicious glare, but still, he didn't seem too thrilled to see the Prince back at his doorstep. Not when he knew Rumple was sending bounty hunters after him.

Killian was protective of Ella, and now with a baby on the way, the man would no doubt be on edge for the rest of his life. He knew Tristan was no longer a threat to them, but Killian didn't trust easily, and with their history, Tristan knew it would take time, even if they had come to an agreement.

"Come in," Killian said, sheathing his knife. "Ella is just dishing out a rabbit stew."

When Tristan walked inside the small cottage, he

followed the juicy scent of meat and onion to find Ella busy in the kitchen. Her blonde curls were stuck to her clammy cheeks, and she wiped her shiny forehead with the back of her hand as he entered the room.

"Tristan. To what do we owe another visit?" Ella asked in a sweet voice, but her eyes flashed with worry. She was a smart woman and must have heard of the battles he'd lost against King Midas.

Tristan ran a hand through his hair, knowing she would be less than enthused about getting Killian involved. Taking him away from her while she was due to have their baby any day now would no doubt be the last thing she would want to hear.

But Tristan was desperate and running out of options.

Before he could reply, Killian strode in and took a seat at the table, filling his tankard with beer. "Come. Sit with us. Eat."

They fell into a polite conversation as they ate the stew.

"So…" Ella finally cut in, her voice carried a light tremble. "What brings you back here?"

Tristan set down his spoon and let out a deep sigh. "King Midas' army has proven too strong for my men. I need help."

Killian's right brow lifted as he glanced in Ella's direction, but then he mopped his mouth with a rag and picked up his beer. "Go on."

Tristan took in a breath as he steeled himself to request the favor he had no right to ask. "Our new soldiers are common men from the villages, they're unskilled. They will not last two days on the battle-field." Tristan gave Ella another nervous glance. "If we don't put a stop to his army, he will kill them all."

The words seemed to strike Ella like a blow to the gut. She held her bump with both hands and blinked the glistening tears from her eyes. She and Killian held eye contact for several heartbeats, and Tristan wondered if they were having a secret conversation.

"What exactly are you asking me?" Killian asked Tristan, although his eyes never left Ella's.

Tristan cleared his throat and leaned forward. "I need you to train those men and lead them into battle. If you do this for me, I will gladly give you any form of payment you wish. But if you don't, Midas will win. Then it will only be a matter of time before he moves to attack a different kingdom."

Killian tore his gaze from Ella, who sank in her seat. "What kingdom?" Killian asked.

"I have heard rumors that he has set eyes on the Chanted Forest," Tristan went on. "Snow is a new queen, and Midas will not hesitate to take advantage of that."

Killian slammed his fist on the table. "Over my dead body will that maniac overtake my home."

Ella began to cry. "Why would you say such a thing?"

Killian's hard expression softened, and he reached for his wife. "Don't cry, love. Nothing will happen to me."

"You don't know that!" She shoved him away, then turned her red eyes toward Tristan. "I'm sorry, Tristan, but he will not be going into battle."

"Ella—"

"No, Killian! You are not immortal anymore!" She turned to face him with a glare, but as their eyes met, her shoulders slumped and she began to sob. "If anything happens to you, Hades will have your soul. Did you forget that?"

"No, I didn't forget that, sweetheart." Killian wrapped her in a tender embrace. "But if I can help stop him before he even thinks to come into our kingdom, then I'll know that you and our baby will be safe. That will always come first."

He held her for as long as she sobbed, then he leaned down and whispered in her ear. She pulled back, suppressing a hint of a smile then wiped her tears.

"Okay, then." Giving Tristan a bashful glance, she offered a slight bow of her head. "If you'll excuse me."

Killian's eyes sparkled as he watched her go. Like a man deeply in love. Tristan felt a pang of jealousy at the possibility he might never find such love.

"I'm sorry for causing so much trouble," Tristan said.

"She's just been extra emotional since the pregnancy." Killian reached for two beers and placed one in front of Tristan. "Feelings aside, she knows it's the right thing to do. She'll come around. We'll help you."

"I cannot thank you enough," Tristan added.

"I will need a few guards to stay with Ella while I'm gone," Killian replied. "I cannot leave her here by herself. Unprotected."

"She's welcome to stay at my castle," Tristan offered, hoping he wouldn't have to lose more skilled men.

"She will not want to stay in your castle. Too many bad memories," Killian said. "Perhaps one or two trustworthy guards would be enough."

Tristan nodded. "In case you change your mind, I

have a cottage by the lake. It's on castle grounds but isolated. If Ella decides to join you, I'll make sure to have guards nearby at all times. You're both welcome to stay there for as long as you like."

A hint of a smile tugged at the corner of Killian's lips, and he cocked his head. "I'm starting to see why Ella fought so hard for me not to kill you."

Tristan lowered his eyes, ashamed of his past actions. "Ella has always seen the good in people. She has a kind heart."

"Yes," Killian agreed, taking a swing of his drink. "Her heart is indeed one of a kind."

"I wish I had half of her fighting spirit," Tristan admitted, gulping his drink and feeling the fizz tickle down his throat. "It would make me a much better king."

Killian narrowed his eyes, studying Tristan for several breaths. "It's not the weight of the crown that's the problem. It's your conscience. I may not be able to smell the scent of guilt anymore, but it doesn't take special abilities to see that it's done a number on you."

Tristan's heart felt like an anvil in his chest. "How does one get rid of it?"

"Let it go," Killian said simply. "If you can't change it or control it, let it go."

Tristan let out a humorless chuckle. "Easier said than done. You didn't kill your father."

Killian shrugged. "Sometimes there is no way around it. You must go through it, destroy it, and bury it." Killian placed his empty canter on the table. "And I may not have killed my father, but the man did try to kill me. If it weren't for Ella, he would have succeeded. She saved my life. Now, she *is* my life and nothing else matters."

Tristan wanted that—someone in his life to take his attention away from all the suffering around him. To soothe his pain. "My attention is currently on defeating Midas. Everything else can wait."

"We will defeat him. I will give it my best effort," Killian assured him. "There's nothing I hate more than a puny little human acting like a bully."

Tristan offered a grateful bow of his head. "Thank you again for your help. Now, I must get going. I try to avoid traveling at night." He rose from the table with a grateful nod. "I will send my royal guards first thing in the morning."

"I would rather have maids." Ella appeared at the threshold with her arms crossed. "And a midwife since I'm only weeks away from giving birth."

Tristan bowed his head respectfully. "I will provide that right away," he said. "I'll also make sure to have a ship docked at the marina for you, Killian."

"That won't be necessary." Killian stood and went to stand next to Ella, planting a kiss on top of her head. "I'll be taking my horse, Azul."

"As you wish." As Tristan prepared to leave, he gave Ella one last look. "While I am here, may I have some more sundrop flowers?"

Ella shook her hair away from her shoulders. "We gave you all we had when you were here last time. And to be honest, I do not wish to have them anywhere near me or my family."

Deflated, Tristan nodded. "I see." He made to turn away but a thought had him stop by the door. "When you were in the Dreamworld, did you remember seeing a blonde woman who went by the name Aurora?"

Ella nodded. "She saved me when I was in danger. I do not know who she is, only that she's been trapped in the Dreamworld for a long time."

"Trapped?" Tristan's brows lifted in surprise. "Are you saying she exists in our world? And she's simply trapped in there?"

Ella shrugged. "Like I said, I don't know much about her at all. Except that she went into that world like most of us, but never made it out."

Tristan thanked Ella and left the cottage, his mind spinning. Now it made sense why she seemed so angry that he had returned. Perhaps it was that he could leave when she couldn't. That he seemed to be using her prison as an escape.

But the thought that consumed him like fire, setting his heart ablaze, was the fact that she was from his world—that at that moment, she was sleeping somewhere in a nearby kingdom. And if she was merely sleeping, then certainly, she could be awakened.

AURORA

*A*urora sat in a treehouse suspended high above the forest floor, honing the edges of her blades while a rusted lantern in the corner cast a faint glow over her work. The treehouse was not overly spacious, but it served as a secure storage for her weapons. Knowing the value of being prepared, she distributed her arsenal throughout the forest. She never knew where the dense fog would take her, but with her weapons stashed away in multiple locations, she could always arm herself when needed. Aurora was not one to leave things to chance. She had learned the hard way that being caught off guard could be deadly.

As the bell tower echoed through the forest, Aurora's senses heightened. She knew that the Dreamworld had been breached, and her instincts were on high alert. She looked around, scanning the forest for the dense fog, but instead, what she saw was the filtered light of the morning sun streaming through the leaves, casting a golden glow over the forest.

Tristan had returned, she knew. And to her surprise, her heart raced with anticipation at the thought of seeing him again. As much as she wished he didn't come back, she couldn't bring herself to reject the light and warmth he brought with him.

As the sun warmed her skin, Aurora closed her eyes and breathed in deeply, taking in the sweet scent of the morning dew mingled with the salty tang of the sea. The sound of waves crashing on the shore echoed in the distance, leaving no doubt in Aurora's mind as to where she would find him.

With the warm rays of the sun on her face, it was as if every cell in her body had awakened from a long, cold sleep. She never thought she would miss the warmth of the sun as much as she did. In fact, she had no idea how much she had missed it until that first day on the beach. It was such a small thing for most people, but yet, it meant so much to her.

Midnight's hooves pounded against the ground, breaking Aurora from her reverie. When he neighed from the base of the tree below, she jumped to her feet. After sheathing her newly sharpened sword, Aurora climbed down and mounted Midnight. Searching for the dense fog that usually served as a portal, she scanned the forest. Instead of the usual ominous fog, a bright mist sparkled in the sun's reflection, swirling between the trees.

Aurora studied the mist, mesmerized by this stranger's ability to shift the elements of that realm in ways she had never seen before. Without another thought, she galloped through it, feeling the cool, wet mist tickle her cheeks as she emerged at a spot where the forest met the beach.

The sand was white and pristine, and the water was a deep shade of blue that seemed to stretch on for miles. And there, sitting on the sand, was the man responsible for all of it. His blond hair was tousled from the wind as he gazed into the distance.

It wasn't until Aurora drew closer that she realized he wasn't lost in thought—he was watching something. She followed his gaze to the end of the beach by the rocks and spotted yet another memory taking place. A younger version of himself was walking alongside a man who bore a striking resemblance to him. Aurora guessed it might've been his father, recalling how Tristan had mentioned having lost him recently.

Her heart ached for his grief, yet Aurora couldn't help but be intrigued by the way Tristan was able to illuminate the world around him even while grappling with such a dreadful emotion.

Thoughts of her own father flooded her mind, and her heart squeezed. It had been ages since she last laid eyes on him, but she remembered their last encounter all too well, every excruciating detail etched in her mind. The shouting, the tears, the hurtful words that spewed out of her mouth as she left him to finish his dinner alone.

If she had done things differently that night— perhaps tried reasoning with her father instead of defying him—she would never have drank from the sundrop flower.

She would never have gone into the Dreamworld.

Aurora pushed the thought away, reminding herself that regret was a useless burden—it weighed like an anvil, but never changed anything. The past couldn't be altered, so dwelling on it only sapped her energy and messed with her focus.

Dismounting Midnight, she stepped onto the sandy beach. The breeze was soothing and refreshing, and just what she needed to ease the pain that still ached from the night before from not having been able to save the village man. She could still feel his blood on her hands, even though she had scrubbed it all off.

Still, it was reckless of Tristan to have returned. She stopped a few feet away, not trusting that she wouldn't hit him upside the head if she got too close. "You're stubborn," she said, startling him.

He staggered to his feet. "Please," he said, lifting his hands, "don't electrocute me again. I come in peace."

She crossed her arms and narrowed her eyes at him. "I didn't electrocute you because I was threatened. I did it to wake you up."

"Wake me up?" he asked, sounding interested. "Like a jolt? Is that how everyone leaves this realm?"

Everyone but me. "Yes. It's the only way," she said.

He must've sensed the edge in her voice because his eyes softened. "I'm sorry to keep intruding into your world. I don't mean to be a nuisance."

He was a nuisance, but not for the reasons he might've been thinking. His presence was a much-needed break from the horrors she often encountered, but regardless of how warm he made her feel, he was still taking his freedom for granted, and that was what bothered her most.

"What brings you back this time?" she asked,

turning away from his soft gaze to look at the man still strolling with his son near the shore.

Tristan followed her line of sight with a heavy sigh. "I'm in desperate need of advice," he confessed. "I thought maybe if I replayed some of the things my father had said to me, I would find some hidden wisdom somewhere."

"Have you found anything yet?" she asked.

He shook his head, then ran a hand through his hair.

"I wish there was a way I could talk to him," Tristan said, watching his father. "I have so many questions."

"You could," she said. "But he wouldn't tell you anything you don't already know."

Tristan gave her a side glance. "Is there a way around that?"

"Not with memories, no." She watched his shoulders sag, and in that moment a lonely cloud covered the bright sun above them. Aurora wasn't surprised that the elements around them reflected his mood. "Illusions might have a bit more to offer, though."

Tristan perked up, and the sun immediately peeked out from behind the cloud, brightening the sky once more. The corner of Aurora's lips curved slightly at how transparent he was. It was refreshing not having to decipher riddles for a change.

"What's the difference?" he asked eagerly. "Between memories and illusions?"

Aurora scanned the woods behind her, as if merely saying the word *illusion* aloud would somehow make things materialize. "Memories are familiar. Events that actually happened and are recreated in fine detail. Illusions, on the other hand, are more abstract."

"What does that mean?" he asked.

"Take that memory, for example." Aurora pointed at Tristan's father in the distance. "If you were to engage with him right now, he would have to respond using words he'd spoken in that precise moment. Nothing different, nothing new. But if that were an illusion…" She arched a brow. "He wouldn't be restricted to any specific conversation because it never actually happened."

Tristan's eyes widened with a mixture of excitement and hope. "Then how do I find an illusion?"

"You don't *find* them. You *create* them. But trust me, you don't want to do that."

"Why not? If it has the answers I seek, I must find one," he insisted. "Tell me, what do I need to do?"

Aurora shook her head, her long, blonde braid

draped over one shoulder. "You don't know what you're asking for."

"I may not understand how this world works, but I came to get answers, and if an illusion of my father is what I have to create in order to get what I need, then that's what I'll do."

"Do you think you could just create an illusion, invite it for tea, and get all the answers you want?" she snapped, taking a forceful step toward him. "Illusions are manipulative. They have all access to your mind, they know your weakness, and they will not hesitate to prey on them until you lose your sanity."

Tristan puffed out his chest. "I'm not afraid."

"You're not afraid because you're not *aware*," she explained. "Look around you. This serene beach your mind created is a reflection of just how naive you are. There is no rip current in that ocean, no fallen leaves at the edge of those woods, not even ragged edges on the seashells. Everything on the beach is pure, honest, and unguarded."

"Those all sound like good qualities to me," he said.

"In this world, being unguarded and trusting will get you killed," she said firmly. "You wouldn't last a day with an illusion."

"Then help me," he begged.

Aurora gave him an incredulous look. "What part of 'they will kill you', do you not understand? And if you die in here, there is no waking up from that."

"All the more reason why I need your help," he insisted. "You have made it abundantly clear that you don't want me here, but I also will not leave until I find what I'm looking for. So, if you want to get rid of me for good, help me find the answers I need. Then, I promise, I will leave and never come back."

Aurora gave him a skeptical look. "You promise?"

Tristan lifted a hand, his blue eyes meeting hers. "You have my word."

Aurora considered his request. Though she wasn't sure he was giving her much of a choice. If she didn't help him, she was fairly certain he would try it on his own. And that was no doubt going to be a lot more dangerous. At least if she kept a close eye on him, she could awaken him before anything terribly bad happened to him.

And as an added bonus, she would acquire new planks for her bridge. She had already woken him up twice without even breaking a sweat. With Tristan, there was no darkness to fear, no creatures to slaughter, no enemies to battle. If she could keep waking him up, she could potentially complete her bridge much faster.

Then she would finally make it into the golden tower.

"Fine. I'll help you," she said, ignoring his wide smile. "But you have to listen to everything I say."

He nodded. "I will. Thank you."

"What answers are you looking for, anyway?" she asked.

"Well, you know…" Tristan trailed off, his gaze falling to the sand beneath his feet. "Answers," he finished lamely.

Aurora narrowed her eyes at him. "You have no idea what you're looking for, do you?"

"No, but trust me, I'll know when I find it," he said, his confidence unwavering. "So… how do we create this illusion?"

"Normally, you could will it to appear with your mind. But…" She studied him briefly. "It might be different with you."

He straightened his posture, seeming unsure of whether or not he should be offended. "Why would it be different with me?" he asked.

"Because you're different," she said, motioning around them once more. "Your mind isn't dark. What you see here… this isn't just a memory. This is a reflection of who you are at your core."

Tristan snorted. "I guarantee you, I am not this sunny and chipper."

"Maybe not. But you are hopeful. And where there's hope, there's light." And Aurora didn't need to look at the beach to know that. His soft blue eyes gave it away.

When several heartbeats passed, Aurora realized they had just been holding each other's gaze. She quickly cleared her throat and looked around the beach again.

"Whatever the case, staying here won't work," she said. "You already attached this location to a memory, so detaching from that will be harder if you're not used to shifting your thoughts."

"Where else can we go?" he asked.

"If you're looking for advice from your father, then the best place to start would be somewhere he has spent most of his time," she explained. "Preferably a place he was most vulnerable. Sometimes, the location itself could contain a well of information."

Tristan's eyes darted toward the end of the beach, beyond where his father was walking. His gaze landed on a majestic castle looming at the top of a hill, overlooking the ocean.

"Will that work?" he asked, his voice barely above a whisper.

Aurora blinked several times. "Uh, yeah…" She figured it was high enough for her to jolt him awake by shoving him off a ledge. "But why would your father be in a castle?" she asked.

Tristan turned his head with a shy smile. "That's where he worked."

It took Aurora a few heartbeats to realize Tristan had already started walking, and she trailed after him.

Tristan led the way with an effortless grace, his long strides carrying him up the hill with ease. Aurora found herself watching the way he moved, his muscles rippling beneath his shirt as he led the way up the cobblestoned path.

There were no guards in sight, which could only mean one thing: that was Tristan's home.

Aurora knew from experience that if he had any guilt about trespassing, or the slightest sense that he didn't belong there, the property would be swarming with guards. But there were none at any post. And when Tristan pulled open a set of ornate French doors overlooking a small garden, it wasn't locked.

As he was about to step inside, Aurora put a hand on his shoulder. Her touch must've interrupted his thoughts because he blinked at her as though he was seeing her for the first time.

"Don't be so trusting," she warned, peering warily into the castle. "Always anticipate traps."

He nodded, then took a careful step into the castle. With a hand on the hilt of her sword, she followed him inside. They entered a grand ballroom, the marble floor decorated with seashell designs that sparkled in the sunlight. The walls were lined with paintings of mermaids, their beauty captured for all eternity.

Aurora couldn't help but feel a sense of awe at the grandeur of the place, even as she remained vigilant for any signs of danger.

"Cousin Tristan!" A little girl in a dress and golden locks ran down the elegant staircase and leaped into Tristan's arms. He caught her with ease, but by his puzzled expression, Aurora could tell that it wasn't a memory.

"Lily?" he whispered, staring at the little girl as though he couldn't believe she wasn't real. That was precisely what made illusions so dangerous.

"Grandfather is at the study, waiting for you," she said in a sweet, melodic voice. "Everything is ready. Everyone is waiting."

Tristan's brows furrowed, and he put the little girl down on the floor. She giggled and scampered away, disappearing into one of the corridors. "Was that…?"

"An illusion, yes," Aurora replied.

"What did she mean by 'everything is ready'?" he asked, turning to Aurora.

She let out a sigh. "That's another thing about illusions. They love blasted riddles," she grumbled. "Now, she did say your father was waiting for you. Where would he be?"

"Right." Tristan shook off his initial shock and started toward one of the hallways to the left.

Aurora's heart thumped in her chest as she followed Tristan down the narrow hallway, trying to push aside the unease that settled in the pit of her stomach. She didn't like enclosed spaces. It didn't take much for a door to disappear, leaving them with no way out.

When they reached the mahogany door, Tristan hesitated, his hand trembling as he pressed it against the wood. Aurora placed her hand on his shoulder, her fingers lightly grazing the soft fabric of his shirt.

"Take a deep breath," she whispered. "Whatever happens, don't lose control of your emotions."

Tristan nodded, and with a deep breath, he pushed the door open, revealing a spacious room filled with bookshelves, a large oak desk, and a roaring fireplace.

Seated at the desk was a tall, imposing man with

dark hair and even darker eyes. It was the same man from the beach, but older. He looked up as they entered, a faint smile playing at the corner of his lips.

"Step inside and close the door," he said, his eyes intense. "We have much to discuss."

Tristan swallowed hard, his gaze locked on the man. "Father," he breathed.

For a long moment, there was silence as the two men regarded each other, each lost in their own thoughts and emotions.

Finally, his father spoke. "Is it guidance you seek?"

Tristan nodded, his expression grim. "Yes," he said, his voice shaking. "I'm ready to face the truth, no matter what it may be."

As both men locked eyes, Aurora wondered if she could have prepared Tristan better for this. Dealing with an illusion was much more intense than simply reliving a memory. And judging from the tremble in his voice, she could sense that he was shaken to his core. Her only hope was that he could keep his emotions under control.

"You are no longer a child," his father said, rising from his seat and moving toward the window.

Aurora couldn't help but notice how the once-bright day had turned cloudy, and the wind outside had picked up, making the branches scratch against the glass. She looked at Tristan with concern.

"You have a duty to your kingdom, Tristan."

Kingdom? Aurora shot Tristan a glance, but his eyes were fixed on his father.

"And to be a good ruler, we don't always have the luxury of preference. You know that," the king continued, his expression hard.

"Why is it always one or the other?" Tristan's voice was thick with sadness. "Why can't I have both?"

The king's face contorted with disdain, his gaze turning dark. "The day will come when you'll have to step into my shoes," he hissed venomously. "But you don't have what it takes to lead a nation. Your ideals are misguided and will only lead to your downfall. Fortunately, I won't be around to watch you destroy everything I've worked so hard to build."

Aurora's jaw dropped as she stared at the king. Even if he was a figment of Tristan's imagination, the hurtful words must've stung like a thousand bee stings. But what was even more disconcerting was seeing Tristan's calm reaction to his father's brutal words. Had he heard them all before?

Suddenly, a raging storm erupted outside, the rain lashing against the windows like an army of drums.

Aurora's eyes flickered to Tristan's white-knuckled fists and clenched jaw, realizing that he was not as calm as he seemed. He was hurting, and her heart trembled like a bolt of lightning at the sight of a single, angry tear tracing down his cheek.

As the walls shook, Aurora's hand found her sword, the hilt gripped tightly between her fingers. "He's not real," she reminded Tristan, her voice low and steady. "He's just trying to provoke you, to make you lose control. You have to stay calm."

Aurora watched as the king's icy gaze pierced through Tristan, his tone rigid as though the weight of the kingdom rested solely on his shoulders. "You have a duty to your kingdom," he said, his words booming with authority. "No matter the cost, you must fulfill it."

With that, the door was thrust open, and two guards rushed in. "Everything is ready, Your Highness," they announced.

The king's lips curved into a sly smile, and he motioned toward Tristan with a dismissive wave. "Take him away," he ordered.

The guards grabbed Tristan, one on each side, and Aurora's hand immediately flew to her sword. In a swift movement, she drew the blade and plunged it into the chest of one of the guards. The man disappeared in a puff of smoke, and Aurora turned her fierce gaze toward the king. She knew he was the root of Tristan's emotional turmoil. If she could eliminate him, Tristan's turbulent emotions would subside.

She raised her sword and charged toward the king.

"No!" Tristan cried, punching one of the guards in the face before lunging at Aurora and tackling her to the ground. Her sword slipped from her grasp and clattered to the floor.

"What are you doing?" she snarled.

"That's my father!" he protested.

"He's not real!" Aurora shouted back, pushing Tristan away and scrambling to retrieve her sword. But before she could reach it, the king picked it up and held the sharp blade to her face.

Aurora raised her hands as she stood.

"Father, please." Tristan stepped in front of Aurora, his eyes pleading. "I'm the one you're angry with. I'm the one who disappointed you."

"You need to kill him, Tristan," Aurora's voice was barely audible, but it must've landed on Tristan's ears like a lightning bolt because he shot her a horrified glance.

"You don't need to tell him twice, my dear," the

king said, a wicked glint in his eye. "He's more than capable. Aren't you, son?"

The walls shook with a violent tremor, and Aurora was thrown against the desk, her senses reeling as books toppled off the shelves.

"Tristan, control your emotions!" she warned, trying to steady herself. "Don't let them overwhelm you!"

"Guards!" the king bellowed over the tremors. "Escort your prince!"

Several guards burst into the room and seized Tristan once again. The quake subsided, and Tristan locked eyes with his father.

"Where are you taking me?" he demanded through gritted teeth.

The king's lips twisted into a wicked grin. "To your worst nightmare, my son."

TRISTAN

The line between reality and illusion became blurred as Tristan began to lose sense of what was real. He was dragged by the guards through two heavy doors and pushed into the main hall of the castle.

He looked up at the high vaulted ceilings and the familiar rays of golden sunshine pouring in through the stained glass windows.

Rows upon rows of guests were seated, waiting, and their gazes burned on him as he walked down the aisle to a priest at the front of the hall.

Hushed voices surrounded him, but he could hardly hear them over the sound of his thumping heartbeat. He swallowed nervously as he turned on his heel, but a string quartet struck up a familiar tune from his childhood—a melody his mother would hum as she rocked him to sleep.

Ryke stepped into view and squeezed Tristan's shoulder. "Stand with me and wait," he instructed, motioning for Tristan to join him in front of the priest.

Suddenly, the doors opened again and a bride entered the hall, her face veiled in layers of white lace. The music turned into a triumphant anthem and Tristan's stomach did backflips as he watched the bride gliding down the aisle.

A rush of panic flooded his senses, rooting his feet to the ground, and no matter how much he wanted to move, he couldn't. His jaw tensed and his breaths grew shallow as a rising sense of doom took hold of him. He glanced around at the guests who stood waiting in hushed excitement, some rocking back and forth on their heels, others clasping their hands together in anticipation.

Tristan watched with a heavy heart as the bride continued slowly down the aisle, her delicate figure illuminated in the flickering candlelight. His mind fogged by a sense of dread, it was like the hundreds of eyes watching him were pressing against his skin, suffocating him in silence. He stood rooted to the spot, unable to move.

As the bride drew closer, Ryke murmured in Tristan's ear, "Your duty is to your kingdom, cousin."

Finally, the bride reached him, and as though he was a puppet, he automatically reached forward and lifted the thick veil.

Tristan's heart pounded furiously as he watched in horror as the face staring back at him revealed his darkest fear. There before him stood Neri, her cold eyes glinting maliciously as a cruel smirk spread across her face. From beneath the fabric of her dress emerged writhing tentacles that seemed to reach out for Tristan.

He had barely blinked before a thick tentacle was coiling around his neck, squeezing out his breath. He gasped for air and clawed at the rubbery limb, but the creature's grip was relentless. Suddenly, the sound of steel slicing through the air filled his ears, and he had a rush of relief as Aurora appeared, her sword gleaming in the sunlight.

She slashed at the tentacle without hesitation, watching with silent satisfaction as it dropped to the ground.

"You need to keep your fear under control!" she barked. "Your mounting terror is causing your illusions to turn on you and fight back!"

She was a force of nature, standing strong, eye

blazing and determined while she hacked at another tentacle.

Before Tristan could grapple with his raging emotions, King Midas stepped into view, his steely glare on Tristan.

"Guards!" he yelled in a commanding voice. "Bring him to me!"

Tristan's ears rang and the hairs on the back of his neck stood on end as he watched the guards draw their swords and start to march toward him.

Aurora exploded into motion, a whirlwind of fury that whipped through the air. Every blow echoed with an intensity beyond her physical form as she threw herself at the guards. Every hit she landed was delivered with enough force to make even the strongest man stumble and shake in fear.

Watching her in action lit a spark, and suddenly Tristan came to life. He punched one of the guards and took his sword.

With a roar, Tristan lunged forward, slashing and stabbing with an intensity he'd never known he possessed. With every swing of his sword, the fear and rage that had been burning inside him intensified until no amount of force could contain it.

The battle raged on as Tristan pushed himself beyond what he thought was possible. Finally, in one last surge, he drove his sword straight through Neri's heart.

Tristan watched in amazement as, one by one, the people in the grand hall disappeared, quietly fading into the shadows until it was just Aurora and him left standing in the center of the empty hall. Silence descended upon them like a cloud.

Aurora looked at him, concern etched on her face. "Are you okay?" she asked breathlessly.

Tristan shook his head, dropping the sword with a clang, unsure whether it was fear or fury that had him trembling. "I need to wake up," he said, his voice shaking.

Aurora gave him a firm nod. "Come with me."

They marched up the winding stairs of the castle, their feet thudding heavily against the creaking steps. On each landing, they paused to catch their breath, tasting the smoky air. When they finally reached the top, Aurora opened the heavy doors that led onto the roof.

As soon as Tristan stepped out, the rain cleared. Even though the sun was shrouded by gray clouds, it was still light out.

Tristan looked up to the gloomy sky, feeling a twinge of residual dread. He glanced around, wondering if there were more illusions coming his way. His heart raced as he sat on the parapet wall, his thoughts running wild with the events that had just unfolded.

Seeing his father again stirred up so much emotion. He had been pushing them down, trying to ignore them, and they festered. All of his confusion, hurt, and fury concocted something terrible—a wretched kind of turmoil that created his worst nightmare.

If it wasn't for Aurora's intervention, he was certain that he would have died. And for a splinter of a moment, he thought that might not have been a bad thing. At least death would bring an end to all of his suffering.

The sky darkened above them, covering the roof in a deep shadow. By the look on Aurora's face as she glanced up, he could tell the weather was mirroring his emotions.

Aurora eased herself onto the parapet next to him, her eyes flickering from his furrowed brows to his downturned mouth. She reached out a hand and gently rested it on his arm. "Breathe in," she whispered, sucking in her own deep breath. "Then out."

Tristan did as she said, and a soothing calm washed over him. His heartbeat slowed, and his swirling thoughts cleared like a sunny day. "Thank you," he breathed. "And you were right, that was absolutely wretched."

A small smile tugged at Aurora's lips. "For what it's worth, you were very brave," she said, searching for his eyes. "Most people run scared, but you faced your fear head-on."

Tristan lowered his eyes to where her hand was still resting on his arm, her touch warm and comforting. But then she drew it away as though she hadn't realized how long she'd lingered.

"Sorry," she murmured, her cheeks reddening.

"No, *I'm* sorry," Tristan said, running a hand through his disheveled hair. "I should've just listened to you and left. But no, I had to go on ahead and put both of us in danger. And the worst part is that while I'm here, fighting illusions, my kingdom is out there, fighting and dying at the hands of King Midas."

Aurora tensed next to him. "I noticed he was in your nightmare," she said. "What makes you so afraid of him?"

Tristan exhaled in despair. "My army is not strong enough to win the war against him. He's too powerful. And he's been relentless in invading our land."

Tristan had dedicated his life to fighting for his kingdom, but the odds were against him. As much as he wanted to believe they could win, deep down he knew there was no way his people could come out victorious.

The thought of failure weighed heavily on him, yet he was determined to keep fighting until the end. "My kingdom is my responsibility, and I just…" He trailed off, the words bundling up in a hard lump at the bottom of his throat.

Aurora edged closer, her small hand barely covering his shoulder. A rush of heat shot through him as her mouth inched toward him. "My father always told me that in order to win a war, you don't need to be stronger. You need to be smarter and know when to strike."

Tristan arched a curious brow. "Care to elaborate?"

Aurora glanced up at the solar eclipse above them in the sky. "I don't have time to explain it all now, but I have an idea. If you come back, I'll show you something that just might help you get the upper hand on Midas."

Tristan narrowed his eyes. "But I thought you wanted me to leave and never come back?"

"Yes, but that was before I knew you were up against Midas," she said, her expression serious. "This world may not have much to offer, but when it does deliver, it's powerful. Trust me, your only weapon against him is here. Come back and I'll show you."

Tristan nodded, his heart lifting with a momentary sense of hope. "Thank you," he said, his eyes dropping to her lips. A flurry of nerves nipped at his insides as he thought about how plump they looked. They were so close, it would have been easy to just lean in and discover the taste of them.

But without warning, Aurora shoved him hard with both hands, and he tumbled off the roof. His heartbeat roared in his ears as he hurled toward the rock-hard ground.

AURORA

*A*urora sat by the half-built wooden bridge, sharpening the tip of her arrows. Her legs hung over the edge. Heavy fog covered the abyss below, which made it seem like she was sitting above the clouds. Thoughts of Tristan lingered in her mind. She hadn't stopped thinking about him since he'd left.

She had misjudged him.

Just because he brought light to that darkened world didn't mean he didn't struggle with his own darkness. However, it was the first time she'd ever seen someone's nightmare manifest as a wedding. Normally, weddings were beautiful and an event so special, people lived their whole lives dreaming of when the day would come. She surely had her moments growing up. The thought of dancing to an orchestra of classical music in the middle of a ball wearing a beautiful, bejeweled gown glistening like diamonds had been at the center of her dreams ever since she was a little girl. She hadn't thought about that for what felt like an eternity. There was no need to dwell on thoughts that would never happen for her.

But why were weddings a nightmare for Tristan? He was a prince, and a very handsome one at that. His eyes sparkled with the vibrancy of the bluest summer sky, revealing not just his keen intelligence, but also his unending warmth. The contours of his face were finely carved, featuring a jawline that would draw any sculptor's envy, all softened by a radiant smile that held the power to melt the coldest of hearts. Any woman would be lucky to be chosen by him.

The distant chime of the bell tower broke through the silent gloom, and Aurora's mind jerked back to the present. *Tristan.*

She rose from the ground and craned her neck to peer up at the sky, searching for any hint of the sunlight. But it seemed as though it had decided to stay hidden away, much like Tristan had retreated into the depths of his own mind during his nightmare.

Aurora wondered if what he'd experienced might've changed his perspective of that world. Had that event finally opened his eyes to the true danger of the Dreamworld? Was that the reason the sun had chosen to not appear this time? She knew all too well that the Dreamworld was not to be underestimated. Its twisted illusions had a way of bringing out the worst in people, unearthing the darkest parts of their souls and leaving them exposed in ways they never thought possible.

And Tristan had finally experienced that firsthand.

A pang of sadness tugged at her heart. If it was truly him who had entered the Dreamworld, then she would surely miss the sunshine that often came with his presence.

With a swift whistle, Midnight came galloping out of the woods, his hooves pounding against the ground like a drumbeat. Aurora mounted him with ease, and urged him forward without hesitation into the blinding fog. The mist swirled around them, obscuring her vision, and Aurora firmed her grip on the reins.

As Midnight navigated through the thick haze, Aurora's breaths came out in frosty puffs, and her cheeks stung with the cold. The air was so frigid that it felt like tiny icicles were forming in her nostrils with every inhale. Aurora tightened her cloak around her thin frame, her leather garments doing little to shield her from the sudden freezing temperature. Finally, they emerged into the heart of a snow-covered forest, and Aurora couldn't help but marvel at the winter wonderland surrounding them. The trees were coated in a thick layer of white, and the snow sparkled like diamonds with the reflection of the lunar eclipse high above her.

The sounds of approaching footsteps shattered the peaceful silence, and Aurora squinted, searching for the source of the sound. A young girl came running out of the trees, her oversized brown cloak billowing behind her like a cape. Her eyes were wild with fright, and when she stopped in front of Midnight, Aurora could see the panic etched into every line of her face.

Midnight whined and pawed the ground anxiously, sensing the danger lurking in the shadows. Aurora's heart pounded in her chest, and she gripped her bow and arrow as the girl took off running ahead of them. Suddenly, a snarling wolf burst into view, its teeth bared and its eyes gleaming with hunger.

"Help!" the girl screamed, her voice ringing out over the snow-covered terrain. "Somebody help me!"

Aurora urged Midnight forward, closing the distance between herself and the terrified girl. In one swift motion, she reached down and scooped the girl up, propping her onto the horse in front of her. The girl was trembling and out of breath, and her heart raced as she clung to Aurora for dear life.

"Where am I?" she asked, her voice shaking. "How did I get here?"

Aurora spared a quick glance over her shoulder, and her heart nearly stopped as she caught sight of the giant wolf chasing after them. Its eyes glowed like red-hot embers, fixated on the girl as though she were its prey.

"What's the last thing you remember?" Aurora asked, her voice strained as she urged Midnight to go faster.

"My brother," the girl said, her eyes scanning the snowy terrain frantically. "He was sick. He had a fever. Then he transformed into a wolf." Understanding dawned on her face, and she turned to Aurora with wide eyes. "Did he kill me?"

"No," Aurora assured her. "You must've just fainted."

The wolf growled ominously behind them, and the heat of its breath was too close for comfort. "I need you to hold on tight," Aurora instructed the girl, thrusting the reins into her shaking hands. "Can you do that?"

The girl nodded, gripping the reins so hard that her knuckles turned white. Aurora leaped to her feet as Midnight thundered forward, his hooves pounding against the snowy ground. The wolf was hot on their heels, its growls growing louder and more frenzied with every passing moment. Then, with gritted teeth, Aurora launched herself into the air, grabbing hold of a tree branch overhead. Midnight made a sharp turn, leaving Aurora dangling precariously from the branch. She pulled herself up quickly, then with a steady hand, she nocked an arrow on her bow and took aim at the snarling wolf.

The wolf charged past her, his eyes glowing. Aurora's heart pounded with adrenaline as she pulled back her bowstring and released the arrow. It flew through the air, striking the wolf's leg with a satisfying *thunk*. The animal howled in pain. With lightning-fast reflexes, she reached for a second arrow and drove it into the wolf's shoulder. The animal screeched, then whipped around, its glowing eyes locking onto Aurora's. He snarled, puffing air out of his nostrils.

Aurora whistled, summoning Midnight from the woods. The horse positioned himself perfectly beneath her, and Aurora mounted him with ease, keeping the girl in front of her. But before they could take off, the wolf charged toward them, his sharp teeth bared.

The girl screamed, but instead of letting the panic consume her, Aurora placed a calming hand on the girl's shoulder and closed her eyes.

With a deep breath, Aurora focused all of her energy on the wolf. She pictured him slowing down, losing momentum, and eventually stopping dead in its tracks.

When she opened her eyes again, another giant wolf had come into view. Its fur was as white as snow, and it barreled into the red-eyed wolf with full force. The two animals crashed onto the snow, sliding until a large tree brought them to a halt. The red-eyed wolf whimpered while the white wolf towered over him.

"That should buy us some time," Aurora murmured, taking back the reins from the trembling girl.

"How are there two of them?" the girl asked, staring at the wolves in shock.

Aurora hesitated for a moment, not wanting to confuse the poor girl with needless details. "Let's just say I have a few tricks up my sleeve," she said with a small smile. "But right now, we need to find a safe place for you."

Midnight charged through the snow, leaving the wolves behind, their snarls echoing in the distance.

Aurora could feel the fear radiating off the girl, and she knew that for as long as the girl was afraid, the wolf would keep chasing after them. As they approached the edge of a cliff, Aurora slowed Midnight to a halt.

"Wait! What are you doing?" the girl said in a frantic voice. "You said a safe place. This is not a safe place. He'll find us here."

"If you want him to disappear, this is the only way," Aurora said. "Trust me."

After dismounting from Midnight, Aurora offered the girl a hand. The girl took it, and Aurora helped her down. Once her feet touched the snow, Aurora tapped Midnight's hind, and the horse galloped off into the woods, leaving them alone.

The girl turned her frightened gaze toward Aurora. "What's the plan?" she asked.

Aurora sucked in a breath, then turned toward the dark forest. "We wait for him to come."

The girl's eyes stretched wide. "And then what?" her voice trembled.

Aurora puffed out her chest, bracing herself.

"Then you face him head-on because you're not afraid of him."

"What?" the girl screeched and stepped back. "But I am. I am very afraid of him."

"You shouldn't be," Aurora said, her voice steady and confident. "He's just an illusion, a manifestation of your own fears. The more afraid you are, the more power you give him. But if you face him head-on and tell him that you're not afraid, he'll lose his hold over you."

"But the size of his mouth…" The girl gaped. "He can swallow me whole."

"He won't."

"How do you know?"

Aurora touched the girl's shoulders and looked into her frightened eyes. "The only way for you to make it out of here alive is to stop viewing that wolf as a monster, and instead start seeing him for who he really is. Your brother."

The girl stared at Aurora as her mind processed everything. "What is this place?" she asked.

Aurora softened her expression, hoping the friendly demeanor would help calm the girl's nerves. "This is a place where you can rise above your fears and come out stronger on the other side."

"But I'm not strong," she whimpered.

"Of course you are," Aurora said, offering an encouraging smile. "You are as strong as your love is."

"What does that even mean?"

A low growl ripped through the stillness of the forest, and the hair on the back of Aurora's neck rose. She turned her head and saw the red-eyed wolf lurching out from behind the trees. His movements were jerky and uncoordinated as he pushed through the pain of his injured leg and shoulder.

"Don't be afraid," Aurora whispered. "Just remember, he's your brother."

The girl's eyes widened in shock. "My... my brother," she stuttered.

Aurora nodded, trying to keep her voice calm as the wolf drew closer. "He's not your enemy," she said, her voice barely above a breath. "He won't harm you."

The girl hesitated for a moment, then took a deep breath. "Okay," she said, her voice still shaking.

The wolf inched closer, his mouth salivating. He walked past Aurora, his focus entirely on his sister. "Annie?" he growled, his voice barely recognizable as human. "Is that really you?"

The girl recoiled at the distorted sound of his voice, but Aurora stepped forward, placing herself between the girl and the wolf. "It's okay," she said. "He's just confused."

But the wolf kept coming, his snarls growing louder and more desperate with each step. Aurora knew she had to act fast. With one swift motion, Aurora plunged her sword into the wolf's jugular, watching as the blood gushed out onto the snow.

Annie screamed in horror, her eyes locking with her brother's. "Ollie!"

The wolf collapsed on the snow, and Annie dropped to her knees beside him, her hands trembling as she cradled him in her arms. "Ollie," she whispered, tears streaming down her face. "I'm so sorry."

Aurora yanked out her sword, allowing the wolf to gasp for air. Annie looked up at Aurora, horrified. "Why did you do that?" she screamed through her sobs.

Aurora sheathed her sword without a word. Even if she were to explain, it wouldn't have made a difference. But it was the only way to get Annie to see the wolf as her brother. As Aurora had guessed, Annie's fear of losing her brother was far greater than her fear of the beast. And that was the emotion Aurora needed to force out of Annie, because that was the emotion she would need to take back with her to the real world once she woke up.

The wolf's body shuddered one last time, and then he was gone. In his place appeared a young man, his face pale and haggard, but unmistakably her brother. "Annie?" Ollie stammered as he struggled to breathe. "What happened?"

Annie's tears slid down her face. "You were sick," she said. "And then you transformed into a wolf."

Confused and disoriented, he blinked several times as Annie cradled him in her arms. "I don't remember," he murmured.

"It's okay," she reassured him. "You're okay now."

He gazed at her with a penetrating stare. "You were afraid of me," he breathed out in a low voice that sent shivers through her arms.

Annie shook her head frantically, trying to dispel any fear that still lingered within her. "I'm not," she said, trying to sound confident. "Not anymore."

Ollie's face broke into a relieved smile, and in the blink of an eye, he vanished into thin air, leaving Annie staring at her empty arms. "Where did he go?" she asked, searching the area frantically.

Aurora placed a comforting hand on Annie's shoulder. "That was just an illusion. Your brother is safe at home, waiting for you," she reassured the young girl.

Annie got up, her mind in a haze, and stumbled forward. "I get to go home now?" she asked.

Aurora nodded, then gestured toward the edge of the cliff. "Yes, now you go home," she said.

Annie approached the cliff's edge, her toes dangling over the precipice. She looked down, a sense of vertigo clearly taking hold. "Is this the only way?" she asked.

"I'm afraid so."

Annie took a deep breath. "It was nice meeting you," she said before leaping into the air with a gasp.

And just like that, she was gone. Aurora smiled to herself, proud of the courage that young girl had just displayed. If only she had been as brave in her youth, Aurora would never have ended up trapped as she was.

"It was nice meeting you, too," she whispered into the wind, hoping that if nothing else, at least a faint sound of her voice would reach the real world.

TRISTAN

*T*ristan blinked his eyes open to find himself sprawled on the sandy beach. As he slowly rose to his feet, the gentle lull of the waves crashing against the shore filled his ears, blending harmoniously with the distant cry of seagulls soaring across the cerulean sky. The air carried a soft, salty tang, and a warm breeze whispered through his wavy hair, instantly refreshing his weary spirit.

His gaze swept across the horizon, taking in the vast expanse of the Dreamworld. The beach stretched out endlessly, its pristine sands meeting the sparkling sapphire waters that seemed to shimmer with a life of their own. A sense of tranquility washed over him as he realized that this place held no trace of the burdens he carried in the real world.

In this ephemeral paradise, he wasn't king. The weight of his heavy crown was nonexistent. Here, he was liberated from the shackles of his regal lineage, no longer bound by the ceaseless expectations of a kingdom in turmoil.

The rhythmic sound of approaching hooves reached his ears. Tristan turned toward the forest that lay just beyond the beach. Emerging from a thick haze, a figure appeared. It was Aurora, mounted gracefully on her white stallion, her blonde braid draped over one shoulder, and her brown eyes alight as she watched him from a distance.

She drew close, then stopped next to him. "Took you long enough," she said, a hint of impatience in her tone. But her eyes carried an irresistible allure.

"How long were you waiting for me?" he asked, curious as to how differently time moved in that world.

Her eyes shifted upward, and he followed her gaze to the lunar eclipse in the sky. "We don't have much time," she said, extending her hand toward him, her voice much gentler than before. "Come with me."

Without hesitation, Tristan reached out and clasped her hand, feeling a surge of energy course through his veins as he swung himself onto the horse's back. Nestling in behind Aurora, he gripped her waist.

Her back stiffened against his chest.

"Is this all right?" he asked, his lips so close to her ear, he could smell the floral scent of her hair.

"You might need to hold on tighter," she said with a nervous gulp.

He wrapped his arms around her. "Like this?"

"Sure," she said hastily, as though trying to keep from entertaining thoughts that might've been triggered by his touch. Or perhaps that was simply his own wishful thinking.

Without another word, she sprang the horse forward, its hooves pounding against the soft sand, propelling them toward a thick fog that enveloped the forest. Its tendrils caressed his skin like ghostly specters, concealing the path ahead of them. Tristan's vision was momentarily obscured, then the fog lifted, and they emerged in the heart of the forest.

Towering trees stretched skyward, their branches interlocking like the hands of ancient giants, filtering the morning light that seeped through the verdant canopy above. Sunbeams danced amidst the gentle sway of the leaves, casting dappled patterns on the forest floor.

Despite having seen the darkness this world had

to offer, there was still so much light. In that world, Tristan was unburdened by the weight of responsibility that plagued his waking hours. There was no throne to ascend, no crown to bear, and no wars to wage. It was a realm untouched by famine and destruction, where the suffering of his people was but a distant memory.

Here, Tristan was free. Free to be a regular person without a care in the world. In this realm, he could revel in the simplicity of existence, where the only obligation was to embrace the beauty that surrounded him. The warmth of the sun. The cool tickle of the breeze.

A profound sense of peace settled deep within him, and his heart swelled with gratitude for the temporary escape he was granted from the harsh realities of his waking life.

But then a dense fog manifested ahead of them, casting eerie shadows on the trees. A tolling bell began to resonate through the woods, its reverberations slicing through the thick silence like a spectral echo.

"What is that?" Tristan asked, his voice barely more than a hushed murmur.

"That's what happens when someone enters the

Dreamworld," Aurora explained. "I'll have to handle this before we continue. Hold on tight."

He tightened his arms around her waist even more as Midnight galloped into the dark mist. The cold air tickled Tristan's cheeks as they emerged from the shadowy veil, leaving him momentarily disoriented. The sun had vanished, plunging the Dreamworld into an eerie nocturnal state. Above them, a full moon cast its silvery glow on a moonlit clearing, painting everything in shades of silver and green.

Aurora's head swiveled from side to side, scanning the surroundings in search of something. "Where is it?" she asked, her voice a soft murmur in the hushed stillness.

Tristan's brows knitted together in confusion. "Where is what?"

But before he could receive an answer, a piercing scream split the tranquil night air, shattering the silence. His eyes darted toward the source of the sound, his heartbeat quickening.

A young man, clad in navy-blue armor emerged from the dark woods, his face contorted in fear. Gripping a gleaming sword, he fled from an ominous trio of guards in glistening gold armor.

"Midas' men," Aurora hissed, her voice laced

with anger as she swiftly nocked an arrow on her
bowstring.

"Wait!" Tristan called out, but Aurora had
already released her arrow. It sailed through the air
with deadly precision, striking one of the golden-
armored guards squarely in the chest. The man disin-
tegrated into a swirling puff of smoke, just as Tristan
had witnessed in his own nightmare at the castle.
They were illusions.

Aurora didn't hesitate, sending two more arrows
streaking through the moonlit clearing, each hitting
its intended target. The remaining guards vanished
into thin air.

The young man who had entered the Dreamworld staggered to a halt, his breaths coming in
ragged gasps. Recognition dawned on Tristan as he
noticed the seashell engraving on the young man's
armor. He was a soldier from Tristan's army.

"Prince Tristan!" the young man exclaimed, his
voice quivering with a mixture of shock and fear.
"You shouldn't be here, sir! We're losing the battle!
We're losing our men! Go, save yourself!"

Before Tristan could formulate a response, more
screams pierced the air, the ominous tolling of a bell
ringing out incessantly. More soldiers from his army

began materializing in the clearing, one by one, each with a look of terror etched on their faces.

Aurora's voice cut through the chaos. "Wait! Don't run! They're illusions! You have to fight them!" She released a barrage of arrows, each finding its mark in the golden armor. "Stop running!"

Tristan's mind whirled in confusion and disbelief. "These are my men," he muttered, his gaze flitting between the frantic soldiers. "What is happening?"

"Midas got to them," Aurora explained, her words laced with a grim certainty as she continued to unleash her arrows. "When he turns someone into gold, they enter a sleep stasis and wake up here."

The nightmare grew even more chaotic as more of Tristan's men appeared, accompanied by their own harrowing nightmares. Panic and terror gripped the soldiers, causing them to drop their weapons and flee in all directions.

"Don't panic!" Aurora pleaded. "You'll make them stronger!"

"Prince Tristan!" another young man called out. "Run! Save yourself—" His warning was abruptly silenced as a golden sword pierced his chest from behind. The gruesome sight propelled Tristan forward. He leaped off the horse.

"Tristan, don't!" Aurora called out. But it was too late.

In a fit of rage and desperation, Tristan hurled a fallen sword at the soldier responsible for the death of the young man. The blade struck its mark, and the soldier vanished from sight. Tristan retrieved the sword from the ground, slashing at another illusory soldier.

Aurora leaped from her horse, rushing to join him at the center of the clearing. Her voice was frantic and breathless. "We have to go! If you're killed here, you die in reality!"

Tristan, his muscles burning from the relentless fighting, continued to swing the sword with unwavering determination. "I will not leave my men!"

Together, they stood back-to-back, fighting harmoniously amongst the avalanche of illusions. Their swords cleaved through the golden-armored soldiers, but with each enemy vanquished, more seemed to materialize from thin air.

"Tristan!" Aurora yelled, her voice strained from the never-ending battle. "Your men are panicked, frenzied. The illusion is gaining too much strength."

But Tristan refused to relent, his rage fueling his every strike. He watched as his men fell one by one, their fates sealed by the inexorable nightmare. Tristan's vision blurred with a maelstrom of silver and green, each swing of his sword a desperate attempt to protect those who were fighting for his kingdom.

As the final golden-armored soldier vanished, Tristan's frenetic assault slowed, his breaths heavy and labored. He surveyed the aftermath, his eyes filled with a harrowing realization.

All of his men lay defeated, their lifeless forms sprawled across the moonlit clearing. Not one had survived the onslaught.

With trembling hands, Tristan released the sword, allowing it to fall to the ground with a hollow thud. He collapsed to his knees, the physical and emotional toll of the battle sapping all of his strength.

Aurora crouched beside him. "Are you all right?" she asked between ragged breaths.

Tristan couldn't find the words to respond. He was numb, engulfed by a profound sense of failure. His men had not only fallen in their battle with Midas in the real world, but they had also succumbed to the relentless onslaught of their own fears and night-mares in the Dreamworld.

And in both realms, Tristan had proven himself inadequate to protect them. He had failed as their prince, as their leader. He was ill-prepared to ascend the throne, and his army's devastation served as a brutal reminder of his shortcomings.

"Tristan," Aurora began, her voice soft and reassuring, "there were too many of them. You did what you could."

Guilt gnawed at Tristan's soul. While he had sought to escape into the Dreamworld, his men had faced the horrors of reality head-on, laying down their lives for him and his kingdom.

But there was no escaping from the harsh reality of his responsibilities any longer. Tristan had a kingdom to protect, and it was time to confront the source of his despair.

Tristan rose to his feet, his voice a low, resolute rumble. "Show me," he demanded, his gaze locked on Aurora's, "how to defeat that wretched Midas."

*A*urora guided Midnight to slow as they reached a cliff. Tristan dismounted from the horse and went to stand by the edge. Before him stretched a half-built bridge suspended in mid-air, its construction seemingly caught between completion and decay. Tristan's eyes traced the path that led to the other side, where a gleaming golden tower stood tall and proud, its spires reaching toward the heavens.

"This is it," Aurora's voice broke the silence. "If you want to defeat King Midas and bring an end to his tyranny, you must get into that tower."

Tristan's heart quickened at the prospect of discovering the key to Midas' downfall. He turned to face Aurora, his mind swirling with a mix of resolve and uncertainty. "What will I find in there?" he asked.

"The only weapon that can defeat Midas," Aurora said, her stern gaze fixed on the tower. "His deepest, darkest secrets. His secrets lie within the confines of that tower."

"I don't understand," he muttered.

"It's simple. Having that secret in your possession will give you leverage," Aurora explained. "And with that upper hand, you will be able to force him to retreat and take his army with him, and in turn, win the war once and for all."

Tristan stared at the tower, remembering how Ella had talked about entering a golden tower when she came into the Dreamworld. "Is that the same golden tower that Ella came to when she was here?" he asked.

"Yes," Aurora said. "But it was Ella's illusion, so

when she entered the tower, she found her own secrets inside. Remember that the Dreamworld and its illusions adapt to our perceptions."

Tristan thought back to his own illusions in the castle, then all the illusions of his men on the battle-field. His chest ached at the memory, and he shook his head, forcing himself to focus.

"If that is true, then how can we possibly find Midas' secret without him being here?" Tristan asked.

"The Dreamworld is malleable," Aurora explained with a knowing look. "As long as we possess something that belongs to the person whose secrets we seek, their truth may be unveiled to us."

"And what do we have that belongs to Midas?" Tristan asked.

Aurora pulled something out of her pocket. Tristan's gaze fell on a golden ring with an engraving of a bee, held delicately in Aurora's palm. The symbol seemed to buzz with a hidden energy.

"How did you come by this ring?" he asked.

Aurora's face softened, revealing a vulnerability that Tristan hadn't seen before. "I stole it from him many moons ago," she confessed, her voice carrying the weight of past sorrows. "I took it so I could get into that tower. So I could set the women free."

Tristan's mind whirled with a torrent of questions.

"So, it's true?" he asked, struggling to comprehend the depths of the tyrant's wickedness. "Midas... he takes young women and imprisons them in his castle?"

"He took them many years ago," Aurora clarified, her voice tinged with bitterness. "They're grown women now, but still not free to live their lives. He took them from their fathers and collected them like rare trinkets, wielding them as instruments of power and control. By snatching them away from their families, he gained leverage over those who opposed him."

Dread clawed its way up Tristan's spine, mingling with the fire of righteous fury that burned within him. "And what has become of these innocent women? What has he done to them?"

"He has used them as servants, as maids, denying them the freedom they deserve." Aurora's voice grew somber as if she was recounting the horrors of her past. "Locked away within his golden walls, their lives wither away, trapped in an endless cycle of servitude and despair."

A shudder ran through Tristan's body, his fists clenching involuntarily at the mere thought of the atrocities inflicted upon those innocent souls. His gaze met Aurora's, an unspoken revelation passing between them. He understood now the depth of her resolve, the desperation to reclaim what was stolen from her.

"You…" Tristan whispered, his voice soft and careful. "You were one of his prisoners, weren't you?"

Aurora's eyes dimmed, but her voice remained steady. "Since I was a little girl," she confessed, her voice tinged with defiance. "Midas took everything from me, so if there's a chance to dismantle his reign and liberate those who suffer under his control, I will give everything to help you."

In that moment, Tristan knew that he and Aurora were bound by more than mere circumstance. They shared a common purpose, driven by a desire to confront the darkness that had plagued their lives.

Tristan's resolve solidified. Midas' reign of tyranny would end, and Tristan would see to it that all those imprisoned within his golden castle would taste freedom once again.

His heart burned with determination as he turned toward the tower once more. The allure of its mysterious grandeur ignited a flame of resolve within him, an irresistible pull that urged him to uncover whatever secrets would lead to Midas' demise.

"Then what are we waiting for?" he asked, his voice brimming with newfound courage. "Let's go inside and uncover his secret once and for all."

"It's not that simple," Aurora said, her gaze shifting uneasily toward the abyss before them. "The bridge isn't complete." But then her eyes landed on something that drained all blood from her beautiful, porcelain face.

"Aurora…" Tristan whispered, his tone laced with caution. "Are you all right?"

"The bridge…" she murmured, her eyes widened in disbelief. "It's gone."

"What?" Tristan followed her gaze to find that the bridge that had been there only moments ago had disappeared.

"No…" Aurora crumbled to her knees, burying her face in her hands. "No, no, no!"

Tristan knelt beside her and placed a comforting hand on her trembling shoulder. "It's all right," he murmured. "We'll find a way to cross. We won't let the shifting nature of this realm deter us."

Aurora raised her tear-streaked face, her eyes searching his for what seemed like a glimmer of hope. "How?" she asked.

"Didn't you say that this world is malleable, that it adapts to our perceptions?" he asked, his voice brimming with possibility. "Then why can't we will a completed bridge into existence?"

Aurora's brows furrowed, skepticism etching its

way across her features. "If it were that easy, don't you think I would have done that by now? The Dreamworld may be unpredictable, but it does adhere to its own set of rules and logic."

"Perhaps…" Tristan nodded. "But it's worth a try."

Tristan rose to his feet, then extended his hand toward the abyss, envisioning a bridge materializing before him. With every ounce of his being, he willed the illusion into existence, pouring his determination and hope into the haze surrounding them.

"What are you doing?" Aurora asked, shaking her head.

Tristan blew out a breath. "That," he said, pointing toward the space where the previous bridge once stood.

Aurora's breath hitched at the sight before her. There, spanning the distance to the other side, stood a brand-new bridge. It was so resplendent that it seemed to shimmer with a life of its own. The bridge had elaborate carved designs, glinting with hues of gold and silver, its path stretching all the way to the base of the tower.

"You did it…" Aurora breathed as she rose from her kneeling position, her eyes tracing the contours of the bridge. "It's… it's incredible."

Tristan's lips curled into a triumphant smile as he stood beside her. "Shall we?" he asked, extending his hand toward her.

Aurora met his gaze, a fire reigniting within her eyes. With a newfound sense of purpose, she placed her hand in his. Together, they stepped onto the bridge. As they reached the other side, Tristan's eyes fixated on the towering door that guarded the entrance to the golden tower. A surge of anticipation coursed through his veins, urging him to unlock the mysteries that lay within.

He reached out to grasp the doorknob, only to find it locked. He turned to Aurora and found her looking down a deep well in the middle of the yard.

"Find anything?" he asked.

"I'm not sure," Aurora said, the tip of her fingers brushing an engraving etched onto the stone of the well. "I think it's a riddle."

Tristan joined her by the well as she read the engraved words aloud.

"In a golden tower, where secrets reside, A golden coin, a mystery to hide. Whispers abound, in hushed tones they say, The coin holds secrets, concealed away."

Aurora looked at Tristan. "What do you think it means?" she asked.

Tristan wasn't sure, but as he looped the words in

his mind over and over again, only one thought took hold. "Do you have a gold coin with you?" he asked.

Aurora reached into her satchel and pulled out a gleaming gold coin. Without hesitation, she flung it into the depths of the well. In that instant, a rusty, metal box materialized next to the door, its hinges creaking open.

Aurora sprinted toward the metal box, and Tristan followed after her. Eagerly, they peered inside, allowing him to look over her shoulder.

"A gold ring?" She pulled it out and held it up to the sunlight. It was different from the one she had shown him before. The engraving wasn't of a bee.

"May I?" Tristan asked, holding out his hand. Aurora placed the ring in his palm, and he held it up to the light to examine it. It was no ordinary piece of jewelry. It bore the markings of a parchment seal. "There should have been a small parchment roll with this," he said, looking at Aurora. "Could Ella have taken it?"

Aurora shook her head. "No. Ella didn't come here seeking Midas. She wouldn't even have seen any of this."

Confusion knitted Tristan's brows together. "Then who could've taken it if there was no bridge there before?"

Aurora's gaze shifted toward a distant mountain peak. "Someone with wings," she grumbled.

"Who would that be?" Tristan asked.

Aurora's voice carried a hint of annoyance as she uttered, "A vengeful fairy."

He glanced up, and a chill ran down his spine as a dark shadow cast over them, obscuring the light of the sun. Aurora's gaze turned skyward, her eyes widening in alarm.

"The solar eclipse... it's nearly at its apex," she said. "You must go."

Tristan's heart sank. Time seemed to slip through his fingers like grains of sand in an hourglass. His window of opportunity was rapidly closing, and a headlong hike up a treacherous mountain was impossible within the limited time he had.

Aurora placed a gentle hand on Tristan's shoulder. "Don't lose heart," she said, her words carrying the weight of an unspoken promise. "I'll get a head start, and you just meet me when you return."

Tristan's gaze met hers. "How will I find you?"

"Do you trust me?" she asked.

He nodded, acknowledging that if there was anyone he could rely on to complete the task swiftly and efficiently, it was Aurora.

"Here." Aurora pressed a piece of jewelry into

Tristan's hand. It was a golden necklace, fashioned in the shape of a spinning wheel, glinting in the muted light. "Take this. It will create a tethered connection between us. Wear it when you next drink from the sundrop flower, and you will be transported to my location."

Clasping the necklace around his neck, Tristan felt a surge of energy coursing through him, binding him to Aurora.

With one final look, Tristan watched as Aurora mounted her stallion, her figure silhouetted against the darkening sky. The majestic creature leaped forward, its hooves thundering against the stone as they raced back across the bridge.

Tristan took a deep breath, gathering courage. The necklace, Aurora's precious gift, glimmered against his chest, a tangible reminder that she was real.

He propelled himself off the bridge, the Dream-world swirling around him in a kaleidoscope of colors and sensations. As he descended through the veil of dreams, he could feel the pulse of the sundrop flower beckoning him back to the real world.

AURORA

*A*urora immersed herself in the soothing waters of a secluded lake, delicately cleansing her long, golden locks as they gracefully flowed down her back. The sky above hung heavy with brooding clouds, casting a pall of solemnity around her.

"Strange," she murmured, her voice barely audible against the backdrop of rustling leaves. She turned to Midnight. "Why do you think the sky isn't dark today?" she asked. "Tristan isn't here, yet there is light."

Tristan's absence should have dimmed the Dreamworld, but instead, it flickered with an eerie luminescence. A world draped in gloom and gray, yet ablaze with an enigmatic light.

Midnight, with his knowing eyes, turned his head toward her and nudged the bee ring adorning her finger—the gold ring she had stolen from Midas. Aurora considered Midnight's gesture.

"What about my jewelry?" she asked.

As if understanding her question, Midnight gently prodded her chest where her spinning wheel necklace used to rest. Aurora's eyes widened as the realization hit her. "You think it has something to do with Tristan having my necklace? Could it be that the weather is reflecting both of our emotions, even when he is not physically present?"

A soft neigh escaped Midnight's lips, and Aurora sighed. "We uncover more about this realm with each passing day, don't we?"

The horse neighed softly, as if in agreement, his warm breath mingling with the misty air. Aurora waded farther into the cool lakewater, feeling its embrace against her skin as she pondered the intricacies of the world.

Closing her eyes, she relished the tranquil moment, but her mind still churned with relentless questions. Would she have the strength to climb the treacherous mountain peak? Millie, the vengeful fairy, had deliberately chosen that remote location to ensure her solitude, knowing that the Dreamworld fed on the fears and insecurities of those who dared to enter. That made it almost impossible to reach the summit unscathed.

Aurora had attempted the hike numerous times before, only to be ensnared in Millie's cunning traps. The negative energy that plagued Aurora had served as a magnet for disaster, thwarting her progress time and again. Frustrated and battered by failure, she had reluctantly accepted defeat, leaving the fairy to revel in her isolation as she wished.

But circumstances had changed, leaving Aurora with no other choice. Millie stole the parchment, the key to entering the golden tower. Aurora's resolve hardened like steel. She would stop at nothing to retrieve what was rightfully hers.

Aurora also had Tristan, who radiated an aura of positivity and strength that bolstered her own spirit. With his unwavering determination to defeat Midas, perhaps they stood a chance of braving the mountain's path, its dangers diminishing in the face of his optimism.

The stakes were high, and Aurora knew she would have to confront her fears head-on. The climb would demand every ounce of courage she possessed, but the reward—the retrieval of the parchment and defeating Midas—loomed like a beacon of victory in her mind.

Taking a deep breath, Aurora opened her eyes, her gaze steady toward the mountain peak. She should get going so that by the time Tristan came back, they didn't waste his limited time hiking, but instead would arrive wherever Millie was. Perhaps Millie would grant them a fleeting audience, even if only to hear Tristan's voice. The bright energy he brought with him had the potential to sway even the most hardened of hearts. Aurora pushed aside the doubts that threatened to creep in and clung to the possibility, however small.

Aurora dried herself, shedding the lingering droplets of her bath. She then slipped into her leather garment, ensuring that each piece clung to her form with a snug and secure fit. It was a race against time, and she refused to be slowed down by trivialities such as improper garments.

With a graceful stride, Aurora mounted Midnight. The horse seemed to sense the urgency in her movements, and together they set off toward the towering mountain. As they ascended, each breath mingled with the crisp, thin air. The sky overhead darkened, casting an eerie pallor over the landscape.

Unnerving sounds reverberated through the air,

echoing from the depths of shadowed corners. At first, Aurora tried to dismiss them, to focus solely on the uneven terrain. But as the sound grew louder, her senses sharpened, and a chill settled over her like an invisible shroud. The hairs on the back of her neck stood on end.

Aurora urged Midnight to quicken his pace. The horse's muscles flexed beneath her as he broke into a gallop. The thunder of hooves against the rugged terrain echoed through the surrounding silence.

Then a monstrous scorpion, its size rivaling that of a wildcat, lunged from the shadows with a hissing sound and its tail ready to strike. Aurora pulled out her sword, and with a swift thrust, she drove the blade into the creature's heart.

The force of her strike sent Aurora tumbling from her horse, the ground greeting her with an unforgiving impact. Midnight galloped onward, leaving Aurora alone in the dark forest. Gritting her teeth against the pain radiating through her body, she pushed the fallen scorpion aside, then freed her sword from its lifeless corpse.

Just as she rose to her feet, three more scorpions emerged from the shadows, their menacing presence encircling her like vengeful creatures. Panic surged through her, and she fled on foot. Desperation fueled her steps as she raced away from the encroaching predators, every muscle straining in a desperate bid for survival.

Drops of sweat glistened on Aurora's brow, mingling with the streaks of dirt that marred her skin. Each heartbeat hammered in her chest as she fought against exhaustion and fear. With a swift swing of her sword, she severed the tail of one of the scorpions, eliciting a shrill cry before it scampered away. Aurora's foot stumbled on an overgrown root, and she hurtled down a steep slope. Her body jolted with each thud to the ground until she plummeted into the depths of a pit. She groaned as her bruised body ached from the impact. The air grew thick, and panic gripped her heart as she realized she had fallen into a trap.

"No, no, no..." She grasped at the walls, clawing, but the slick surface was of no help. "Midnight!"

Her mind raced, analyzing every possibility. She refused to surrender to the suffocating despair that threatened to consume her. Inch by inch, she clawed her way to the top.

With a final surge of strength, Aurora's fingertips grazed the edge of the pit, her body trembling with exertion. She pulled herself up, her muscles protesting the strain. Breathless and battered, she emerged from the trap.

But then echoes of more scorpions filled the air, and she lost her grip, tumbling back down. She grimaced as a sharp pain shot up her arm. Aurora crawled to the corner and curled into a protective ball, hugging her legs tightly as the menacing sounds of scorpions crawling grew nearer. Fear enveloped her, its icy tendrils snaking around her mind.

She closed her eyes and buried her face between her knees. "Tristan…" she whispered. "Where are you?"

In the depths of her mind, she conjured his image —the warmth of his smile, the gentle strength in his eyes. She visualized his return, knowing with absolute certainty that with his arrival would come light and peace, and she would be safe. It was a conviction that ran deeper than reason, a steadfast belief that filled her with hope even with danger still lurking above.

As thoughts of Tristan invaded her consciousness, a shift occurred within her. The world around her seemed to quiet, its dangers melting away like shadows before the dawn. The scurrying of scorpions vanished, replaced by a tranquil stillness that wrapped around her like a comforting cloak.

In that moment, thoughts of Tristan became a

lifeline, grounding her. The fear that had threatened
to consume her consciousness lost its grip, weakened
by the unwavering strength of her trust in Tristan.

The weight of her burdens momentarily lifted,
and Aurora allowed herself to bask in the serenity
that washed over her. Her heart, once burdened with
fear, now floated with newfound lightness. It was a
fleeting peace, yet within that stolen moment, she felt
an undeniable connection to Tristan.

The air hung motionless, as if nature itself held
its breath, recognizing the significance of that
moment. Aurora's breath came easy, her mind clear
once again, untethered from the worries that had
plagued her only moments ago. In the presence of
Tristan's memory, she not only found peace but also
caught a glimmer of something else—an emotion she
struggled to remember because of the relentless darkness that lived within her.

Hope.

Hope had become a stranger to her, a distant
memory buried beneath layers of despair. Yet, in that
precise moment, its familiar touch brushed against
her spirit.

As if in response to such a delicate awakening, the
sky above brightened, casting a solitary beam of
sunlight into the pit. No bells tolled, which revealed

that the radiant glow had sprung forth from within her.

The glimmer of hope flickered within Aurora, much like a small, fragile ember. It breathed life into the depths of her being, casting its gentle light on the darkest corners of her soul.

TRISTAN

*T*ristan sat in the throne room, surrounded by his advisors who were going through all of the royal matters of the day. After their lengthy meetings, his advisors thrust endless pieces of parchment before him, of which he was expected to read and sign.

The castle bustled with activity, but the movement blurred in his peripheral. He tried to draw a mental portrait of Aurora's face. Her intense, distrusting eyes were the deepest shade of brown. He was certain that he could drown in those eyes. And it would not be a terrible way to die.

Then there was the flush of color staining her cheeks, like strawberries. His fingers flexed as he imagined the touch of her satin skin as he caressed her face. Then there were her lips. The bottom fuller than the upper. Everything about her was a sight for sore eyes.

The palace was abuzz with activity, but Tristan had retreated into the recesses of his own mind. He couldn't muster any enthusiasm for the grand ball preparations or the intricacies of political negotiations. Not while the looming war with Midas was still at full swing. As night descended on the kingdom, he excused himself from the council and retreated to his chamber, his heart pounding with a strange anticipation.

In the solitude of his room, Tristan took the sundrop flower drink from the ledge of his window, the silver glow of moonlight reflecting across the polished surface of his bowl. He carried it to his bed, downing the contents in a single gulp. A wave of serenity washed over him, and a faint smile curled his lips as his limp body sank into the silk sheets. He closed his eyes, welcoming sleep's sweet embrace.

Just as his consciousness began to slip away, a violent jolt yanked him back to alertness. Blinking, he found himself no longer on the familiar shores of his dreams, but within the heart of a dense forest. His heart lurched when he noticed Midnight, Aurora's horse, standing alone and looking almost as confused as he felt. Tristan's fingers found the pendant hanging from his neck, the spinning wheel that had transported him there.

"Where is Aurora?" he murmured to the horse, his hand gently stroking its mane. Midnight huffed and pawed at the ground, as though attempting to convey a message. An uneasy sensation crawled up Tristan's spine. He couldn't shake the feeling that Aurora had ventured into danger alone.

He had to find her.

He started along the winding trail until he came onto a pit trap, its mouth gaping wide open—ready to swallow anything that stepped too close. Taking a deep breath, he planted a firm foot by the edge and peered into it.

"Aurora?" he called out.

"Tristan?"

His eyes widened with relief as he spotted her sitting rather disgruntled at the bottom of the hole. Her golden hair glinted in the sunshine as she looked up at him.

"Is that you?" she asked.

A surge of joy filled Tristan's heart. She was alive, at least. "Yes, it's me. Hold on."

He turned to find Midnight had cantered to his side, the end of a rope hanging in his mouth. *Good horse.* Tristan pulled the rest of the rope from the saddle and wrapped it around a tree trunk, securing it with a tight knot.

"Here," he called down to Aurora, tossing the rope into the pit. "Take this, and I'll pull you up."

The tension in his shoulders eased as Aurora grasped the rope and began to ascend. Tristan gripped the rope tightly, muscles straining as he hauled her out of the pit.

As she emerged, he knelt beside her, placing a reassuring hand on her shoulder. "Are you all right?"

She rolled over, eyeing him with both irritation and relief. "What took you so long?"

Tristan couldn't help but smile. "It's not as if I have a kingdom to run or anything," he teased, offering her a hand.

Aurora allowed him to pull her up. Once on her feet, she slapped the dirt from her pants. "We still have a ways to go," she said.

Curiosity gnawed at him. "What happened down there?"

"Scorpions," she grumbled, her cheeks flushing. "Disgusting creatures."

Tristan suppressed a chuckle. Even in her disgruntlement, she was still beautiful. Yet, as he watched her, he noticed her blush deepening. It wasn't anger but embarrassment that colored her cheeks, and it only made her more endearing.

Aurora's head snapped up, catching his amused expression. "What?"

Tristan shook his head. "Nothing." But he couldn't erase the smile from his lips.

She rolled her eyes but then, to his delight, a smile spread across her face. Her gaze dropped. "Great. I'm making a fool of myself in front of a prince."

Stepping closer, Tristan met her eyes. "Here, I'm just Tristan," he said, his voice soft. "And you could never be a fool in my eyes."

Her gaze held his, and Tristan wished he could discern her thoughts. Was she pleased to see him, or had he become an unwelcome intrusion in her life?

"Thank you," she finally said. "For rescuing me from the pit."

Tristan waved it off. "It's the least I could do considering how you've been helping me."

"Oh, don't thank me yet," she said, blowing out a breath as she walked past him. "You haven't met Millie."

"Who's Millie?" Tristan asked, quickening his pace to keep up with her.

"She's the fairy who stole the parchment," Aurora

said irritably. "And I'm fairly certain she won't give it back without a price."

"What kind of price?" he asked.

Aurora shook her head. "No idea. But I'm sure we'll find out soon enough."

Crows circled the skies above and beads of sweat clung to Tristan's temples as they traversed higher up the mountain. The forest grew denser, the towering trees casting a dappled shade over the forest floor. Patches of sunlight scattered like gold on the ground, contrasting with the eerie stillness that settled over the place, broken only by the distant cawing of crows against the azure sky.

Approaching a gaping chasm, Tristan eyed the vines hanging down from above. They hung like boas, curled around the branches of the unfathomably tall trees. He grabbed one and gave it a firm tug. "Seems secure," he said, looking back at Aurora.

She regarded the vines skeptically, her eyes scanning them as if they were serpents poised to strike. "How can you be sure?" she asked.

Ignoring her doubts, Tristan wrapped the vine around his forearm and swung across with ease. Turning back to Aurora with a triumphant smile on his face, he tossed the vine toward her, then watched as she tugged on the vine one last time.

Aurora took a deep breath and leaped into the air, soaring over the chasm. "See? I told you—" But the vine snapped mid-swing, sending her plummeting. Tristan's reflexes kicked in, and he snagged her hand as she went down. His knees hit the ground to brace against the force.

"Tristan!" she screamed.

"I've got you," he assured her, his grip firm. "I won't let go."

She exhaled shakily, then nodded.

"Come on. Grab onto me," he urged, straining as he pulled her up.

Once she was back on her feet, she staggered forward and landed on him, her weight pinning him to the ground. Their breaths came in ragged gasps as they locked eyes, a charged silence stretching between them. Tristan's hands remained fixed on her hips, fingers pressing into her soft flesh.

Her warmth enveloped him, and for a fleeting moment, he wished he could savor it longer. But then, Aurora blinked and scrambled off him.

"I told you," she grumbled as she brushed dirt from her pants. "Her traps are based on negativity. She knows that's my weakness. These traps are designed to keep me from reaching her."

Tristan got to his feet, patting himself down. "How could traps be based on negativity?"

"I was skeptical of that vine," she explained. "I doubted it. So, it snapped."

He looked ahead at the trail they'd been following. "Then how are we supposed to get to the top?"

"You'll have to lead the way," she replied. "You're positive and hopeful, so... the elements won't turn on you like they will on me. I'll just have to trust you and follow your lead."

Tristan couldn't resist a teasing smile. "And here I thought you brought me along because you enjoyed my company."

That made her smile, and it was like a ray of sunlight breaking through the forest canopy.

"Well, lead the way," Aurora said, gesturing toward the winding trail.

Tristan took the lead. The hike progressed smoothly until they encountered what looked like a wall of thorns. Large thorns crisscrossed over one another, forming an impenetrable barrier that blocked their path.

Stepping back, Tristan assessed the thicket. "May I use your sword?" he asked, extending his hand toward Aurora.

She handed it to him without hesitation.

With a deep breath, Tristan began to cut and chop through the thorns as if their only way out was through that prickly maze. Thorn after thorn fell at their feet, the sharp edges gleaming dangerously.

"Why would this fairy go through all this trouble to keep you away?" he asked, his voice strained by the effort.

Aurora moved cautiously, tracing Tristan's steps to avoid the thorns. "Because I'm the reason she's stuck here," she confessed. "I needed a fairy who could retrieve the sundrop flower and make the drink for me. She warned me of the dangers, but I didn't listen. And now she blames me for getting us stuck here."

"Does she also want Midas' secret?" Tristan asked, glancing over his shoulder at her. "Is that why she took the parchment?"

Aurora hesitated briefly, then shook her head as if dismissing a troubling thought. "She most likely knows I'm helping you. So, she knew I would come looking for the parchment. She took it to get back at me."

"Perhaps she took it to reconnect with you," Tristan suggested. "To entice you to visit her."

"Trust me, I'm the last person she would want to see."

"Does she know what his secret is?" he asked curiously. "Perhaps we might not even need to get into the tower."

"We'll need to get into that tower," she said firmly. "There's no way around it."

Tristan kept cutting the thorns. "Do you even know what to look for?"

Aurora's expression grew pensive. "I'm not entirely sure, but I have a feeling it has something to do with his ability to turn things into gold."

Tristan had heard of the phenomenon and witnessed the aftermath of Midas' touch in countless destroyed villages. But he had never seen it with his own eyes. "Has he ever demonstrated his power in front of you?"

She nodded gravely. "Many times."

"How does it work?" he asked, partly horrified, partly fascinated. "Is it truly everything he touches?"

"It's everything his *blood* touches," she clarified.

"So, we're hoping his secret is connected to his powers?" Tristan asked, pondering the implications of their mission.

"If we can't uncover the source of his power, we might find a way to neutralize it."

"And free you," Tristan added.

Aurora's eyes saddened. "I'm afraid it's too late for me."

"Nuh-uh. No negativity, remember?" Tristan chided gently as he cut through the final layer of thorns barring their way. As much as he relished the Dreamworld, the idea of Aurora leaving that realm warmed his heart. He clung to the belief that she was merely sleeping in a hidden corner of his world, waiting to be awakened.

"Can I ask you a question?" Aurora asked.

"Sure," he replied, handing her sword back to her.

"Your nightmare was a wedding. Why?"

Tristan hadn't thought about it since. "I'm being pressured to find a wife, and marrying without love isn't something I ever thought I would do."

"Who's pressuring you?" she asked.

"I made a deal with Rumpelstiltskin," he confessed. "It was a trap, and I fell right into his snare."

"What kind of deal?" she asked, genuinely curious.

Tristan frowned. "If I die without an heir to the throne, my kingdom will become his. If my father were still alive, I would already be married."

"What are you waiting for?" Aurora asked, her voice almost hesitant.

Tristan glanced at her, wondering the answer

himself. But he knew the answer. He'd always known the answer. "True love," he said simply. Then he continued on his way.

They resumed their way in silence, the rhythmic huffing of their breaths and the occasional snap of twigs under their boots the only sounds around them. The forest's secrets hung heavy in the air as they ascended the mountain.

Finally, as they reached the mountain's summit, they came face to face with a petite fairy. Her narrow hips and dainty hands made her appear almost fragile. A cascade of purple hair framed her face, and her beady eyes sparkled with a mischievous glint. She was adorned in garb fashioned from green leaves and yellow petals, and behind her, a humble wooden hut nestled between two towering oak trees. A wreath of pinecones and roses hung on the front door.

"Welcome to my humble abode," Millie greeted them, her voice a curious blend of warmth and hostility. Tristan tilted his head, studying her carefully. Despite her apparent capriciousness, there was an undeniable childlike aura about her.

Tristan leaned closer to Aurora and whispered, "She doesn't look so scary."

"Don't let her fool you," Aurora whispered back. As she took a cautious step forward, a sudden snap pierced the air. In an instant, a net sprang up from the ground, ensnaring her and leaving her suspended from a nearby tree.

Millie skipped forward, her demeanor switching between amusement and annoyance. She settled beside Tristan, her gaze shifting between him and the dangling Aurora.

"Why, hello, old friend," she chirped, her attention now solely on Aurora. "Long time no see."

AURORA

*D*angling from the net, Aurora glared at Millie as she grinned from below, her vibrant purple locks shining with the reflection of the solar eclipse, which hadn't yet reached its apex.

"You must be starving," she said, placing a gentle hand on Tristan's shoulder. "Please, come inside. Have something to eat."

She guided Tristan toward her hut. Aurora's gaze darted toward the open door, catching a whiff of savory pot roast wafting through the open windows. The tantalizing aroma teased her senses and fueled a growl deep within her stomach.

A moment later, Tristan returned with a knife in hand. With a swift stroke of the blade, he sliced through the net's entangled threads, setting Aurora free.

She tumbled toward the ground, bracing for impact. But before her body could collide with the hard earth, strong arms wrapped around her, enveloping her in a protective embrace. Tristan's grip tightened, his touch grounding her.

Flutters coursed through her veins like wild butterflies as she looked up, meeting his concerned gaze.

"Are you all right?" he asked.

"Y-yes," Aurora said, her voice barely audible.

Once he lowered her to the ground, she wriggled from his arms and brushed off invisible dirt from her clothes because she had no idea what else to do with her hands.

"We should…" She motioned toward the opened cottage door. With her mind refocused, a surge of frustration propelled her forward and she stormed into Millie's home.

The fairy was standing over a table, arranging the settings for supper, seemingly unperturbed by their visit.

Impatience tinged Aurora's voice. "Where is it?" she demanded.

Millie's gaze remained fixed on her task. With a

touch of indifference, she replied, "Does this table meet your expectations? Forgive me, for I have long been without the pleasure of company."

Aurora's tone softened, her frustration dwindling at the double meaning in Millie's words. She sounded just as lonely then as she did the last time they'd spoken. "Just give us the parchment, Millie, and we'll be on our way."

"*We*." Millie's words were laced with a familiar bitterness. "Always dragging people down with you, I see. You haven't changed a bit."

A pang of hurt resonated within Aurora. "That's not fair."

"What's not fair," Millie's voice grew stern, "is dragging your friend to a mountain's peak, then denying him food. Now, have a seat." Her tone brooked no argument.

With a heavy heart, Aurora sank into a chair. Tristan settled beside her. Aurora could feel the tension crackling in the air as she and Millie engaged in a bitter exchange. Candlelight flickered between them as they sat across from each other, their faces mirroring the loneliness within their hearts.

"Millie—"

"It's because of you that I'm stuck here," she spat, her voice dripping with resentment. "Because of your meddling, I will never fulfill my dreams of having a family, of being a mother to eleven beautiful children."

The accusations flew like arrows on a battlefield, and Aurora winced at the sting of each word.

Tristan leaned forward, his voice soft. "If you didn't want to help her, why didn't you simply show her how to make the drink on her own?"

Millie's eyes flashed with anger. "Because I wasn't given that option. She didn't afford me the opportunity to be anything but her accomplice."

Aurora winced again, memories of that time flooding back into her mind like a tsunami.

"I was blackmailed," Millie continued. "My family's heirloom was taken and threatened to be destroyed if I didn't assist her."

Aurora felt the weight of guilt settle on her shoulders as she listened to Millie's words. It had been a desperate move, and one she'd wished had never happened.

"I've already apologized for everything I've done, Millie. I know it doesn't change what happened, but I truly am sorry."

"No apology in the world will change the fact that we are stuck here forever," she hissed, her words cutting through the air like a sharpened blade.

As silence settled upon the room, the weight of their unspoken truths threatened to suffocate them both.

"There must be a way to escape, even after time runs out," Tristan said, his eyes darting between the two women. "Millie?"

The fairy's eyes narrowed, her lips curling into a bitter smile. "Even if there were, I would never divulge it to her," she replied. "She is untrustworthy, and I have no intention of aiding her ever again."

"It's me who needs your help," he said, his eyes meeting Millie's.

Curiosity sparked in the fairy's eyes as she tilted her head, intrigued by the change in focus. "You? What could you possibly need from me?" she inquired.

"King Midas has come against my kingdom." Tristan went on to paint vivid images of Midas' insatiable thirst for power, his relentless conquests that left the land scarred and its people oppressed. He spoke of the innocent lives that were torn apart, of the cries of despair that echoed through the ravaged towns.

"I have a duty to protect my kingdom, and my only hope lies inside that golden tower. But we can't enter without the parchment," he said.

Aurora watched as Millie's expression shifted

from curiosity to surprise. Tristan's words seemed to awaken something within her, like a dormant ember of interest flickering to life. "You intend to stop Midas?" she murmured.

Tristan nodded. "Yes. If we can find a way to eliminate Midas' golden touch, we can weaken his power and protect my kingdom."

Millie's eyes widened, amusement swirling within them. "Aurora is helping you *kill* Midas?"

"No one said anything about killing him." Aurora's tone was low but firm. "Uncovering Midas' secret will simply give Tristan leverage to stop the war. He seeks a peaceful resolution, not bloodshed."

Millie studied Aurora, her gaze piercing through the layers of doubt and mistrust between them. "If I were to help you," she said cautiously, "I have a condition."

"Anything," Tristan hurried to say.

But Aurora didn't respond. Instead, she stared Millie down as though they were competing on who blinked first.

"No more manipulations. No more using people as a pawn in your schemes," Millie said with an air of defiance. "Tell Tristan the truth."

Aurora's heart dropped to her stomach at Millie's

demand, and a tense silence settled on them, hanging heavy in the air.

"We don't need your help," Aurora spoke through clenched teeth. "All we need is for you to give back what you stole."

Millie flashed a sarcastic smirk. "Well, I have learned from the best."

"Millie, please," Tristan interjected. "I understand that there's bad blood between you two, but in the end, we all share the same goal."

Millie's laughter rang out, a bitter and hollow sound that reverberated in the room. "Bad blood," she scoffed, her eyes glinting toward Aurora with a touch of amusement. "If only he knew the irony of his words."

Aurora could sense Tristan's gaze darting between her and Millie, searching for some sort of clarity, but Aurora couldn't bring herself to meet his gaze.

"Why don't we shift our focus toward our common goal?" he continued. "We all want to defeat Midas."

"Except, that's not what Aurora wants," Millie blurted out, her voice sharp. "In fact, she couldn't care less about what happens to Midas because she knows she's never getting out of here."

Tristan's brows furrowed, and he turned to

Aurora, his eyes imploring her for an explanation. "What is she talking about?" he asked.

Aurora's silence lingered, a heavy weight tensing her muscles. She grappled with the decision to reveal the truth, knowing that it would irrevocably alter the course of their plans.

"A little word of advice, Tristan," Millie said, a glimmer of warning shining in her eyes. "If you continue to blindly believe everything she says, you're destined for a tragic end. They always do."

Aurora shook her head, unable to recognize the fairy who had once been her friend. "When did you develop such a mean streak?"

Millie's lips curved into a bitter smile as she picked up a dagger from the table, twirling it with a calculated grace. "Loneliness has a way of shaping a person. You should know that better than anyone."

Aurora's heart sank, the memories of her past eroding her resolve. She fought to regain her composure, unwilling to be consumed by the darkness that threatened to swallow her sanity. "Just because I have my own reasons for pursuing that secret," Aurora hissed, "doesn't mean Tristan won't be able to wield it to his advantage as well."

Millie's eyes narrowed. "Why are you filling his head with false hope? You and I both know that you're the only one capable of getting close enough to Midas to truly defeat him," she argued. "If Tristan so much as breathes a word of blackmail to Midas, he'll be turned into a lifeless statue of gold and sent right back here with no hope of return."

"You underestimate him," Aurora insisted. "He possesses a strength that surpasses all of our expectations."

Millie's response was firm, her gaze unwavering. "He still deserves to know the truth."

Tristan rested his elbows on the table. "You don't have to talk like I'm not here, you know?"

Millie's grip tightened around the dagger still in her hand, her gaze shifting toward Tristan. "Fine," she replied with a dismissive shrug. "If you insist."

Aurora's muscles tensed as she stared at the dagger. "What are you doing?" she asked.

The fairy's indifference sent shivers down Aurora's spine. "What? He's as good as dead anyway," Millie said callously.

At that, the fairy hurled the dagger toward Tristan's chest. Time seemed to slow as panic seized Aurora's mind. Acting on instinct, she reached out, her hand closing around the blade just before it could pierce Tristan's skin. Pain radiated through her palm as the sharp edge sliced into her flesh, but her grasp prevented the knife from reaching his beating heart.

Blood dripped from Aurora's hand, the crimson droplets pooling onto Tristan's plate. Tristan's eyes stretched wide, his body frozen in shock.

Then, it happened.

The plate before him transformed into solid gold. He glanced toward the dagger, still clutched in Aurora's bloodied hand, only to find it had undergone the same transformation. "Are you…?"

Aurora blew out a defeated breath. "King Midas' daughter. Yes."

Her gaze then locked onto Millie with a piercing glare as the golden hue shimmered in the candlelight.

The fairy's smile grew wide as her features relaxed. "Would anyone like dessert?"

TRISTAN

*T*ristan's mind whirled, struggling to grasp the enormity of what he'd just discovered. He rose from his seat, a mix of astonishment and anger twisting his features. He turned his gaze from the golden plate to Aurora, searching for answers within her eyes.

But she was too busy digging into her satchel. Pulling out a jar of honey, she drank from it. Then she took a sheepskin bottle and a cloth from the table. After pouring the liquid on the cloth, which Tristan assumed was some kind of medicine, she wrapped it around her bleeding hand. To Tristan's surprise, the cloth did not transform into gold. Instead, a blotchy crimson stain spread across the white material.

The fairy's laughter echoed through the room. "Oh, how fate has twisted your paths," Millie mused, her voice dancing with a mock fascination. "The daughter of Midas and his enemy, united by destiny's cruel hand. Long live the king's legacy."

Aurora's gaze hardened. "If you think I will succumb to the same desires that consumed my father, then you've never known me at all."

Millie twirled a purple strand of her hair between her fingers. "Oh, my dear, how noble your intentions may be, in a world where power tempts even the purest of souls, will you truly resist the allure of *absolute* control?"

Instead of responding, Aurora's eyes shifted to Tristan and she frowned. "Tristan—"

He raised a hand to stop her from talking. His head was spinning. He had a million questions, but darkness covered the world outside and he realized that the solar eclipse was almost complete. He had to leave.

"I will be back," he said. "And when I do, I want the whole truth."

Without another word, he went outside to the edge of the cliff. Giving Aurora one last glance, he jumped off.

Tristan shot his eyes open, and as his consciousness returned, he found himself surrounded by towering trees. The familiar scent of earth filled his senses, and the sunlight filtered through the canopy above, casting dappled patterns on the forest floor.

Confusion swept over him like a gust of wind, and he scrambled to his feet. *How did I end up in the middle of the forest?* he wondered. Uneasiness settled in the pit of his stomach as he tried to piece together the fragments of memory that lingered in his mind.

As he pondered the possibilities, a sudden clip-clop of hooves broke through the silence, drawing his attention to a carriage approaching from a nearby path. Two figures emerged from within, their faces obscured by the hood of their cloaks.

"Prince Tristan!" one of them exclaimed. "We have a message for you!"

They climbed down the carriage, then they each pulled out a knife.

Tristan stepped back, alarmed. "Who is the message from?" he demanded, watching the men carefully.

They flashed him a sinister smile. "From Rumpel-stiltskin."

Before Tristan could react, one of the men lunged

forward and pain exploded in Tristan's side. He grunted, a hand instinctively flying to his ribcage. His fingers came away slick with blood, and his vision swam. The attackers attempted to seize him, their grips tightening around his arms.

"Cousin!" Ryke came into view, launching himself at one of the assailants. His iron hook slashed at the man's face, sending him reeling backward.

Tristan, fueled by adrenaline, fought back against the other attacker. With a swift strike, he disarmed the man, his weapon falling to the ground with a thud.

The commotion alerted the prince's guards, and their thundering approach sent the attackers fleeing into the woods, disappearing like shadows in the fading light. Ryke rushed to Tristan's side, supporting him as he swayed unsteadily.

"Easy now, cousin," Ryke said, concern etched on his face. "You're bleeding. We need to get you back to the castle."

Tristan nodded weakly, his vision blurring around the edges. The world spun, and darkness threatened to engulf him. He fought against the encroaching unconsciousness, clinging to Ryke's shoulder. But Tristan could feel his mind slipping. He was mentally drained and he wondered if it was because of his extended stay in the Dreamworld.

As the prince's guards arrived, their shouts of alarm were muffled in Tristan's ears. Finally, he succumbed to the pull of darkness, his body slumping against Ryke's supporting frame.

When Tristan awoke, he found himself in the comforting embrace of his own bed within the castle walls. Sunlight streamed through the stained glass windows, casting colorful hues across the room. He groaned, gingerly touching his bandaged side.

Then his eyes focused on the figure seated next to him, and he blinked away the remnants of sleep to see Ryke holding the basin with the sundrop flower. The fragrant scent of the flower drifted through the air, adding a touch of tranquility to the space.

"What is this, cousin?" Ryke asked, peering into the bowl to inspect the flower.

Tristan wanted to reveal the truth behind the flower and its connection to the Dreamworld, but he didn't think Ryke would understand. How could he explain the relentless pull of the Dreamworld and the secrets that awaited him there? How could he convey his need for answers?

"It's just a remedy to help me sleep," Tristan replied evasively.

Ryke placed the basin carefully back onto the table, his expression still tinged with suspicion. Still, he didn't press the matter further. Instead, he shifted his attention to Tristan's wound.

"You know," Ryke began, his voice heavy with concern, "I've noticed you've been sleepwalking lately. And in the past few nights, it's become more frequent. Have you considered that this substance you've been consuming might be the cause? They could be affecting your rest and leading to these episodes."

Tristan had no idea he'd been sleepwalking. That would explain how he'd woken up in the forest instead of in his room.

"What happened today was a close call," Ryke continued. "Rumple will not rest until he takes your life. You have to be more careful."

Tristan's gaze dropped to his hands, his fingers unconsciously tracing the edge of the bandage. The weight of his actions bore down upon him, but it was a burden he had to carry alone. "I appreciate your concern, cousin. There are... complexities I can't fully explain. But rest assured, I will address the matter."

"I trust that you will," Ryke conceded, his frown easing. "Just remember, I am here to offer my support in whatever way you need."

A knock came from the door, and a moment later a servant entered the room.

"The tailor has arrived," the servant announced. It seemed that the suit fitting for the upcoming ball demanded Tristan's immediate attention. "They're eager to ensure you make a resplendent appearance at the ball, sir."

Confusion clouded Tristan's thoughts. "The ball? But that isn't for another few days."

Ryke shook his head. "No, cousin. The ball is tonight. The court has been buzzing with the preparations for days."

A jolt of apprehension surged through Tristan's veins, his heartbeat quickening with the realization of his oversight. How had he lost track of time? The Dreamworld had drawn him deeper into its depths, blurring the boundaries of reality.

"Tonight…" Tristan whispered. "The ball where I must find a wife… is tonight."

The allure of the Dreamworld tugged at his every thought, beckoning him to return. He wanted to go back and confront Aurora about her secrets. Yet, duty called, a royal ball that was put in place so as to save his life, as well as his kingdom. Finding a wife would mean having offspring, and as soon as his child came into this world, his contract with Rumpelstiltskin would be nullified. His kingdom was counting on him.

"Very well," Tristan sighed. "Let us proceed with the fitting, then."

Before long, Tristan was standing in front of a full-body mirror. The tailor's deft hands moved swiftly, adjusting the suit fabric around Tristan's frame. However, his mind remained consumed by thoughts of Aurora and the secrets she'd kept from him. She was Midas' daughter. His enemy. Betrayal simmered within him, an ember of hurt lodged in the pit of his stomach.

"Tristan?" Ryke's voice cut through Tristan's thoughts. "I've been talking to you, but it seems you've been elsewhere. Are you all right?"

Tristan snapped back, his eyes refocusing on Ryke's concerned face. He offered a half-hearted smile, his mind still entangled with thoughts of Aurora. "Forgive me. My mind has been preoccupied lately. I'm all right, truly. What were you saying?"

Ryke's features softened, his concern morphing

into a thoughtful expression. "Are you nervous about tonight?" he asked. "About finding a wife?"

Tristan looked deeply at his reflection in the mirror. "A king must do what a king must do," he murmured. "But I do not wish to burden you with my troubles. This must be a joyful occasion, and I will be sure to make it so."

Ryke beamed. "You make a great king, Tristan. And I am positive you will find a great queen to stand by your side."

"Thank you, cousin."

"Now, since you mentioned making the ball a joyous occasion, I was wondering…" Ryke ran a hand through his hair. "Would you consider asking Lexa to sing at the ball? Her voice has a way of enchanting the crowd, and I believe it would make your ball all the more special."

"That's a splendid idea," Tristan replied. "I will extend the invitation to her. Thank you."

As the tailor made final adjustments to the suit, Ryke dropped his gaze to the floor and ran a hand through his black hair. "Also… I'll be leaving in the morning," he said. "The ball will be our last evening here for a while."

Tristan frowned, but he wasn't entirely surprised. "I figured the day would come sooner or later," he admitted. "This kingdom is my responsibility. It wouldn't be right to keep you from living your life, to carry a load I must bear alone."

Ryke touched his cousin's shoulder. "No matter the distance between us, our bond remains unbreakable. Besides, I trust you to make the right decisions. You'll find your path, just as I have found mine. For now, I want to be here to support you in your pursuit of finding our next queen."

Tristan's heart swelled with gratitude. He cherished the loyalty and love Ryke had always shown him. With a nod, he acknowledged the strength of their bond. "Your presence at the ball means the world to me."

The tailor stepped back, surveying his work with a critical eye. The suit, now perfectly tailored, seemed to embody the weight of Tristan's responsibilities and the choices that lay before him.

*L*ater that night, Tristan stood in the grand ballroom, his eyes scanning the elegant crowd that filled the space. The air buzzed with excitement and the murmur of hushed conversations. Chandeliers bathed the room in a warm glow, casting flickering lights on the marble floor. Velvet drapes adorned the walls, their deep blue color a stark contrast to the shimmering gowns and polished suits of the guests.

But because Tristan was still angry with Aurora for lying to him, the notion of finding a wife at the ball didn't seem as burdensome as it once had. Perhaps, he mused, he could bury himself in the pursuit of love and forget about the Dreamworld forever. Maybe he should let Aurora keep her lies, her world, and the shattered remnants of his heart.

The thought lingered as he found himself needing fresh air. He made his way outside and walked toward the castle's gardens. Stepping onto the cobblestone path, his footsteps were barely audible beneath the soft whispers of the evening breeze. As he wandered, his gaze fell on a patch of vibrant flowers. Among them bloomed the sundrop flower, its golden petals dancing in the fading sunlight. Wendy must've brought the flower's root with her and planted them in the garden to keep them alive.

Tristan's mind shifted back to Aurora, recalling their fleeting moments together on top of the castle's roof. She had spoken of the weight of a father's control, of the suffocating grip that Midas had held over her life. Tristan couldn't fathom what it would be like to have someone like Midas as a father, a ruler whose legacy was shrouded in darkness.

Questions brewed within Tristan's mind, intertwining like vines. How long had he left his own daughter trapped in that desolate realm alone? Was she merely a pawn in Midas' cruel game? Was she, too, a victim of his insidious machinations?

A flicker of doubt tugged at Tristan's heart, but he clung to the hope that not everything Aurora had shared with him was a lie. Her words had resonated with a raw honesty, a passion that seemed to bleed from her very soul. When she'd spoken of freedom, her eyes ignited with a hopeful fire, as if she had glimpsed a realm beyond the confines of her prison. And when she'd spoken of rescuing the girls stolen by Midas, her voice held an unwavering determination that could not have been merely to manipulate him.

Tristan knew that there was only one way to uncover the truth. He had to return to the Dreamworld, to face Aurora and peel back the layers of deception that she'd laid between them. But most importantly, he needed to find out what was inside that tower. That was the only way he would be able to defeat Midas, and that plan hadn't changed.

War still loomed over his kingdom like a dark

cloud. Time was slipping through Tristan's fingers like grains of sand in an hourglass, each passing moment amplifying the weight of his choices. The future of his people depended on him finding a solution, but deep within, he knew that unraveling Aurora's truth was an integral part of that puzzle.

AURORA

*A*urora's gaze fixated on the crackling flames, her wounded hand held close to her chest. The sting of Tristan's reaction lingered in her mind, etching itself into her very being. The shock that flickered in his eyes, the revulsion that twisted his features—it was as if a dagger had been thrust into her heart. But what troubled her most was the uncertainty of his emotions. Was he angry at her for withholding the truth, or did his animosity stem from her connection to the very man who was burning down his kingdom? Would he think that she was in cahoots with her father? That she had kept him distracted and away from his kingdom so her father could keep conquering more of Tristan's land?

A knock came from the door, its sound echoing

through the cottage. With cautious curiosity, Aurora rose from her seat and approached the door. As she swung it open, her breath caught in her throat.

Tristan stood before her, attired in regal garments. The sight of him ignited a whirlwind of emotions within her, stealing the very air from her lungs. Relief, longing, and a torrent of unspoken words hung between them. He looked every bit the prince he was, his presence commanding attention and igniting a flicker inside her heart.

Inviting him in, Aurora stepped aside, her gaze unable to leave Tristan's striking figure as he crossed the threshold. The subtle scent of his cologne mingled with the comforting warmth of the crackling fire flooding her senses. Silence settled between them, heavy with the weight of unanswered questions.

Tristan's eyes roamed the room, taking in the modest furnishings and the flickering flames dancing against the walls. Aurora watched him, wondering what was going through his mind. Did he expect a castle, a dwelling befitting the daughter of a king? She knew all too well that she was far from a princess.

That fact had never troubled her before, but in that moment, as she observed Tristan's royal attire and perfectly coiffed hair, a pang of sadness tugged at her heart. He seemed out of place in that humble setting, a bitter reminder of the contrasting worlds they inhabited.

She waited, her gaze yearning for Tristan's eyes to meet hers, to bridge the invisible chasm that had grown between them.

"I... I don't know what to say," Tristan confessed, his eyes searching hers.

Aurora nodded, her heart resonating with the shared sentiment. The weight of their unspoken words echoed louder than any conversation. She held up her injured hand. "I could use some help with wrapping this bandage," she said softly.

Tristan's features softened. He moved closer, his presence bringing a sense of comfort.

Aurora guided him to a seat beside her, then with her other hand, she brought a basin of water with yellow flower petals floating on the surface. She settled it on the small wooden table in front of them. Dipping the bandage into the water, she allowed the petals to infuse their healing essence into the fabric.

Tristan's touch was gentle as he wrapped the bandage around her wound. Each movement carried a tenderness that mirrored the blossoming feelings within her.

As he worked, Aurora's attention turned to a jar of honey resting on the table nearby. She reached for it, dipping into its golden richness before bringing a spoonful to her lips. The sweetness coated her tongue, and she savored the taste.

With a soft sigh, she turned to Tristan. "Honey hastens the healing process," she revealed. "For both my father and for me."

"How come?" Tristan asked.

Aurora shook her head. "I'm not entirely sure. He never explained."

Tristan shifted his attention back to her hand. "Does it hurt?" he asked, his voice gentle.

"Not as much anymore," she replied.

There was a brief pause as Tristan absorbed her response. "So, how did you make it back down the mountain without falling into any traps?" he asked.

"Someone entered the Dreamworld, so I was able to use the fog as a shortcut and leave the mountain peak," she explained.

Tristan nodded as he finished wrapping the bandage around her wounded palm. "Were you able to help them escape?"

Aurora leaned forward, searching for his eyes. "Is that truly what you came here to discuss?" she asked, her words gently pushing beyond the surface of his defenses.

Tristan watched the bandage with a curious gaze.

"How come the bandage is touching your blood but isn't turning to gold?" he asked, a note of genuine curiosity coloring his words.

Aurora wasn't sure where his questions were leading, but it didn't matter. She had decided that she would not keep anything from him anymore. "The water in the basin contains sunflower petals," she answered. "It possesses a unique property that prevents objects from turning to gold. It seems that sunflowers hold a special connection to my powers."

Tristan's eyes sparkled with fascination. "I've heard stories of King Midas and his renowned sunflower gardens at his palace."

Aurora nodded, a wistful smile gracing her lips as memories flickered to life within her mind. "Yes, those gardens were very special to him."

Tristan's voice dipped with curiosity. "I also heard that he would kill anyone who tried to grow their own."

"Only if they took it from his garden," Aurora clarified, then she plucked a single sunflower petal from the bowl and held it up for Tristan to see. The petal shimmered with an ethereal glow, reflecting the flickering fire. "As you can see, these aren't your average sunflowers."

A flicker of realization crossed Tristan's face as he

connected the dots. "Are you saying that your father's sunflowers are from the Dreamworld?"

"Where else do you think my father obtained his golden powers?" she asked, giving him a knowing look. "Many moons ago, my father was an ordinary king, content with a loving wife and a beloved son. But one day, he brought a bag of sunflower seeds for my mother's garden, and she nurtured them into a flourishing field. In time, his blood began turning everything to gold, and he became the most powerful ruler of his time. All of this happened long before I was even born."

"Wait, Midas has a son?" Tristan asked, surprised.

"Yes, he was taken from us when I was just a child," she whispered, her voice heavy with the weight of loss. "He was a victim of someone's vendetta against my father. It was a tragedy that shook our family to its core."

Tristan frowned. "I had no idea."

"After my brother was killed, my father locked me away in a tower, erasing both of our existences from the world," she continued. "He believed he was protecting me from his enemies, but in doing so, he turned me into a prisoner. For many years, I lived in isolation, deprived of freedom."

Tristan's eyes narrowed curiously. "Is that why you came here? To escape?"

Aurora shook her head gently. "No, I came here because the sunflower seeds originated from this place," she clarified. "I had hoped to find a way to break the curse my father passed down to me, to undo the burden that plagues my existence."

"So, you came here seeking something that would strip you of your golden touch?" he asked, his disbelief seeping through his words. "Why would you want that?"

Aurora's expression softened, her vulnerability tethering on the edge. "Growing up as a princess, my deepest desire was to meet a prince and find true love. To live a life filled with happiness, and to bear enough children to fill a castle. But my abilities posed a threat to my father's kingdom. If ever I were to marry outside its borders, it would have to be someone my father deemed worthy of wealth. Soon, I became a transaction of power, and my happiness was no longer of any importance."

Tristan frowned. "I am sorry you had to endure that," he said sincerely. "I can't even fathom what it must have been like for you to go through all of that alone."

"I wasn't completely alone," she confessed.

"Eventually, my father brought girls my age to the castle, ensuring I had companionship. They were the only ones privy to my existence, which meant they were also forbidden to leave. Among them, one girl in particular became my dearest friend. Her name was Rapunzel. She was one of the firsts, enduring the tower's confines for as long as I did."

Tristan's curiosity piqued. "How long did you live in that tower?"

Aurora responded with a humorless laugh. "Let's just say I reached the age when marriage was expected," she replied. "Yet, my father refused to give any other kingdom the power of the golden touch. So, I remained hidden, nonexistent."

Tristan shook his head in disbelief. "And what about in the Dreamworld?" he pressed. "How long have you been trapped here?"

"I honestly don't know," she admitted. "Time holds no meaning in this realm. There are no sunrises or sunsets, only an eternal darkness that encases everything."

As Tristan fell silent, Aurora found herself drawn to his gaze once more. "I'm sorry I didn't reveal my true identity to you," she said softly.

"Why didn't you?" he asked.

"Given what happened to my brother, I didn't

believe it would be wise to disclose that I am related to the most despised man alive," she explained. "I also feared that if you didn't find your leverage within that tower, you would end up using me instead."

Tristan narrowed his eyes. "Did you truly think I would stoop to such actions?"

"A king's duty is to his kingdom above all else," she said, remembering her father's words. "There are times when one must make sacrifices, even if it means sacrificing one innocent life to save the lives of many. It doesn't necessarily make him a bad person, but rather a strong ruler."

"Well, that is not the kind of king I aspire to be," he said.

A gentle smile played on Aurora's lips. "I know that now."

"You do?" Tristan's voice carried a hint of surprise.

"I don't trust easily," she confessed, her words spoken with raw honesty. "But the Dreamworld doesn't lie. It reflects the true essence of a person, and I see the goodness in you."

Tristan's eyes bore into hers, his gaze searching for truth within the intricate web of emotions between them. "I'm glad you trust me, but can I trust *you?*" he asked.

Aurora nodded. "With your life."

She then watched as Tristan reached into his pocket and pulled out a small parchment. Her eyes widened. "Is that...?" she trailed off, her voice filled with hope.

"Millie gave it to me while you were trapped in the net," he explained. "She made me promise not to say anything until the end of the dinner."

Aurora couldn't blame him for not having told her. She hadn't been honest with him either.

"So, now what?" Tristan asked curiously.

Aurora took the parchment and carefully unrolled it. The page was blank.

Tristan leaned closer to get a better look at the paper. He scowled. "That fairy deceived us!"

"No, she didn't," Aurora responded, her voice calm and assured. "The message is hidden."

With that, she stood and dropped to her knees by the fire. She held the paper over the flickering flames of her fireplace, watching as the edges turned black, revealing the hidden words written in a fiery red glow. The lines formed a poem.

With venom's kiss and golden hum,
Scorpions guard while bees gently strum.
For dreams within dreams, a puzzle concealed,
Unlocking secrets yet to be revealed.

· · ·

ith pincers poised and tails upright,
     A cryptic secret it keeps from sight.
In scorpion's realm, and buzzing bee,
Unlock the riddle, and set it free.

Aurora stared at the poem, her mind stumped with its cryptic message.

Tristan crouched next to her. "What does it mean?" he asked.

"I'm not sure," she admitted, tapping a finger to her lips. "But perhaps we can make more sense of its meaning once we return it to the tower."

Tristan's eyes lowered to his intertwined fingers. "I will not be accompanying you this time," he said, his words carrying a weight of responsibility. "There is a ball I must attend tonight."

"What kind of ball?" Aurora couldn't help her curiosity.

Tristan pressed his lips to a tight line as if not wanting to push the words out. "A royal ball where I must find a wife."

A sickening feeling twisted in the pit of Aurora's stomach as the reality of their different worlds sank in. Still, the thought of Tristan with another woman stirred a pang of dread within her, yet she swallowed her feelings, masking them as best she could.

Her voice softened as she found her words. "Thank you for your assistance with my hand," she said, averting her gaze to the flames dancing in front of them.

"I—" Tristan's words were cut off by the distant sound of a bell tower echoing through the air, its mournful toll reverberating within Aurora's chest.

Time was slipping away, and Tristan had his own path to follow. Their eyes locked for a lingering moment, both reluctant to part ways.

Finally, Tristan stood. "I hope you find what you're seeking inside that tower," he said in a gentle voice. "Goodbye, Aurora."

As he walked out the door, a hollow emptiness settled within Aurora's heart, leaving her feeling more alone than ever before.

TRISTAN

*T*he ballroom had been utterly transformed by scores of Tristan's servants and maids. Soft organza in colors of blue and gold swept along the walls, reminding Tristan of the sea meeting the setting sun.

Brilliant bouquets of white lilies and marigolds adorned the long banquet tables. And the food was in abundance. There were more glazed rolls and fine meats than could possibly feed the guests.

Tristan found Wendy in the crowd and nodded to the food. "Have the servants hand out the leftovers to the people in the nearby villages once the ball is over."

Wendy's eyes shined back at him before she gave

a nod of understanding. Then she disappeared in a sea of swishing ball gowns.

Ryke appeared at Tristan's side, dressed in his finest garment. His neatly-trimmed beard along with his regal attire made him appear nothing like the pirate that he had become. To any onlooker, they were two princes, standing side by side.

The thought gave way to the stark realization that this moment was fleeting, and soon, his cousin would be leaving him alone in the cold castle.

"Isn't she beautiful?" Ryke asked, pulling Tristan out of his head. He followed Ryke's gaze to Lexa standing beside the musicians. Her long, black hair fell over one shoulder and sparkled like the night sky in the candlelight.

When she began to sing, everyone stopped musing and turned to watch, enchanted by her melodic voice.

"Indeed," Tristan affirmed. "Lexa is looking lovely as ever. But I think I should be looking at the other ladies in the room, not your wife."

Ryke shoved Tristan playfully, then rose a champagne flute to his lips. "Does anyone catch your fancy?" he said, his eyes sweeping around the room.

Tristan scanned the sea of faces. Many rosy-cheeked women swayed, their fine gowns flowing like flowers in the wind. The motion reminded Tristan of the way the forest plants seemed to sway in the Dreamworld. The fragrant flowers flooded his nostrils in delight. He mentally shook himself and tried to focus on the task at hand.

He was not to think of the Dreamworld. He lived in the real world. With an incredibly important duty to fulfill. He had to be present and do justice to his future wife.

His gaze landed on a woman with long, golden hair pinned to the back of her head. Her locks fell in a mass like a pony's tail, and it curled at the very bottom. The woman had her back to him, and she stood tensely. Tristan ventured through the crowd, eager to reach her. But when he touched her elbow and she spun around, a pair of dull blue eyes blinked at him. His heart sank.

Of course, it wasn't Aurora. He could not understand why even a small part of him wondered if it was. *Hoped* it was.

He forced a smile. "May I have this dance?" he asked, holding out his hand with a bow.

"Why, of course, Your Royal Highness." The woman curtsied. "I shall be most honored to accompany you."

The two danced stiffly and out of sync. It took all

of Tristan's resolve not to stumble on the woman's toes, and her imposing orange gown almost had him trip on more than one occasion.

"How do you find the ball, my lady? Does the music please you?" he asked, trying to break the awkward silence between them.

The woman shrugged and made a strange sound that reminded Tristan of a mouse. "The music is fine enough, but the drinks are less to be desired. The first thing I shall do when I am queen is send whoever is in charge of the wine to the gallows."

Tristan stiffened, bringing their dance to a halt. For a moment, he stood frozen, unsure of what to do next.

"Something wrong, Your Highness?" she said the words as though they took great effort.

Tristan let her hands drop and stepped away. "Thank you for the lovely dance," he said, tilting his head ever so slightly.

As the night went on, more women filled the dance floor. But each one left him more frustrated and annoyed. He found flaws in all of them. Some of them were deserving of his harsh judgments. Especially the ones who acted spoiled and entitled. But there were a few friendly ones who remembered their manners and danced with grace. But even the meek, quiet ones had Tristan wishing he could retreat back to his chambers alone.

He thought up all kinds of unreasonable objections. One was too short, another too tall. Some hair was too curly, others too smooth. A few had beautiful blonde braids, but they smelled of spice instead of flowers.

None of that should have mattered, but it did. And if he was being honest with himself, he knew who he was searching for.

Tristan stopped by the drinks table and gulped down an entire goblet of wine. Unsure of whether it had been the drink or not, he had a moment of clarity. None of those women would do because none of them were *her*.

Gritting his teeth, he shook himself. To indulge in such thoughts was unproductive. Aurora was not at the ball. She was in the Dreamworld, and even if she had been there, she was still the daughter of his enemy.

His father's face surfaced in his mind's eye, accompanied by the all-too-familiar pang of grief. He wondered what his father would do in his position, and the answer came in an instant. He would do his duty. The purpose of that ball was to find a queen for his kingdom—for his people—so Tristan would dance with every single maiden in the room until he found her.

"What a fine piece of gold, Your Royal Highness," a soft-spoken brunette said as he danced with her. She was extravagant in looks, but to Tristan, she had quickly become just another woman with no distinguishable qualities. "Did someone special gift that to you?"

Tristan followed her gaze to the small golden spinning wheel hanging around his neck. He was still wearing the necklace Aurora had given to him.

Memories of that day flooded his mind, along with a forbidden thought. If he were to use the locket to enter the Dreamworld in that very moment, he would wake up wherever Aurora was. *Where would that be?* he wondered. *What was she up to?* Soon, he found himself wondering if it would be possible to slip out of the ballroom and go to her.

But his father's voice entered his mind, and his stomach knotted.

Your priority is to your kingdom. Nothing else matters.

Tristan forced a polite smile at the woman in his arms. "Yes, my lady. Someone very special indeed." Then his smile fell.

"I'm sorry, my lord. I didn't mean to pry…" the

woman added, picking up on Tristan's change in mood.

"No apology necessary," he said, putting on his regal mask once more.

The intermingled fragrances of the various women dancing around him made the knot in his stomach twist even tighter. Still, they continued to dance, exchanging polite remarks on the music and each other's footwork while Tristan's mind spun.

Suddenly, a gut-wrenching realization consumed him. The only way Tristan would be able to find a wife and a queen for his kingdom, was by removing Aurora from his mind completely.

He needed to let her go once and for all.

AURORA

*A*urora rode toward the golden tower, its majestic presence growing larger as she closed the distance. But as she crossed the beach, Midnight slowed to a canter. The sound of crashing waves against the shore filled her with a sense of calmness, then a memory rose from within her mind.

Tristan, waist-deep in the ocean, begging her to hear him out. She couldn't resist the pull to revisit the place where she had once unleashed a lightning bolt to jolt him awake.

She smiled at the memory as the wind whipped through her hair. She looked up at the towering castle, remembering Tristan's nightmare. His wedding to the sea creature. Thoughts of Tristan danced through her mind, and she wondered if he was enjoying the ball. If he'd already found the future queen.

The thought stirred a bittersweet longing within Aurora, but she pushed it away.

Lost in her thoughts, Aurora found herself guiding Midnight to the castle's garden, peering through the window into the darkened ballroom. Her imagination ran wild, envisioning the grandeur and elegance of the scene that was most likely playing in the real world. A part of her, the princess she once was, yearned for the chance to dance at a ball, to feel the exhilaration of being swept away in the arms of a prince. But that life seemed like a distant memory, a fantasy she could no longer grasp.

Turning to leave, the tolling of a bell resonated through the air, capturing Aurora's attention. She gazed around, her eyes searching for the source of the disturbance. A twig snapped behind her, and she spun around to find a figure standing by the garden.

Tristan.

"I thought I would find you at the golden tower, trying to solve the riddle," he said, stepping out from the shadows, the embodiment of regal charm in his royal attire.

Aurora's heart skipped a beat at the sight of him, her cheeks flushing with both surprise and embarrassment. "I... um... I was," she stammered, struggling to find the right words to explain her unexpected detour. "But... I came here... to... well, it's silly, really."

Tristan's eyes sparkled. "Try me," he urged.

Aurora hesitated. "I've always wanted to attend a ball. So, I came here to see if I could... at least imagine one. But I guess it didn't work."

Tristan's warm smile melted her reservations. "Perhaps I can try," he offered, stretching out his hand to her.

Aurora waved off his offer, her cheeks turning even redder. "Oh, no," she protested, shaking her head. "You have a real ball to attend. I couldn't possibly—"

"It won't take long," he insisted. "Indulge me."

His words tugged at her heartstrings, stirring a newfound sense of hope within her. With a deep breath, she finally relented, her gaze meeting his with eager anticipation. "All right," she conceded, dismounting Midnight.

Tristan motioned toward the ballroom, and to Aurora's astonishment, the double doors swung open, revealing a room bathed in a soft, enchanting light.

The air seemed to shimmer with anticipation as the strains of music filled the space. Aurora's eyes widened, captivated by the beauty that unfolded before her.

She took a step forward, but then stopped, her mind whirling. "Wait. What am I doing?" she muttered to herself. "I'm not even dressed…"

Tristan took her hand in his, and in an instant, Aurora found herself swathed in a breathtaking pink and blue ball gown. The fabric caressed her skin, its elegance and grace enveloping her like a second skin. She glanced up at Tristan, her eyes sparkling with wonder.

"How did you…?"

"It's my illusion," he explained. "Come on. Just one dance."

Aurora's heart swelled as she allowed Tristan to guide her into the ballroom. The room, though empty, seemed to come alive with the flickering candlelight and the soft strains of music. The dance floor awaited them, a blank canvas on which their footsteps would paint an ephemeral masterpiece.

Hand in hand, they began to sway to the enchanting melody, their movements harmonizing with the rhythm of their shared dream. They twirled and spun, lost in the magic of the moment. The absence of other guests felt like a blessing, for in that realm of illusions, being by themselves ensured their safety.

For a fleeting instant, Aurora allowed herself to forget the impossibility of it all, as well as the dangers that lurked outside those ballroom doors. Instead, she reveled in the warmth of Tristan's touch and the genuine joy radiating from his eyes.

With a tender smile, he leaned in, his voice barely above a whisper. "You look absolutely breathtaking."

"Have you danced with many women tonight?" Aurora asked.

Tristan's eyes held hers, their gazes locked in a dance of their own. "A few," he admitted.

"And... have you found a wife yet?"

"Not yet." Tristan's grip tightened around her waist, his gaze unwavering. "But the night isn't over."

Aurora's breath caught in her throat. Her heart longed to hear his declaration, to feel the weight of his intentions. But reality set in, a reminder that their connection existed only within the realm of dreams— a fleeting and fragile illusion.

She cleared her throat, her voice trembling as she continued, "Then, why did you come here tonight?"

"I have danced with many women, but none of them felt right," he admitted, his words making her feel like she was levitating and dancing on air. "Besides, I couldn't get you out of my mind."

Aurora's heart soared, her emotions swirling with joy. But she knew the boundaries and limitations that confined them. And that wasn't going to change with one dance. Especially since their connection could never extend beyond the Dreamworld. He shouldn't have come.

Struggling to find the right words, Aurora began, "Tristan—"

"What I meant was... I couldn't stop thinking about the poem and riddle," he clarified. "After all, the answers we need are inside that tower, right?"

Aurora knew the unspoken truth in his words, but she chose not to confront it. Not in that moment, where their dance held a semblance of the magic of stolen time. She didn't want to tarnish the beauty they had found in each other's arms.

Though a part of her reveled in the knowledge that he had not found a spark in the arms of the women at the ball, another part tugged at her conscience. She couldn't give him anything real, anything tangible. The weight of guilt pressed on her, threatening to extinguish the joy she felt in that dreamlike state.

Aurora's frown deepened, her steps faltering as the music played on.

Tristan sensed her distress. "Are you all right?" he asked.

As the final notes of the music faded into the air, they came to a gentle stop, their breaths mingling with the lingering magic of the ballroom. Then silence enveloped them.

"Thank you for the lovely dance," she said softly. "And for giving me a taste of a dream I thought was lost."

"Did I do something wrong?" he asked.

Torn between her desires and the nagging reality that loomed over them, Aurora met his concerned gaze. "You need to go back. You shouldn't waste time dancing in a dream when your true love could be back at that ball. In reality."

Tristan's brows furrowed, a myriad of emotions crossing his face. The depth of his disturbance mirrored Aurora's own internal struggle.

"Like I said, I came because I needed a break," he said, pulling away from her. "But if you don't want to dance anymore, then we might as well head over to the golden tower while I still have time."

With those words, Tristan charged out of the double doors, his strides leading him back toward the garden.

Aurora followed after him, but as soon as she stepped outside, the illusion of the beautiful gown faded away, replaced by her familiar leather attire. Her heart sank as the moon cast a gentle glow on their path. She couldn't shake the ache that resonated within her. She knew she had made the right decision in pushing him away, yet her heart yearned for a different outcome. The echoes of their dance lingered, a melody that reverberated through her soul.

In the depths of her being, Aurora hoped that someday Tristan would find the love and happiness he sought in the real world. She had to reconcile herself with the fact that her role in his life was limited to the realm of dreams.

However, there was no time to dwell on her regrets. With renewed determination fueling her every step, she joined Tristan and mounted Midnight.

Tristan sat behind her. She could feel him breathing near the back of her neck. His warmth beckoned her to press her back to his chest, but she resisted. Without saying anything else, she yanked at the reins, urging Midnight forward.

It didn't take them long to arrive at the bridge. They crossed without a problem. Once they reached the tower entrance, Aurora dismounted her horse, and Tristan followed her.

Pulling out the poem from her pocket, she held it up. Aurora cleared her throat, her voice steady as she recited the poem, its words echoing in the stillness of the night. With a haunting creak, the door swung open.

The empty expanse of the tower stretched before them, its hollow depths echoing with a haunting stillness. Aurora led the way as Tristan followed closely behind. She ascended a spiral staircase, twisting higher and higher, her anticipation mounting with each step. This was it. Her father's secret was at the very top, and she was finally going to get the answers she'd been seeking.

But as they reached the midway point, their ascent came to an abrupt halt. The staircase ended, leaving them suspended in mid-air, their progress halted by an unfinished path. Aurora studied the last step, trying to make sense of its meaning.

Her mind raced, and then it hit her like a bolt of lightning. The number of steps on the staircase mirrored the exact count of the planks on her bridge.

It was a puzzle, a reflection of all her hard work and the lives she had saved along the way.

"Tristan, can you use your imagination to finish the staircase like you did with the bridge?" she asked.

Tristan focused his thoughts, his brow furrowed in concentration, but to their disappointment, nothing changed. "It's not working," he said, confused. "Why isn't it working?"

In that moment, Aurora came to another sudden realization. The completion of the staircase was her responsibility alone. It was tied to her father's secret, her lineage.

She turned to face Tristan. "It has to be me," she said. "My father's secret is at the top of this tower, and only I can unlock it."

Silence settled between them as the implications sank in. Aurora knew the truth—her ability to manifest the missing steps relied upon saving lives within the Dreamworld. Each soul she rescued, each person she guided back to reality, brought her one step closer to completion. The realization weighed heavy on her, a burden that threatened to smother the only ember of hope she had left.

"For every life I save, I will earn one step," she explained. "It could take years before I'm able to complete this staircase and reach the secrets hidden at the top."

Tristan's gaze held a spark of hope. "Maybe not," he said, his words tinged with a quiet excitement. "I may have an idea."

TRISTAN

*T*ristan awoke with a start, the hard stems of flowers tangled around his legs. He was outside, lying in his garden. The bright light of the moon shined over him, casting a silvery glow over the metal buttons of his jacket. He sat up, rubbing his temples, the remnants of the dream fading away. The ball. The guests. The music. It all came rushing back.

Even the memory of Aurora that had driven him back to his room mid-dance to down the sundrop drink in one gulp. He'd been in his room when he drank the silver liquid. But yet, he'd woken up in the garden. He sleepwalked again.

Looking around, a wave of relief washed over him. No one had noticed. That meant he could continue with his plan. With a swift motion, he rose to his feet, brushing the dirt from his clothes. A single petal of sundrop flower clung to his jacket, and he stared fondly at it as it rested on the palm of his hand. It amazed him just how a simple flower had turned his entire world upside down. He shoved it into his pocket and hurried back inside.

On returning to his room, he approached his desk. There, in a basin, lay what was left of the sundrop drink, its petals shimmering with a gentle luminescence. He carefully poured the water into a crystal decanter, the liquid shimmering with a silver hue.

Making his way to the kitchen, he found Wendy and pulled her aside. His eyes swept over the hall to make sure no one had followed them. "I need your help," he signed, handing her the decanter. "Pour a drop of this mixture into every champagne glass, for every guest present."

Wendy nodded, her fingers delicately gripping the vessel. She responded with a bow.

Once she disappeared into the kitchen, Tristan sucked in a deep breath before returning to the banquet hall. Lexa was still singing. Her beautiful voice wove a tapestry of emotions, each note pulling at the listeners' heartstrings. It was as if time had stopped, and every soul in the room was transported to a world of pure emotion and beauty.

While he acknowledged the beauty of Lexa's performance, a restless energy bubbled within him. His heart raced, not from the music, but from the weight of the plans he had set in motion. His fingers tapped rhythmically against his thigh. As the room remained enraptured by Lexa's song, Tristan's thoughts raced, preparing for his next move.

As the final haunting notes of Lexa's song began to fade, Tristan weaved through the crowd. Each step was deliberate, his movements fluid yet filled with a tension that anyone observant enough could sense. The applause and chatter that followed faded into the background, replaced by the pounding of his own heart in his ears.

With a practiced hand, he selected two champagne flutes from a nearby tray, their crystal stems catching the ambient light, making the golden liquid within them sparkle. He went to stand next to his cousin, who was just as mesmerized by Lexa as everyone else. After handing him a flute, Tristan turned to face his guests.

Then, turning to Ryke and Lexa, he held out the champagne flute. "To true love," he said, raising his glass high.

The crowd echoed his sentiment, glasses clinking in unison. And as the liquid touched their lips, their whole world shifted.

In an instant, the opulent chandeliers, the royal blue drapes, and the echoing laughter of the ball-room vanished. Tristan found himself standing on the edge of an endless beach, the transition so abrupt that it left him momentarily breathless. The once solid marble floor beneath his feet was replaced by the soft, cool embrace of wet sand. The rhythmic waves, like nature's own orchestra, crashed onto the shore, their frothy tips brushing against his ankles.

The air was thick with the scent of salt and seaweed, and the wind, more forceful than any dance partner, whipped around him, pulling at his clothes and sending his hair into a frenzy. The vast horizon stretched out before him, the sky painted in hues of oranges and purples, signaling the sun's descent.

A distance away, a lone figure sat astride a majestic horse. Aurora, with her hair flowing like a cascade of molten gold, was a delight to see against the fiery backdrop of the setting sun. Her horse, Midnight, stood still, its black coat gleaming, absorbing the last rays of the day.

Panic and confusion reigned as the guests, once lost in the revelry of the ball, now found themselves waist-deep in the encroaching tide. Their elegant gowns and tailored suits were drenched. Their faces painted with disbelief and fear. Tristan thought it must have been a most disorienting experience for them, having no idea about the Dreamworld and what had just happened. Though he supposed they would simply put the experience down to having too much wine, rather than assuming that any of it was real. Their voices, once filled with laughter, echoed with cries for help, jolting Tristan to move.

He darted toward Aurora, each step weighed down by the wet sand beneath his shoes. But before he could get far, Aurora raised a hand, her eyes boring an intensity that rooted him to the spot.

"Stay in the water," she urged. Her voice, though soft, carried an undeniable authority.

"I am not letting you go alone," he said. The mere thought of anything happening to her made his stomach twist in knots.

"Tristan—"

"I am not leaving you, Aurora." He studied the soft contours of her face, willing himself to memorize every single part. From her glittering eyes, shining at him, to her soft, rose-plump lips, pulling him to her. Even if they didn't have a future together, he still wanted to spend every remaining second by her side.

Her pink cheeks rounded as she gave him a smile. Then, with a flick of her wrist, she summoned a bolt of lightning. The sky thundered above their heads and a flash of blinding light shot toward the ocean. It struck the water, and the guests screamed.

In a blink of an eye, the guests were gone, leaving behind vapor and the echoes of their collective scream. The night grew still once more.

Tristan's gaze returned to Aurora. "Do you think it worked?" he asked.

"There's only one way to find out." She reached out her hand and pulled him up onto Midnight with her, then galloped into the forest toward the golden tower looming in the distance.

AURORA

*U*pon returning to the golden tower, Aurora sprinted up the newly formed stairs, her steps fueled by excitement and urgency. Aurora led the way, her heart pounding in rhythm with each step. Tristan followed close behind, his pace matching hers. Upon reaching the upper landing, her eyes were met not by an imposing door, but by an intricately etched engraving just below the doorknob.

Drawing a breath, Aurora retrieved her father's golden ring, the tiny bee ornament fitting perfectly within the groove of the engraving. With a twist that mimicked a key turning in a lock, she felt the door yield, granting them access.

As the door swung open, their gaze fell upon an

interior that mirrored Aurora's hazy recollections. It was her old bedroom, painstakingly recreated down to the minutest detail. The bed stood against the wall with a figure concealed beneath the blankets.

Without hesitation, Tristan stepped forward, his fingers inching toward the covers, ready to unveil the mystery concealed beneath.

A scorpion, poised to strike, erupted from its hiding place, its venomous tail directed straight at Aurora. Time seemed to pause as she locked with its beady eyes.

Tristan lunged between them. The scorpion's venomous stinger buried itself into Tristan's back. An agonized gasp escaped his lips, his body contorting in a grimace. Aurora's scream pierced the air, a desperate cry of fear and anguish.

A wave of heat began coursing through her body. Then a grim realization dawned on her as she looked down and saw that the stinger had gone through Tristan and into her. It had impaled them both.

A searing jolt of pain raced through their bodies as the scorpion retracted its stinger. The venom's fiery touch seared through her body like molten lava, and a relentless current of pain overwhelmed her very soul.

As the scorpion slunk away through an open window, Aurora and Tristan collapsed to the floor. Their breaths labored and chests heaved as they grappled with the searing agony coursing through their veins.

Aurora clung to Tristan's arm, as if he could anchor her to consciousness. Yet, darkness encroached like tendrils of an inky abyss, a relentless force that sought to engulf her. As her vision blurred, Tristan's voice emerged like a lifeline in a storm.

Desperate to stay awake, she clung to the sound of his voice. But her efforts were futile. Darkness beckoned, pulling her into its depths.

Panic etched across Tristan's face as her strength waned, her consciousness slipping through her fingers like grains of sand carried by an unforgiving wind.

Diving deeper into the blackness, Aurora's mind was a canvas on which layers of dreams converged. Whispers of memories danced like fireflies, illuminating fragments of her life. Her father's enigmatic presence, the burden of her curse, and the newborn desire of a future with Tristan—all wove a symphony of emotions that echoed through her soul.

When consciousness finally reclaimed her, Tristan was gone and Aurora found herself in an unfamiliar room. Her surroundings were different, the transition so smooth that for a moment she questioned if she had truly awakened.

She lay on a sofa, her surroundings bathed in the soft glow of a warm fire. Its warmth cast flickering shadows on the walls. The surroundings bore an uncanny resemblance to her father's study, a place she had frequented in her distant past.

A figure stood before the hearth, exuding an air of authority. Aurora's heart quickened as her gaze settled on him. Recognition dawned. An illusion of her father, King Midas, stood before her.

Aurora sat up, her body protesting as the scorpion's venom burned through her. "How did you get your gold?" she asked, biting back the pain.

The figure raised a jar of honey nectar, the golden bee ring she had once taken from him still adorning his finger. "Would you care for some honey, my dear?" His tone held an air of false geniality.

Setting her discomfort aside, she pressed, "What I want is an answer from you."

He gave a humorless chuckle. "Straightforward, just like your mother."

The revelation stirred a whirlwind of emotions within Aurora, but she wasn't about to be sidetracked.

"Tell me how to rid myself of this curse you've bestowed upon me."

Midas turned to face her fully, his eyes locking onto hers, and for a moment, she felt stripped bare, as if her thoughts were an open book before him. "You didn't come here solely for that answer, Aurora. Another question burns within you."

Her heartbeat quickened, her emotions exposed to a degree that left her feeling vulnerable. Still, she wouldn't play into his manipulative game. "All I want is to know how to remove my curse."

A knowing smirk curled at the edges of her father's lips. "So, you don't wish to know where your precious prince has vanished to? Your search for him has driven you across this world, hasn't it? Your desire to enter this tower was fueled by him. And I know precisely where he can be found."

From his pocket, Midas produced a parchment scroll, its surface blank and unmarked. With a swift, practiced movement, he pricked his finger, allowing a drop of blood to fall on the paper. Instantaneously, the parchment transformed into a golden plate. Even Aurora couldn't see the sudden inscription on its surface, by the look in her father's eyes, she supposed it contained the answer she sought.

Aurora rose to her feet and took the plate, her

gaze tracing the names engraved into it. On one side, Hendrick's name gleamed, a memory from her past. Flipping the plate, she found Tristan's name. Confusion knitted her brows.

"What is this?" she asked.

Midas spoke with a calm finality. "Hold the plate over a flame, and the answer you desire will be revealed. But you must choose: either you discover the path to Hendrick, your former love, or you assist your newfound beloved in defeating me."

Aurora's heart drummed against her ribcage. Her fingers trembled as she tucked the golden plate into her satchel.

"What about my gold?" Her voice sliced through the tension-laden air. "How can I rid myself of it?"

Her father's illusion waved a dismissive hand. "The answer rests within you, my dear. You need only to look within to find it."

"Enough with the riddles!" she demanded, her words sharp. "Tell me!"

Her father regarded her with an enigmatic smile, his eyes holding a depth of knowledge that eluded her. And then a glint of metal caught her eye. In his hand materialized a golden dagger, its blade glimmering with an otherworldly light. Before she could react, the blade pierced her abdomen, pain searing through her like another shot of venom.

Gasping for breath, Aurora felt the world around her dissolve into darkness. Her father's voice, a haunting whisper, brushed against her ear. "The answer is inside you."

A sharp intake of air jolted Aurora back to consciousness. Her surroundings were a haze, like a half-remembered dream. She was back in her bedroom within the golden tower, her body drenched in a cold sweat.

Beside her, Tristan lay still, his face contorted in pain. She crawled toward him, wincing with every movement, her own pain an echo of his. She rolled him onto his back, her heart a drumbeat of concern.

His eyes fluttered open, the effort visible on his haggard face. His voice, hoarse and laced with pain, pierced the silence, "Have you ever been stung by a scorpion before?"

Aurora shook her head, her eyes locked onto the blood that trickled from his nose. "You're bleeding," she murmured.

His touch smeared blood across his skin, the crimson stain a stark contrast against his pale complexion.

"The bell tower must have rung, and we didn't

hear it," she muttered. Panic welled within her chest, the sight of his life slipping away sent her mind reeling. "You're out of time. You must go. Now!"

Tristan pushed himself onto his elbows. "I can't leave you like this."

Aurora met his gaze. "If you die here, you'll never awaken. But if you go, heal, and return, we can face whatever lies ahead together."

Tristan's nod felt like a promise, a silent understanding that passed between them like a whispered prayer. His hands cupped her face, a fleeting touch that conveyed a world of emotion that reached her very core. "I won't be long. I promise."

Aurora nodded, her breath shaky as her consciousness wavered on the edge of an abyss. "Hurry," she breathed, her voice a fragile thread in the stillness.

With a determined push, Tristan hoisted himself up, his movements fueled by a blend of purpose and urgency. Staggering toward the window, he perched onto the ledge, a lone figure against the eclipse-lit landscape. His gaze returned to her, a beacon of hope that kindled the embers of her spirit.

"Hang in there," he urged. And she hung onto his words like a lifeline.

She nodded, even though she could feel the edges

of her consciousness succumbing to an encroaching darkness. As he propelled himself from the window, she pressed her cheek to the cold floor. And then, as if the world itself had surrendered to the void, everything plunged into blackness.

TRISTAN

Tristan's eyes flew open, heart pounding against his chest like a caged bird. The luxurious comfort of his bed, the familiar scent of his chambers, and all other trappings of comfort were cruelly absent. Instead, he was met with the cold, unyielding embrace of stone beneath him and the stifling dampness of a dungeon. Panic surged within him, a tidal wave threatening to drown him.

He jumped to his feet. "Hello? Anyone!" he cried out, his voice echoing off the walls, sounding more desperate than he intended. He clutched the bars, the cold metal biting into his palms. But as he strained to hear any sign of life, a sickening dizziness gripped him. The world spun, and a nauseating feeling rose, threatening to spill over. He staggered to a corner, emptying his stomach into a bucket. The venom's aftertaste was vile, but the burning agony had mercifully faded.

The distant sound of footsteps grew steadily louder. When Ryke's familiar face came into view, a rush of relief surged through Tristan. "Ryke! Oh, thank the gods. Please, you have to get me out of here."

But Ryke's face was a mask of stoicism, his eyes devoid of their usual warmth. The stillness, the silence between them, was thick with tension. "I thought you were suffering from insomnia. But now I see it is so much more than that, isn't it?"

His cousin's words sat heavily on Tristan's chest as he processed them. Tristan shook himself.

"Ryke, I don't understand," his voice quivered. "Did I sleepwalk again? I promise, whatever you think happened—"

"Don't." Ryke interrupted, his voice cold as he held up the decanter Tristan had given to Wendy. "I suppose you thought you were being discreet, didn't you?"

A cold dread settled in Tristan's stomach. "Ryke, please. I can explain everything. But first, I need what's left of that drink."

Ryke's gaze was unwavering, his voice firm. "That will not happen."

Tristan gripped the bars with all his strength. "I am your prince. I command you to hand it over right this instant!"

Ryke's response was filled with a mix of pain and defiance. "And I am your family and I'm saying over my dead body."

Emotions swirled within Tristan, a tempest of fear, desperation, and guilt. "Ryke, please," he whispered, his voice breaking, "I'm begging you."

Ryke's eyes, once filled with brotherly affection, now shimmered with tears of anger and sorrow. "I lost my parents too, you know? I know what grief can do to you. But *this*... this isn't the way to cope."

Tears clung to Tristan's eyes as he gripped the steel bars of the cell until the whites of his knuckles were on show. He clenched his teeth and looked darkly at the dusty floor. But his surroundings faded from view, and all he could see was Aurora's paled face.

"I have to go back. She was poisoned. She'll die if I don't return!" Tristan's voice cracked with raw emotion.

Ryke's brows furrowed. "Return where? Who are you talking about?"

Tristan paced around, wiping cold sweat from his brow as he shook with frustration and worry. When he didn't reply, Ryke banged the bars with his fist to draw his attention back to him.

"Do you hear yourself? You have lost sense of what is real and what is not. You're spiraling, Tristan. If you can't see that, then you leave me no choice."

Tristan's desperation reached a fever pitch as Ryke tilted the decanter, its silver liquid threatening to spill over the edge. "Stop! I don't owe you explanations for what I do in my private time."

Ryke's voice rose. "But you owe it to your kingdom! They're terrified, thinking their prince was poisoned at his own ball, all because you've been secretly drugging yourself with *this*!" In his agitation, he brandished the decanter. Waving it in the air, the liquid sloshed about, and Tristan's heart sank as a few drops spilled from it.

"Stop that! Give it to me!" he grunted, lunging forward and reaching through the bars.

Before Ryke could jump back, Tristan's hands collided with Ryke's, knocking it from Ryke's grasp. Time seemed to slow, and Tristan watched, frozen and helpless, as it fell and splashed onto the stone floor.

The sundrop mixture seeped away, and Tristan

screamed internally as he watched each droplet disappear. He sank to his knees, the weight of his actions, the magnitude of his loss, pressing down on him.

Ryke panted and took a few steps back. But then he rounded his shoulders and puffed out his chest. "This ends now, Tristan. You've become lost to a disease. You won't leave this cell until that poison is purged from your system."

With those final words, he turned and walked away, leaving Tristan in the suffocating darkness, grappling with the thought of losing Aurora forever.

AURORA

*A*urora's eyelids fluttered open, and for a fleeting moment, disorientation clouded her senses. Then, as her vision cleared, a familiar face came into view.

Millie.

Aurora found herself in a bath, the soft embrace of a sunflower-scented bathwater surrounding her. Her mind churned, trying to piece together the fragments of her memories, a puzzle that refused to align.

Millie sat across from her, a copper dagger twirling in her hand, mirroring the same gesture she had made during their dinner.

"How did you do it?" Millie's voice pierced through the haze of Aurora's mind.

What was she talking about? Aurora's head spun,

trying to remember her arrival home, disrobed and immersed in a sunflower bath. "Wait." She shot her eyes open again. "Did you bring me home?"

Millie's gaze held an intensity that matched her words. "How did you get rid of your gold?"

Confusion clouded Aurora's senses. "I didn't," she muttered. "My father's illusion rambled something about looking within, and then he… he stabbed me with a knife."

Millie leaned in, the copper dagger gleaming in her hand. "This is the dagger you turned to gold at my house."

Aurora drew out a tired breath. "If you plan to stab me with it, at least let me stand up first. Fair fight, you know."

"Aurora." Millie's fingers closed around Aurora's wrist, the dagger's tip breaking the skin of her palm. Aurora winced as blood welled up.

"Ouch." She withdrew her hand, rinsing away the blood in the water. "What was that for?"

"Look." Millie held the dagger before Aurora's eyes, droplets of her blood staining the blade. "No gold."

Forcefully, Aurora blinked away the remnants of exhaustion, her focus sharpening on the blade. She had missed it before, but now she saw it—the dagger's tip still bore droplets of her blood, its metallic hue unmarred by a trace of gold.

Aurora's heart raced as she held her hand to the light, watching as her blood stained the water. She blinked, disbelief mingling with hope. "Are you saying it actually worked?"

"Not only did it work, but whatever you did, it reversed the transformation," Millie added. "It seems that everything you've turned to gold has returned to its original state."

Aurora's gaze shifted from the dagger to her surroundings. The golden hue that had once painted every corner of her home had vanished. The bathtub, the bed frame, even the mirror—all were free from the imprisoning touch of gold.

"I was in my kitchen, using this very dagger, and I saw it change," Millie explained in amazement. "That's when I knew something must've changed with you."

A weak smile curved Aurora's lips. "You were concerned about me."

Millie's eyes rolled dramatically. "Don't flatter yourself. I came mostly out of curiosity. Now, spill it. How did you manage it?"

Aurora's laughter was a cathartic release, the irony of it all not lost on her. "I was stung by a scorpion," she explained between chuckles. "The venom acted as the antidote."

Millie joined her laughter, the absurdity of the situation too vivid to ignore. "The creatures that have been trying to sting you all along were the key to your freedom?"

"Yes, the very creatures I've been avoiding like the plague."

Millie's tone grew hopeful. "So, does that mean if your father gets stung, he'll lose his gold too?"

"Seems so." Aurora met Millie's gaze with fondness. "Life has a strange way of weaving its threads, doesn't it? The answers we seek are often right under our noses, hidden within the unexpected."

Millie tapped a finger to her lips, her eyes dancing with newfound hope. "Aurora, if your father takes the venom, and everything he's ever touched is restored, that means…"

Aurora frowned. "I'm sorry for all you've endured because of me."

Millie brushed off the apology. "Focus, Aurora. This could be my way out. I didn't drink the sundrop flower, remember? My sleep stasis isn't internal like yours. It's solely based on his gold. If he loses that, I can wake up again."

Emotion welled within Aurora, and she longed to

offer Millie a comforting embrace. But her body protested every movement, aching to her bones. "I'm genuinely happy for you, Millie. But without Tristan, there will be no freedom."

Millie's expression shifted to worry. "Are you certain he'll return?"

Aurora nodded. "He promised."

"Very well, then." Millie clasped her hands together. "Stay put. I'll return with a few supplies from the house. Oh, and here." She handed Aurora a cup. "Drink this."

Aurora eyed the concoction with suspicion, wrinkling her nose at its pungent odor. "What is it?"

"Real medicine," Millie replied. "Since you've lost your gold, the honey won't help you heal anymore."

With a hesitant sip, Aurora swallowed the bitter liquid. "Gross." Then an icy wave coursed through Aurora's body, and she shivered. "What on earth is that?"

Millie flashed a triumphant smile. "That, princess, is the taste of freedom."

TRISTAN

The oppressive silence of the dungeon was only broken by the rhythmic clang of metal against metal. Tristan banged an empty decanter against the bars of his cell. Each echo seemed to mock him, amplifying the solitude that surrounded him. But beyond the immediate confines of his cell, his thoughts were consumed by Aurora.

Visions of her, pale and writhing in pain from the scorpion's sting, haunted him. The memory of her agonized cries echoed louder in his mind than the sound of the rain outside. He had to return to the Dreamworld, to be by her side, to rescue her.

Every fiber of his being, every atom, yearned to hold her close, to soothe her pain, to whisper promises of safety and cover her face in healing kisses.

His throat felt parched, every swallow a painful reminder of his thirst. The empty cup in his hand seemed to taunt him, its hollowness mirroring the void he felt inside. As his fingers traced the cold, smooth surface of the decanter, a memory surfaced—the flower petal that had clung to his jacket from the castle gardens earlier that night.

With trembling hands, he retrieved the slightly crushed petal from his pocket, its once vibrant color now wilted. Carefully, he placed it inside the cup, its delicate fragrance filling the air, a stark contrast to the musty odor of the dungeon.

His eyes, adjusting to the dim light, were drawn to a small window near the ceiling of his cell. A faint glimmer of hope ignited within him. He leaped onto the bed, stretching his arm through the narrow opening. The sensation of cool raindrops caressed his skin. Beneath his fingertips, he could feel the soft, wet earth of what seemed to be the garden.

Carefully positioning the cup on an iron stand over a candle at the edge of the window, he listened intently as the gentle patter of rain began to fill it. The sound was almost musical, a soothing lullaby in the midst of his despair. He left the cup there, bathed in the soft glow of the moonlight, the passage of time marked only by the steady accumulation of water.

Finally, when it began to boil and the petals turned silver, he retrieved the cup, now filled with rainwater infused with the essence of the sundrop flower. Holding it close, he took a moment to savor the scent, a mix of rain and the flower's unique aroma.

With a silent prayer, he took a sip, the cool liquid a balm to his parched throat. But more than physical relief, he sought a passage back to the Dreamworld, to Aurora. The urgency to protect and heal her was a fire that wouldn't be quenched.

The sensation of soft fabric beneath him roused Tristan from his slumber. Blinking away the remnants of sleep, he found himself on a plush sofa. The familiar surroundings of Aurora's home greeted him, yet something felt amiss. Without a moment's hesitation, he sprang to his feet, a sense of urgency propelling him toward her bedroom. The sight of the empty bed sent a jolt of panic through him.

"Aurora!" His heart raced as he moved through the house. The opulence he remembered was gone. The rooms, once ornamented with gold and intricate designs, now appeared simpler, almost unrecognizable. The change was jarring, adding to his growing unease.

As he approached one of the rooms, the soft sound of water caught his attention. Pushing the door open, he was met with a sight he hadn't anticipated. Aurora, her skin glistening with droplets, stood there, momentarily frozen in surprise. A yelp escaped her lips as she hastily grabbed a towel, wrapping it around herself.

Mortified, Tristan spun around, his hand instinctively covering his eyes. "My apologies," he stammered, his cheeks burning with embarrassment.

A quivering chuckle came from behind him. "It's all right. You can turn around."

Taking a deep breath, he slowly turned to face her. While she was now modestly covered by the towel, the flush on her cheeks was evident. He stepped closer, the relief of finding her safe overwhelming him. Gently cupping her face, his eyes peered into hers. He then tangled his fingers through her hair.

"I was terrified something had happened to you,"

he whispered, touching his cheek to hers. Her skin was as cold as ice, and he pulled back.

Her lips quivered, and only then did he notice it turning a deep shade of purple and blue. "I'm so cold," she said, shivering.

Tristan wrapped her up in his arms, trying to warm her with his body heat.

"The venom was burning, but now I'm freezing," she continued, her voice shaking.

With gentle hands, Tristan helped Aurora into a soft, dry robe, ensuring she was covered and warm. The wet towel was discarded carelessly to the side. He quickly arranged a makeshift bed in front of the roaring fireplace, using cushions and blankets from the nearby sofa. He gently laid her down, the warmth from the flames casting a golden glow on her face. Pulling a thick blanket over them, he nestled close, wrapping her securely in his arms.

Despite the warmth, Aurora's body shivered against him. The alarming shade of blue tinging her lips grew deeper, and panic welled up within him.

Feeling her weak tug on his shirt, he looked down to meet her eyes.

"I need... your skin," she murmured, her voice quivering from the cold.

Without hesitation, Tristan began to unbutton his

shirt, discarding it to reveal his toned chest. He then stripped down to his undergarment, his every action driven by the need to warm her. Pulling her close once more, he enveloped her in his embrace, their bodies pressed together.

Aurora's voice, soft and weak, broke the silence, "I think... this might be a side effect of Millie's medicine." But as she nestled her face against the warmth of his neck, her tense muscles began to relax, the comfort of his presence covering her.

The intimate proximity, the thin barrier of her robe against his skin, sent Tristan's heart racing. Every beat echoed the depth of his feelings, the intensity of the moment.

Aurora's soft whisper reached his ears. "Is it time for you to go already?" she asked.

He tightened his hold on her, his voice a low rumble as he said, "Not yet."

She shifted slightly, her fingers tracing patterns on his back. "Then why is your heart racing so fast?"

Images flashed through Tristan's mind: the fear of losing her, the relief of finding her, the sensation of her body pressed against his. Out of all the women he had ever held, none had ever stirred such raw emotions within him. "You gave me quite a scare today," he admitted, his voice cracking.

"I know. Sorry about that."

Gently, Tristan lifted Aurora's chin, his fingers brushing against the softness of her skin. The alarming blue hue of her lips had faded, replaced by a healthy pink.

"What happened at the tower?" he asked.

A slow smile spread across her face. "It worked."

His eyebrows shot up in surprise. "It did?"

She gestured around the room, her smile widening. "Look around. The gold is all gone."

Taking a moment to truly observe his surroundings, Tristan realized the stark difference. The gold that had once covered every corner of Aurora's home was nowhere to be seen. "Does this mean...?"

She nodded. "The scorpion's venom cured me of my curse."

His fingers traced the curve of her cheek, the warmth of his touch making her lean into his hand. "You did it. You got what you wanted."

Aurora's gaze locked onto his, gratitude evident in her eyes. "I couldn't do it without your help. Thank you."

He chuckled softly. "We made a good team."

"I think so too," she murmured, her eyelids growing heavy. But as he brushed a stray strand of hair from her face, her eyes fluttered open once more.

"You're tired. Why don't you sleep for a bit?" he whispered.

She gave him a weak smile, determination shining through her fatigue. "And miss out on the little time I have with you? Not a chance." She paused. "So, tell me about the ball. How was it?"

He exhaled deeply, the weight of the evening's events pressing down on him. "It was going very well until I decided to drug everyone, then electrocute them back to life."

A soft laugh escaped her lips. "Yeah. Even I thought that was crazy. And that's saying a lot coming from me."

The sound of her laughter, light and melodic, warmed his heart, bringing a smile to his face. "You weren't the only one to think that. My cousin thinks I'm going insane and has decided to lock me up."

Aurora's playful demeanor shifted instantly, her eyes widening in alarm. "What?"

Tristan's expression grew somber. "The sundrop flower has been causing some side effects on me in the real world. My cousin is worried."

She leaned closer, her voice filled with concern. "What kind of side effects?"

He sighed. "Sleepwalking. Losing sense of time.

What feels like only a few hours here, turns out to be days over there."

"You can't blame him for being concerned," Aurora pressed.

Tristan nodded. "I know."

Aurora's gaze softened, her fingers reaching out to trace the lines of worry on his face. "Tristan, you can't come here anymore. The side effects... It's not safe."

"I know," he murmured, his fingers gently tracing the curve of her lips, feeling their softness beneath his touch. "But the thought of leaving you, of never seeing you again... it's unbearable."

She chuckled softly, a hint of teasing in her tone. "What about your grand bachelor ball? Did no woman catch your eye?"

Holding her gaze, he replied with unwavering sincerity, "None of them were you."

A soft smile played on her lips, her eyes shimmering. "Having a Prince say those words to me is like a fairy tale. But that's all it will ever be for us, Tristan. A dream. Now, it's time for you to wake up and embrace reality."

He shook his head. "You don't understand. Every time I've tried to stay away, something pulls me back to you."

Aurora's fingers gently caressed his cheek, her touch sending a warmth through him. "Then you need to find a woman in your world, someone who anchors you, makes you want to stay there."

He looked away. "How can I marry without love?"

She tilted his face back toward her, her gaze searching his. "Sometimes love comes later. Sometimes it surprises you."

He swallowed hard, his voice barely above a whisper. "What if I'm already in love... but with someone I can never truly be with?"

Aurora lowered her eyes. "It is possible to move on. And love again."

"How can you be so sure?"

She offered a sad smile. "After years imprisoned in that tower, Rapunzel and I devised a way for me to escape. She had this incredibly long hair, and she would throw it out the window for me to climb down. During one of my escapades, I met a Prince named Hendrick. He was kind, honorable, and he loved me without knowing my true identity."

"What happened to him?" Tristan asked.

A shadow crossed Aurora's face. "My father discovered our secret and, in his rage, turned Hendrick into a statue of gold right before my eyes. I never saw him again. And to deepen my despair, he did the same to Millie."

Tristan's heart ached for her. "I'm so sorry you had to endure such pain."

She gently caressed his face again, her touch comforting. "The reason I'm sharing this with you is to show that even after such heartbreak, I found love again. I never thought I would, or even could, but life has a way of surprising us."

The soft glow of the fireplace painted the room in a warm, amber hue, casting dancing shadows on the walls.

"Tell me more about this new love of yours," Tristan pressed.

Aurora's voice was a whisper, vulnerable yet resolute, her confession hanging between them like a fragile thread. "I tried to convince myself that it was nothing. That it meant nothing, but deep down, I knew it wasn't true. You brought light into my darkness, Tristan. And infused hope into my heart." She glanced away, her gaze lost in the dancing flames of the fireplace. "And then you kept coming back... at the beach, at the castle, and now here."

Tristan's heart thrummed in his chest. His thoughts swirled like autumn leaves, each one a testament to the complexity of their situation. Her honesty was like a mirror to his own feelings.

"Every time I'm with you," she continued, "I tell myself that I shouldn't, that we should stop seeing each other. That you should leave and never come back." She paused, her breath shaky. "But every time I even think about not seeing you again, it makes it hard to breathe."

The silence that followed was charged, a void brimming with unspoken desires and fears. Tristan's throat tightened. Instinctively, he found his hand reaching for hers, his fingers brushing against her palm. He felt the tension in her grip, the uncertainty woven within her touch.

His heart ached, the weight of their impending separation like an anvil to his soul. "This is goodbye, isn't it?"

She closed her eyes, trying to hide the tears welling up in them. "It has to be."

His fingers, warm and steady, found their way to her cheek, a tender caress that felt both natural and electrifying. "Look at me," he whispered over the crackling of the fire.

Aurora's gaze met his, and he felt a universe of emotions echoing in the depths of her eyes. "Do you want me to leave right now?" he asked.

Emotion trembled on the edge of her voice. Her lips parted as if to speak, but her jaw clenched, the swirl of her thoughts evident in her conflicted expression. "Yes," she breathed, but then, with a shuddering exhale, she whispered, "No."

The fireplace's crackling grew more distinct, the golden light casting a warm glow on her sun-kissed skin—a sun he had brought into her life. Tristan's gaze was fixated on her, on the battle she fought within herself. The depth of his feelings for her surged within him.

He drew closer, his hand moving from her cheek to rest gently on her hip, a connection that seemed to echo the heartbeat of the world around them. He found his arms wrapping around her, their bodies drawing closer, and his heart swelled with longing.

Their proximity was intoxicating, a blend of uncertainty and undeniable connection. Tristan's touch, tender and gentle, explored the expanse of her back, his fingers tracing patterns over the fabric that separated them from the depths of their desires.

Her warmth seeped through the thin material of her robe, a touch that ignited every nerve in his body. She felt real, solid, as if they were both part of the same realm. He breathed in her sunflower scent, the familiarity of it settling within him like a comforting embrace.

"Aurora…" he murmured, his throat constricting. "I don't know how to leave you."

Although their connection was undeniable, he knew that a future with her was as ephemeral as a dream, and yet, in that moment, there was nothing he desired more.

With every touch, every gaze exchanged, their bond deepened, a connection that transcended the boundaries of multiple realms. Tristan's fingers brushed over her cheek as he leaned in, his lips meeting her neck in a tender, exploratory kiss. Her skin was soft beneath his touch, and he felt her shiver, her body responding to his caress.

Something stirred within him. It was a mixture of raw need and excitement. Gently, he brushed his thumb over her soft, inviting lips. "Tell me… if you were in the real world, and I had asked for your hand in marriage…" His fingers tenderly caressed her bottom lip. "Would you have accepted?"

By her expression, Tristan knew she recognized the intensity of what he was feeling. Though it may have frightened her, she didn't pull away. Instead, she leaned into him and twined her arms around his neck. He could feel her chest, soft and full, press against him. She brushed his lips with hers. The feathery touch sent tingles throughout Tristan's body.

"Yes," she said through a breath. "I would have loved being your wife."

An explosion of passion tore from Tristan's heart, flooding him with warmth. She lifted her head as his lips met her neck. Tristan nearly groaned with delight at the taste of her. She was sweet like the ripest fruit from the rarest tree in a secret forest. Her skin felt as delicate as silk under the tip of his tongue. With a groan, she pulled him even closer, and he finally moved his lips toward hers.

As they greedily explored each other's mouths, Tristan marveled that even though this moment was supposed to have been a dream, he had never felt more awake.

The world seemed to fade around them, their desires the only reality that mattered. The sweetness of her lips against his sent ripples of longing through him, a wave of sensations that stirred his very soul. Her tentative response ignited a flame that consumed every rational thought.

His hands trailed down her hip, memorizing every inch of her skin. Through it all, he was conscious of his love for her, coupled with a riptide of desire more powerful than he'd ever felt before.

When he finally pulled back, her eyes were half-closed, her mouth parted in sensual anticipation. As her golden tresses fell over her face, Tristan took in the sight of her as shiny sweat pooled between the swell of her cleavage and the thin robe left little to the imagination. Then, in a motion that felt utterly natural, he rolled atop her. Her eyes stayed on his, and with a gentle nip at her lips, he made a silent vow to worship her entire body until she begged him to stop.

AURORA

*A*urora shuddered with delight as a rush of sensation poured over her. Tristan nibbled at her neck while his fingers left burning trails up her arms. She rolled atop him and straddled his lap. The silk of her robe fell from one shoulder in the most tantalizing way, but Aurora refused to shy away from his gaze as he took in the sight of her.

The intensity in Tristan's eyes ignited a fire deep within her, a fire she had long denied but could no longer ignore. The way his eyes darkened with desire had her heart racing, each beat echoing her own need for him. She thought again that none of this could be real, but as his strength overlaid her, it suddenly felt more real than anything she'd ever experienced.

She could still stop this. She *should* stop it. After

all, in a matter of hours, he'd be a world away, and the physical and emotional bond between them was destined to be broken, leaving them both shattered beyond repair—and yet, she couldn't stop herself. The magnetic pull between them was too strong, a force she could no longer resist. Aurora's senses were heightened, every touch, every glance burned for him. They were tethered to one another, bound by a love that defied reason and reality.

Tristan slipped his arms around her back, his thumb tracing small circles as if tracing the petals of a rose. The fabric of her robe was thin and light enough for her to feel as if she had nothing on at all.

The moment was so sweet, she almost forgot that it was a goodbye. Almost.

The awareness that their time together was coming to an end infused her chest with a bittersweet ache. She knew none of it was real—their real bodies were possibly hundreds of miles apart. But his warmth, his scent, his kisses, they felt more real than reality.

His kiss was exhilarating—liberating—and when he buried his hands in her hair, she heard a soft moan, barely recognizing it as her own, as their tongues came together. He ran his hands over her back and her arms and then her hips, and the sensation was like a trail of tiny electric shocks, a current that pulsed between them, binding them in a world of their own making.

He then traced a finger over her ribcage and her skin filled with goosebumps. He smiled teasingly, and she knew that image would be etched in her memory forever.

Bringing a hand to his cheek, she ran her fingertips over the stubble. Aurora's heart swelled with emotion. She needed him to know, to understand the depth of her feelings. With a gentle touch, she guided his hand to rest over her heart.

As their eyes locked, she bared her soul to him. "From this day forward, every beat of my heart…" she whispered breathlessly, "will beat for you."

The dim light made shadows dance along the walls, but all they could do was drink in the sight of each other. She sensed his desire and allowed herself to soak it in before pressing her lips to his again. As they kissed, she relished their taste.

He lay her back down, alternating between feather-light kisses and rough ones. All the while his hands roamed, as if he was trying to memorize every inch of her. She let out a moan and rolled her head back, savoring each touch as if it were the last.

Reaching for her hands, Tristan placed them

above her head, then kissed her cheek and her nose, and then her mouth again.

"I love you," she whispered against his lips. The corner of his mouth curved, then he kissed her in ways that told her he loved her too. And in that moment, she wanted nothing more than to be connected to him in a way that transcended time and space.

But he pulled back and rested his forehead on hers. "I want to live in this moment forever with you," he whispered. Then he took her in his arms and continued to stroke her back as the fire weaned.

A residual energy swirled around them. It was electric, and Aurora had never felt more alive and connected to another soul. Each caress was a promise, each kiss a declaration of love that defied the constraints of their reality. She sensed his passion, his longing, and in that moment, nothing else mattered.

She rested her head on his shoulder, letting herself drift on the tide of the little time they had left. She felt utterly spent, but it wasn't until Tristan whispered softly into her ear, "I love you, too," that she was finally able to fall into a dreamless sleep.

*T*he reverberating echo of the front door slamming shut jolted Aurora awake. She quickly scrambled to cover herself, pulling the sheets up to her chin. Beside her, Tristan blinked in bleary confusion, his ruffled hair illuminated by the hazy morning light that filtered through the curtains.

"Up! Get up, both of you!" Millie's voice rang out as she strode into the room like a gust of wind. "Up, up, up!"

Through the haze of drowsiness, Aurora squinted to witness Millie's flurry of activity. Bags dangled from her arms as she buzzed about, animatedly discussing plans for her departure from the Dreamworld.

Aurora massaged her temples while Tristan roused himself to a seated position, rubbing the sleep from his eyes.

A flicker of amusement danced in Millie's eyes as she looked at the disheveled pair. "Perfect! I see my concoction worked."

Aurora shot her a pointed glare. "Your concoction almost froze me to death," she grumbled, clutching the sheets around her.

Millie's grin broadened. "Yes, but it got you two to cozy up under the covers, and that only strengthens our chances of leaving this empty void of a world."

"You mean it strengthens *your* chances," Aurora corrected.

"Primarily, yes. Now, hurry up and get dressed. There's no time to waste." Millie turned her back on them, her hands digging into the depths of her bags as Aurora and Tristan scrambled to slip into their clothes.

"Here it is! I knew I had it here somewhere," Millie announced triumphantly, holding up a vial filled with neon liquid from her bag. She handed it to Aurora with a flourish. "Here you go."

Aurora took the vial, turning it in her hands as she examined it. "What is it?"

Millie's eyes rolled skyward in mock exasperation. "What do you think? Scorpion's venom, of course. The last one, by the way. Thanks to you finally getting stung, they're all gone. I didn't see a single one out there. It's as if they've fulfilled some sort of purpose and ceased to exist. I hate the unpredictability of this wretched world."

Aurora handed the venom to Tristan, only to have Millie reclaim it with a swift motion.

"What are you doing?" Millie asked.

"I'm giving it to Tristan since he's the only one of us who can actually leave this world," Aurora said.

Millie's gaze turned steely as she met Aurora's eyes. "You and I both know you are the only one who can get close enough to your father to feed him the venom. This is the last vial, and I'm not taking any chances."

A heavy sigh escaped Aurora's lips. "Well, I don't know if you've noticed, but I'm stuck here for good."

"Actually…" Millie chewed on her lip. "That's not entirely true."

Aurora's gaze snapped to Millie. "Are you telling me you've known there's a way out for me this whole time?"

Millie's shrug held a touch of sheepishness. "We weren't on good terms then. But now we are, so cheer up!"

Aurora huffed, wrapping her thin robe tighter around her body as she shot another glare at Millie. "You're lucky I'm indecent right now, otherwise I would strangle you with my bare hands."

"Now that's the spirit you need to take back to your father." Millie's clapping hands seemed to set the rhythm for a new momentum. "Now, chop-chop. We have work to do."

"Is it true?" Tristan's voice cut through the

tension. "Is there really a way to wake Aurora up in the real world, or is it just some sick joke to get back at her?"

Silence hung heavy in the room, and then Millie spoke. "Okay. I can see why you wouldn't trust me. I did hurl a knife at your heart. But to my defense, there was no doubt in my mind that Aurora would've stopped that blade."

"So, you are telling the truth, then?" Tristan pressed, his voice cautious, hesitant, and hungry for assurance. "There is a way she can awaken?" He needed to hear her say it. Needed that seed of hope to take root in the soil of his doubts.

"Fine. The truth is, it's no guarantee. But I'm hoping that thanks to your shenanigans"—Millie motioned toward the disheveled sheets on the floor—"you both made it that much more possible. Now, let me think, what else will you need…"

"Nothing happened—" Aurora ventured to say, but Millie lifted a finger, signaling for Aurora not to interrupt her thinking process.

"I need to make a list." As Millie delved into the contents of her bag, her attention shifted to the practicalities of their escape plan. Meanwhile, uncertainty flooded Aurora's senses.

Could it be true? Could there truly be a way for

her to escape the Dreamworld's clutches and return to the real world?

Tristan touched her shoulder. "You hear that?" he said softly. "There's a chance you'll be getting out of here."

Aurora nodded, but she couldn't help the twinge of doubt that gripped her. What if this was just another illusion, another layer of deception that the Dreamworld was known for? She didn't trust it.

"I know that look. And no." Tristan's voice grew firm. "We are not going to be pessimistic." He lifted her chin until her gaze met his unwavering eyes. "You are getting out of here. I will make sure of that."

Aurora forced a smile just for him. "Perhaps it's best that we focus on more certain things."

"Like what?" he asked.

Aurora's thoughts shifted to the golden plate she had found at the tower. She reached into her satchel and retrieved it, her fingers curling around its cool surface. With a purposeful stride, she approached the fire, turning the plate in her hands until the engraved writings caught the light. Her gaze was then drawn to Hendrick's name etched into the gold.

But then, she turned the plate around, revealing Tristan's name. She held the plate above the fire, the flames casting flickering shadows that danced across the engraving. And just as the fire's warmth licked at the golden plate, the script on the plate began to emerge, etchings unfolding like a scroll.

Amidst the petals, the bees find their way,

Collecting the nectar for honey's bouquet.

A dance of cooperation, a rhythm divine,

A partnership forged in nature's design.

Aurora's fingers brushed the engraved lines as if she could unravel their secrets with her touch alone.

"What is it?" Millie's voice cut through the quiet.

Aurora glanced at Tristan, then at Millie, her brows furrowing. "Another blazing riddle."

TRISTAN

*T*ristan and Aurora stood outside, hand-in-hand, exposed to the elements. The cliff's edge was a jagged line against the horizon and the vast expanse of the sea below churned with waves that crashed against the rocks.

The wind howled, whipping back their hair and clothes, but nothing could compare to the storm swirling inside of Tristan as he clutched Aurora's hand. Above them, the sky was a canvas of dark purples and reds, the moon slowly moving to obscure the sun, signaling the nearing eclipse. He was torn between the drive to stay and protect her, and the task he was planning to do.

Aurora's eyes, usually so bright and full of life, were clouded with worry. "Are you sure you're okay with this plan?" she asked, her low voice barely audible over the roar of the wind.

For a moment, Tristan's insides knotted with concern. But he shook away his worries, shifting Millie's bag on his shoulder and turning to Aurora.

He reached out, cupping her face. Her skin burned against his cool fingertips. "If this plan works, I'll be able to wake you up. We'll be together, in the real world, Aurora. The thought of that... it's worth any risk."

He spoke the words, unsure if they were for her benefit or his own. It felt unnatural to be parted from her, and if things went wrong, he'd never see her again. The very thought sent his heart plummeting.

Aurora glanced over her shoulder, apparently ensuring Millie was out of earshot before slipping the venom vial into Tristan's hand. The small glass container felt heavy. "Just in case it doesn't work," she whispered, her eyes glistening with unshed tears. "Save your kingdom and free the women."

Tristan gripped the vial tightly until his knuckles ached. "It will work," he insisted. "And when it does, I'll free you, and if you'll have me, I'll make you my queen. This isn't just a dream anymore." He caressed her cheek, his heart warming at the thought of their happy ending, which was almost in sight.

But a shadow crossed Aurora's face as she bit her lip. "About that... there's something I haven't told you."

Tristan's heart skipped a beat. "What is it?"

She looked down, her fingers playing with the folds of her dress.

"Hey," he whispered, lifting her chin gently, forcing her to meet his gaze. "You can tell me anything."

But before she could speak, the distant sound of the bell tower echoed, its chimes resonating with an eerie finality. They both turned to the sky, watching as the eclipse began.

Time seemed to slow as Tristan pulled Aurora close, their lips meeting in a desperate, passionate kiss. It was a kiss filled with promises. "I will see you soon," he murmured against her mouth.

And then, with a final glance at the woman he had come to love, Tristan took a deep breath and threw himself off the cliff.

The sensation of falling was brief, and when he opened his eyes again, he was back in the cold, damp cell. The early morning light was weak as it streamed through the narrow slit in the stone wall. The contents of Millie's bag—tools and potions of various kinds—lay scattered around him. With renewed purpose, Tristan set to work, using the tools to pick the lock of the cell.

The weight of his responsibility to his kingdom and the burning desire to save Aurora waged a war in his heart. But one thing was clear: he would stop at nothing to ensure her freedom and their future together.

Tristan barged into the council room. A long, wooden table, polished to a gleaming finish, dominated the center, surrounded by advisors deep in discussion. All eyes turned to him. Ryke, who was sitting at the head of the table, stood as soon as he caught sight of Tristan.

"Thank you for your concern for me, cousin," Tristan began. "You were right about everything. I'm sorry for putting you in this position. I assure you, I am well and ready to resume my duties."

The advisors exchanged uneasy glances, but Tristan continued, addressing them directly. "Please set a date for my coronation as king as soon as possible. My duty and honor to my kingdom has been delayed long enough."

Ryke's skeptical gaze never left Tristan. "Are you certain you are well?"

"I am better than well." Tristan's smile was confident, almost defiant. "I have found myself a bride—a queen—and I shall wed her at once."

"A bride?" Ryke echoed. "From the ball?"

"I was with her the night of the ball, yes." Tristan's response was cryptic, but he didn't linger on the topic. Turning to one of the guards, he commanded, "Please prepare a carriage for me. I must leave at once."

An advisor, an older man with a graying beard, interjected, "Where are you going, Your Highness? We must discuss more reports of the war. Since your absence, there have been more casualties…"

"There shall be no more casualties after today," Tristan declared, his voice booming with authority. "This war will end, and King Midas will no longer be a threat to us."

The men fell silent, their hollow eyes looking at him wide and alarmed. It seemed as though they were weighing him up, wondering if he had finally come to his senses or given in to madness.

Ryke, however, gave a nod of approval. "Spoken like a true king."

*K*ing Midas' castle was a looming structure. Its tall spires reached for the heavens, and its walls of dark gray stone were impenetrable. The entrance was guarded by two massive golden lions, their eyes set with rubies that seemed to glow with an inner fire. The castle's battlements were lined with soldiers, their golden armor reflecting the sun's rays, making the entire structure shimmer.

As Tristan stepped out of his royal carriage, he noticed a magnificent fountain at the front. In its center stood a golden statue of a horse, its front legs raised as if in mid-gallop. The nameplate read "Midnight." Tristan's heart ached at the sight.

Perhaps, to an ordinary person, the fountain was merely a work of art. An exquisite monument to a beloved horse. But Tristan knew better. That was Aurora's companion in the Dreamworld. He wondered what transgressions the horse might have committed to deserve such a fate. But then, a thought comforted him: in the Dreamworld, Aurora had Midnight by her side.

With determination burning in his veins, Tristan allowed himself to be escorted into the castle by Midas' guards. The walls were lined with rich tapestries depicting tales of conquest and power.

Golden chandeliers hung from the ceiling, their candles casting a warm glow that danced on the marble floors. The air was thick with the scent of burning incense, a mix of sandalwood and myrrh.

As Tristan walked deeper into the castle, he passed several rooms where young women busied themselves with cleaning, their faces pale and eyes vacant. Their hands moved lethargically, as if their soul was slowly withering away. The weight of their task was evident in their hunched shoulders. It was a chilling sight, and Tristan wondered which of them had been captured as children.

Finally, he was announced, then allowed into the throne room. At the far end of the hall, on a raised platform, sat King Midas on a throne gleaming with a brilliance that could only come from pure gold. The very air around him seemed to shimmer with opulence.

As Tristan stepped forward, the soft echo of his footsteps was the only sound that broke the heavy silence. Midas' gaze, cold and calculating, followed him.

"Prince Tristan," Midas began, his voice dripping with false warmth. "To what do I owe the displeasure of your visit?"

Tristan stopped a few paces away from the

throne, his posture straight, exuding confidence. "King Midas," he replied evenly, "I've come to end this war once and for all."

Midas chuckled, a sound devoid of genuine mirth. "And how do you plan on doing that?"

Tristan's hand moved to the small pouch at his side, extracting a vial filled with a dark liquid. "With this," he said, holding the vial up for Midas to see.

Midas' eyes widened slightly, a flicker of recognition passing through them. "Is that supposed to intimidate me?" he sneered, though the tremor in his voice betrayed his confidence.

"It's scorpion venom," Tristan stated calmly. "A single drop can turn all your precious gold to dust."

The atmosphere in the hall grew even more charged. Midas' initial confidence seemed to waver, replaced by a dawning realization of the threat Tristan posed.

"Am I supposed to be scared?" he spat, as though he was insulted more than afraid, but the whites of his eyes said otherwise.

"I am not here to instill fear," Tristan said. "I've come to seek peace."

Midas held out his hand. "If it's the end of the war that you seek, consider it done."

But Tristan didn't take the king's hand. "One

more thing," he said.

"What else could you possibly want?" Midas asked gruffly.

Tristan met his hard stare and stood his ground. He was determined to show no fear, despite the knowledge that with a single touch, the king could turn him into another golden statue for the palace.

"Your daughter's freedom," Tristan finally said.

Midas' eyes widened for a flicker of a moment, but then he scoffed. "You must be mistaken. My daughter has perished. Long ago."

Tension grew inside of Tristan as he gritted his teeth. "Aurora is alive and well, sleeping away somewhere in this castle, while her mind is in a dream world far away."

Midas' face grew blotchy, and he took a step back as though Tristan had struck him.

"How could you possibly know that?" he asked, wavering.

The reaction gave Tristan the strength to press further. So, Aurora was indeed kept in the castle. And Midas knew where she was. It was the confirmation he needed.

"Because I have been there. I have met her. And I have come to awaken her."

Midas opened and closed his mouth like a fish out

of water. Finally, he cleared his throat and wagged a dangerous finger in the air. "You come into my home, threaten my throne, and have the audacity to demand a marriage alliance? Have you gone mad, young man?"

"I am not demanding a marriage alliance," Tristan clarified, keeping calm despite the situation. "I only wish to awaken her and grant her freedom. If she chooses to accept a marriage proposal from me, that will be her choice, not a business transaction."

"My daughter will not leave this castle unless I have that vial," Midas spat.

Tristan rounded his shoulders and gave Midas a furious look. "You will not have this vial until you grant her freedom. Otherwise, you can say goodbye to your powers."

The two kings locked eyes, a battle of wills playing out in the silence of the throne room. The balance of power had shifted, and the outcome of that confrontation would shape the fate of their kingdoms.

But finally, Midas inclined his head. "Fine. I'll take you to her."

The castle's stone walls seemed to close in on Tristan as he followed Midas to Aurora's chamber.

Every step he took echoed back to him, amplifying the weight of the silence that filled the vast hallways.

As he walked, the golden statues became more frequent, each one more lifelike than the last. It was as if they had been frozen in time, their expressions capturing the exact moment of their transformation. A young maiden with her hand outstretched, perhaps reaching for a loved one; a knight with his sword drawn, forever locked in a battle that he would never finish; a child, no older than ten, with a look of sheer terror etched onto his face. The number of them was overwhelming, and Tristan couldn't help but shudder at the thought of the power that Midas wielded.

Here and there, animals too had been turned to gold. A hawk, wings spread as if in mid-flight, its eyes capturing a moment of surprise. A cat, its back arched and fur standing on end. An artistry of nature.

Whispers seemed to emanate from the walls themselves, tales of those who had dared defy Midas and paid the ultimate price. The air grew colder, and a sense of foreboding settled over Tristan. Every corner he turned, he half expected Midas to turn around and strike, adding him to his collection.

But Aurora was within those walls, and he would not leave without her. The thought of her gave him strength. Finally, after what felt like an eternity, they reached her bedroom at the very top—at the tower of the golden castle. The heavy wooden door stood before him, carved with elaborate designs and inlaid with gold. Midas stood aside and looked at Tristan pointedly.

Taking a deep breath, Tristan pushed it open, praying that he was not too late. The chamber was a vision of serenity. High, arched windows let in the gentle glow of the moon, casting a silvery sheen over everything. In the very center, he spotted Millie. Her delicate fairy wings were frozen mid-flutter. Her purple hair, which usually flowed like a cascade of lavender waterfalls, had turned solid gold, capturing each strand in meticulous detail. The expression on her face was one of surprise, perhaps even anger, her eyes wide and lips parted as if she had been caught in the midst of uttering a warning.

But it was Aurora who truly captured Tristan's attention. She lay in the center of the room on an ornate bed with carved posts and draped silks. Her soft golden hair flowed like a river of sunlight, spilling over the silk pillow and cascading down her shoulders, contrasting beautifully with her pale skin. Her hands were placed neatly together on her chest, fingers entwined, as if in prayer. The soft pink gown she wore clung to her form, its delicate lace and intricate embroidery making her look every bit the princess she was. The fabric shimmered with every breath she took, making it seem as though she was encased in a halo of light.

Her face was the epitome of peace. Long lashes rested on her cheeks, and her lips, though devoid of color, held a softness that made Tristan yearn to touch them. She looked so fragile, so ethereal, that for a moment, he was afraid to approach, fearing that the mere act might shatter her.

Taking a deep breath, he stepped closer, the weight of what he had to do pressing down on him. She was the perfect princess—a sleeping beauty of legends—and he'd come to awaken her.

Tristan leaned over her, the scent of wildflowers enveloping him. The fate of their two worlds hinged on that single act. With a deep breath, he closed his eyes and pressed his lips to hers. The room seemed to hold its breath, waiting for a sign, a miracle.

But nothing happened.

AURORA

*A*urora sat perched on the edge of the cliff, her legs swaying over the abyss as the golden hues of the setting sun bathed the landscape in a warm embrace. Aurora smiled as she watched the sun set. Tristan wasn't there, and yet the sun hadn't gone away. For the first time in what felt like forever, the world was bright, and it reflected her own hope. Real, genuine hope.

As the sun descended, its brilliance painting the sky in hues of orange and pink, Aurora's heart swelled. She marveled at the symbolism of this moment, a testament to the light Tristan had brought into her life. He was her beacon, dispelling the darkness that had lingered for far too long. With a soft smile, she closed her eyes, allowing her thoughts to be consumed by images of him.

"The sun is out and Tristan isn't here," Millie's voice interrupted Aurora's reverie as she settled down beside her. "Someone's feeling hopeful again. That's nice to see."

Aurora's smile remained, her eyes still closed. "It's amazing how he makes everything brighter, even when he's not around."

"I never thought I would see you in love again," Millie said, her tone gentle.

Aurora's smile faded slightly as doubt crept in. She opened her eyes, her gaze fixed on the horizon. "Do you really think this plan will work?"

Millie turned to her with a knowing smile. "If you're asking me if I think he's genuinely in love with you, the answer is a resounding yes. But the better question is... are you?"

Aurora's heart clenched, a swirl of emotions cascading through her. "It's more than love," she admitted, her voice barely a whisper. "He lights up my soul in a way I never thought possible."

Millie's words were like a soothing balm. "Then it will work."

As the sun dipped farther, casting longer shadows

across the landscape, Aurora's thoughts turned dark. "Am I a terrible person for leading him to believe that we can be together?" she asked, her voice tinged with guilt.

Millie regarded her thoughtfully. "Why wouldn't you be together?"

Aurora's gaze remained fixed on the horizon, regret and uncertainty weighing on her heart. "I haven't been completely honest with him about Hendrick."

Millie's voice was gentle but direct. "Do you think it would've changed anything if you had told him?"

"Not for me, but for him... I don't know."

Millie leaned in. "If he truly loves you, he should want to save you regardless of whether or not he can be with you."

A soft breeze ruffled Aurora's hair. "I still think I should've told him."

Millie's gaze held a comforting certainty. "I think he'll understand. So much of what has happened to you has been out of your control. He should at least understand that."

"I hope you're right—" Aurora's breath caught in her throat as her chest began to tighten. Then, like a bolt of lightning, panic surged through Aurora's veins, gripping her like icy fingers. She clutched onto Millie as her world narrowed to a terrifying point.

Everything around her began to spin, the edges of her vision blurred as her breath quickened.

"Wh–what is happening?" Aurora choked.

Millie's eyes widened in understanding. "It's working, Aurora! You're waking up!"

Aurora gasped for air, her chest tightening as if an invisible hand were squeezing her heart. She clung to Millie as her consciousness teetered on the precipice of reality.

"Go get us out of here," Millie managed to whisper before Aurora's vision spiraled into darkness.

The world spun, unraveling the threads of Aurora's dreams. As the darkness encroached, Aurora's grip on the Dreamworld slipped.

Her eyes fluttered open, and Tristan's worried expression greeted her. As recognition dawned, his features eased.

"It worked…" he breathed, a relieved smile stretching his lips.

Aurora propped herself up, the sense of disorientation slowly receding. Her gaze swept the room, and there, by the fireplace, stood a man lost in thought, his contemplative gaze fixed on the dancing flames. The familiarity of the scene clawed at the edges of Aurora's memory.

"Father?" The word escaped her lips as memories

surged, unraveling the threads of her fragmented reality. The scene before her seemed so familiar, and yet so distant.

Midas turned, his gaze icy and piercing, a stark reminder of the dark chapters of her past. "Foolish child," his voice dripped with disdain. "You almost cost me everything."

His words hung heavy in the air, a reminder of the years Aurora had spent under his control, enduring his cruelty after her mother's death. The pain he had inflicted on her was an old wound that never truly healed.

As his gaze shifted toward Tristan, Aurora could sense the tension in the air—the past and present colliding in a way she never thought possible.

"You got what you wanted. Now, give me the vial," Midas' demand sliced through the silence.

Aurora's heart raced as she stood. "He won't be giving you anything." She held out her hand to Tristan, her resolve steeling her voice. "Give me the vial, and I'll put an end to this once and for all."

Midas' expression twisted with bitterness. "Betrayed by my own blood. How ironic."

Aurora's spine straightened as she met her father's glare with a steady one. "What can I say, it runs in the family."

Tristan's presence was a comforting anchor beside her, his unwavering support bolstering her resolve.

Midas' attention shifted toward Tristan. "If you're going to give her the vial, you should at least know the real reason she wants to do away with my gold."

Midas' words hung in the air. Aurora's heart clenched as Tristan's calm façade held firm. "The list is endless, I'm sure."

Midas flashed a malicious grin that sent a shiver down Aurora's spine. "True. But the first name on that list is… Hendrick."

The very mention of that name sent a tremor through Aurora's being. Memories surged, a tumultuous sea she had long tried to suppress.

"I already know about him," Tristan's voice was measured. "She told me you turned him into a statue of gold."

Midas' grin only widened, his eyes glinting wickedly. "Did she also care to mention that I did that on their wedding day?"

The revelation struck with the force of a sledgehammer. Aurora's chest tightened, and she struggled to breathe as the weight of her father's words pierced through her.

Midas continued, each word a calculated strike. "And when she found out he had gone to the Dreamworld, she went in there after him. The reason she got trapped there was because she refused to leave without him. And I am fairly certain that while she was in there, she found out that if she took away my gold, that would bring him back to life. Hence, she used you to get her real prince back."

The room seemed to close in around her, the reality of her actions crashing down like a tidal wave. Her throat constricted, and her vision blurred with unshed tears. "Don't listen to him. You know that if I didn't truly love you, your kiss wouldn't have woken me up."

Tristan's gaze turned to her, his expression unreadable. "Is it true? Was there a wedding?"

Tears welled in Aurora's eyes, her heart aching with the weight of her past. "Yes. But it was never officiated—"

"You were promised to a man in front of his kingdom, Aurora." Tristan's words were like shards of glass, slicing through her heart. "He may still be alive, and you led me to believe we could be together."

Desperation clawed at Aurora's chest, her voice trembling as she reached out to him. "We can, Tristan. Please, just listen—"

"Think like a king, Tristan." Midas' voice sliced

through the tense air, a sinister temptation that ensnared Tristan's attention. "Your kingdom is suffering right now. It needs resources to rebuild and restore. I can provide you with everything you need. In exchange for that vial."

Tristan's posture remained steadfast, his voice steady in the face of the offer. "I want an alliance of peace. Your kingdom and mine, joined as one. And you provide all the resources I need to rebuild the villages you destroyed."

Midas' agreement was swift. "You have my word."

Aurora's heart pounded, caught between the hope of a better future and the despair of what it might cost. The weight of the decisions hung heavily in the air, threatening to shatter the fragile balance that had been achieved.

"And lastly…" Tristan's voice held a gravity that stole the breath from Aurora's lungs. She watched, her heart in her throat, as he continued, "I want Aurora to be set free."

Midas reached out his hand. "Done."

Aurora's breath caught as the vial passed from Tristan's hand to Midas', and in one swift move, Midas shattered the glass against the cold stone wall of the fireplace. The liquid within was quickly consumed by the hungry flames before vanishing into thin air.

Midas turned and gave Aurora a hard, narrow look. "If you ever return to this castle, you shall be imprisoned at once. From this moment on, you are no longer my daughter." And with those words, he turned and walked away.

Aurora's heart splintered. His final words hung in the air like a curse, like a final nail in the coffin of their fractured relationship.

As her father disappeared from sight, Aurora turned to Tristan, her heart raw and broken, seeking comfort in his gaze. But was met with a storm that raged within his eyes.

"Was it true what he said?" Tristan asked, his voice barely audible. "The reason you wanted to get in that tower was to find Hendrick?"

"Yes, but it changed," she cried. "The more I got to know you—"

"You lied to me."

"I fell in *love* with you!"

Tristan pressed his lips to a tight line, then he looked away, as though the mere sight of her was unbearable.

"I never lied about my feelings."

Shaking his head, he began pacing. "Everything

we have was built on a lie, Aurora." He stopped and bore his eyes into her. "How could you possibly think that it could weather a storm?"

Aurora's lips trembled as she suppressed the torrent of emotions that were threatening to burst out of her.

"Millie was right," Tristan's voice cut through the heavy silence, his words a frigid accusation that pierced her like a dagger. "You did use me like a pawn."

As he moved toward the door, she reached for him. "Tristan, please…" she cried.

But he pulled his arm away so as to avoid her touch. "I've granted your freedom," he said, barely glancing back at her. "Do with it as you wish."

Aurora's emotions surged, a maelstrom of regret, fear, and the searing agony of her past choices. The room around her seemed to close in, the walls a suffocating reminder of her secrets and their consequences.

As Tristan's footsteps receded down the hall, it echoed like the beat of a funeral drum. With a heavy heart, Aurora sank to her knees among the ruins of the shattered fragments of her heart.

TRISTAN

*T*he musty scent of the council chamber permeated the room. It was a scent that had clung to Tristan's memory since his early childhood, a mixture of old wood, ink, and the presence of countless rulers who had convened before him. As he sat at the head of the table, absorbing the atmosphere, the voices of his advisors reverberated like echoes of history.

Sir Harwick, a stout man with a graying beard, was the first to speak. "Your Highness, the reports from the borders are promising. King Midas has indeed withdrawn his forces. Our towns and villages, once desolated, are now buzzing with renewed vitality. The reconstruction is well underway."

Tristan nodded, acknowledging the positive development. The turmoil of war had given way to the industrious hum of progress, a testament to the resilience of his people. But he knew that this was just the beginning, a single brushstroke on the canvas of his reign.

Sir Cedric, a younger advisor with sharp features, chimed in, "Furthermore, sire, King Nathaniel of the White Rose Kingdom has sent a ship laden with provisions. It's a tangible symbol of the alliances we're forging."

"And Queen Snow White of the Chanted Kingdom has made an offer that extends beyond mere words," Harwick continued. "She's pledged troops and resources to safeguard our kingdom's future."

Tristan nodded, taking in all the reports. The kingdom was healing, and hope was no longer a distant dream. "This unity, this collaboration, it's what our kingdom has needed for so long. My father believed in self-reliance, and while I respect his views, I believe in the strength of unity. We are stronger together."

A wistful smile tugged at the corners of Tristan's lips as he looked around the room. It was a smile tinged with acceptance, a sign that he was growing into the role fate had thrust onto him. He would never be the ruler his father had been, but that was not a mark of failure. It was a testament to his adaptability, his willingness to learn, and his capacity to evolve.

As the council members filed out of the chamber, their discussions concluded, Tristan lingered for a moment. He moved to stand by the window, allowing the warm sunlight to wash over him. The grandeur of the day ahead—his coronation day—cast a shadow over his thoughts.

A breeze rustled the ornate curtains, bringing with it the scent of blooming flowers from the castle gardens. He found himself lost in the view, as the castle bustled with activity. His coronation was soon to take place. He knew that he needed to stand tall, to wear the crown with confidence, but his heart remained a battleground of scars.

Tristan's thoughts inevitably turned to Aurora. The memories of Midas' words stirred within him like embers fanned to life. The revelation of Aurora's marriage to Prince Hendrick had been a blow that had struck at the core of his emotions. The sacrifices she had made, her willingness to endure for the sake of love for someone else, had left him utterly broken.

But despite the pain that gnawed at his chest, despite the turmoil that raged within him, Tristan's heart still yearned for her. Her absence, the hollow void that she left behind, was a pain that cut deeper than any wound he had ever known. It was a pain that defied reason, a pain that made him question everything he thought he knew about himself.

He pondered the true depths of Aurora's feelings. The true love's kiss they had shared was a testament to her love for him, an undeniable proof that their connection ran deeper than circumstance. Yet, the specter of Prince Hendrick's existence loomed like a shadow over their relationship. If Hendrick were truly alive and returned, where did that leave Tristan in Aurora's heart? The question plagued him, a constant whisper in the back of his mind that he couldn't escape.

He had questioned his own emotions countless times, grappling with the complexity of his feelings. The tangle of his heartstrings, the longing that pulled him toward Aurora, was undeniable. Yet, uncertainty clawed at him, a persistent shadow that refused to be dispelled. He had been raised to believe in duty and honor, but love was a wild and unruly thing that defied logic.

"Tristan."

A deep voice sliced through the silence, pulling Tristan from his reverie. He turned to find Killian entering the room. A smile tugged at Tristan's lips as he met the eyes of the man who had fought at the front lines for his kingdom.

"Killian," Tristan greeted him, the warmth in his voice mirroring the camaraderie that had formed between them. "What can I do for you?"

"Ella sends her love," Killian began, his voice a deep rumble that resonated with sincerity. "She believes you'll make a great king."

Tristan appreciated the sentiment, but he knew that Killian's visit carried more weight than a simple message of well-wishing.

"Ella would've come for your coronation," Killian continued, "but with the newborn baby, the journey would have been too much for her. Aurora has been of great help to Ella the past few weeks. Ella also insisted that I bring Lily a new dress. I gave it to Wendy when I arrived."

Tristan nodded, his respect for Ella's character deepening. Her compassion and thoughtfulness toward Ryke's little sister were qualities that had endeared her not only to Killian, but to Tristan as well. During her time working in the castle, Ella had taken very good care of Lily. The mention of Aurora, however, was a bittersweet reminder of the woman who had taken root in his heart, despite the thorny path their relationship had taken.

Tristan turned to gaze out the window. "Will Aurora be attending the coronation?" he asked.

"She believed you might prefer her absence," Killian said as though repeating Aurora's own words. "Should I tell her otherwise?"

Tristan's heart clenched at the thought of Aurora's selflessness, her ability to sense his inner turmoil even when he tried to mask it. He knew he had been distant, grappling with emotions that were as delicate as the tapestries that lined the castle walls.

"No," Tristan finally said. "Distance is best for us at the moment."

"She seems to agree," Killian continued. "She's mentioned traveling north soon."

Hendrick's kingdom was to the north. The realization struck Tristan like a bolt of lightning, illuminating the shadows of doubt that had taken refuge in his mind. Before he could dwell any further on it, he shifted the conversation.

"Killian," he began, his voice earnest, "your service to the kingdom has been invaluable. I want to show my appreciation, as well as to ensure that you and Ella are well taken care of. That being said, I offer you an expansion of your land as a token of gratitude for your support."

Killian responded with a nod. "Your offer is generous. However, I wish to request something else."

Tristan raised an eyebrow, intrigued. "Speak your mind."

"Ella," Killian said, his voice softening as he mentioned his wife's name. "She is a talented dress-maker. I've seen her create beauty from plain fabric. If it pleases you, could you provide her with a place in the royal square to showcase and sell her dresses?"

Tristan smiled, his respect for Killian growing even more. "Consider it done. Ella will have a place in the royal square, where her talent can shine for all to see."

As Killian took his leave, a sense of accomplishment washed over Tristan. He knew that the decisions he was making were molding the future of the kingdom, and it was a responsibility he had to bear with grace.

Before he could dwell further on his thoughts, the sound of footsteps heralded a new arrival. Turning, Tristan found his cousin Ryke approaching, pride and admiration shining in his gaze.

"Tristan," Ryke said in greeting, his voice warm as they clasped hands in a firm handshake.

"Ryke. You've been scarce lately."

Ryke chuckled, a knowing glint in his eyes. "I've been giving you space to grow into the king I've always known you could become."

Tristan gave his cousin a knowing look. "That sounds like something Lexa would say."

"Why, yes." Ryke smirked. "And she can be very persuasive."

Tristan laughed. "Well, whatever it is she is doing, tell her to keep it up."

A mischievous glint shined in Ryke's eyes. "I most certainly will. King's orders."

"Ah, but I'm not king yet," Tristan corrected.

Ryke placed an encouraging hand on Tristan's shoulder. "To me, you have been king from the moment Uncle drew his last breath. You may not have believed in yourself, but I always did."

Tristan's heart swelled with affection for his cousin, who had always understood him in ways that others couldn't. As they embraced, the unspoken bond between them spoke volumes.

"You've done exceptional work," Ryke commended, pulling back to meet Tristan's eyes. "The kingdom is on its way to healing, and it's all because of you."

Tristan's lips curved into a wry smile. "The work is just beginning."

Ryke ran a hand through his thick, black hair. "There's another reason I've come to see you," he said, his voice tinged with a slight weariness. "I shall be leaving after your coronation. I'm afraid it's time for me to return to the seas."

Tristan felt his heart tug a little, but he knew Ryke hadn't returned to stay. He was just grateful his cousin had hung around long enough to see him finally embrace the throne.

"I'll miss you," Tristan admitted.

Ryke's smile held a promise. "I'll only be a message away, cousin. No matter the distance, our bond remains."

A tiny glimmer of pride rose from within Tristan, but still, their separation would leave a void. "Your guidance and concern have been my anchor, Ryke. Thank you for that."

They embraced once more, the gesture a testament to the depth of their connection. As Ryke departed, Tristan was once again left alone, the weight of the crown he was about to wear already pulling him down. But more than that, the crushing pressure of a heart yearning for a love that seemed just out of reach.

But as he stood there, surrounded by the echoes of his past and the promise of his future, Tristan knew that destiny was weaving its intricate patterns. He was no longer a prince grappling with uncertainties. He was a leader, a man forging a path through uncharted territories, and with each step, he was determined to shape a kingdom that would thrive, united under his reign.

"Tristan?" A voice, soft and melodic, came from behind the door connecting his study to the library.

He turned toward the sound, a sense of familiarity and comfort washing over him. "Aurora?" he called in response.

"Tristan…" Aurora's voice spoke through the door. "Where are you?" she called out, her voice gentle.

A smile tugged at Tristan's lips as he crossed the study. He reached for the door, his fingers wrapping around the copper handle. With a deep breath, he pulled it open.

AURORA

*B*athed in the soft glow of the morning light filtering through the windows, Aurora stood before a tri-fold mirror, draped in a delicate dress that Ella was meticulously working on. The newborn baby girl lay sleeping nearby, a picture of serenity within the quiet room. Aurora's gaze was fixed on her reflection, but her thoughts were far away.

As her fingers traced the fabric of the dress, she couldn't help but imagine what it would've been like to have a family with Tristan. Her heart ached at the thought of the life they might have shared, the children they could've raised together. In her mind's eye, she pictured their kids—golden hair and brown eyes, a perfect blend of their love.

But amidst her hopeful daydreams, a shadow of reality lingered. Tristan's deal with Rumple still haunted her thoughts. If he were to die without leaving behind an heir, the kingdom would fall into the clutches of that conniving monster. The weight of the responsibility he carried for their kingdom's future was a burden she couldn't ignore.

The sting of a needle on her leg pulled Aurora back to the present. Ella, kneeling at her feet, offered an apologetic smile. "Sorry, my eyes are a little blurry. I didn't get much sleep last night."

"Killian's to blame?" Aurora teased, hoping to lighten the mood.

Ella's cheek reddened, and a shy smile tugged at her lips. "Mostly the baby, but yeah, Killian too."

Aurora met her own gaze in the mirror and couldn't help but admire the beautiful dress Ella was working on. "This dress is lovely."

Ella's eyes lit up with excitement. "Killian is going to ask Tristan if I could have my own store in the square. I want to have brand new designs to display if he agrees."

"He'll agree," Aurora replied with a small smile, though her countenance fell at the memory of Tristan's kindness. The thought of no longer having him in her life, of losing the possibility of a future together, made tears threaten to spill from her eyes. "Well, your designs are stunning. Seems like you and your sister have more than just looks in common."

Ella paused in her work, looking up at Aurora curiously. "You know my sister?"

Caught off guard, Aurora pressed her lips together, but it was too late, the words had already spilled out. "I did, yes," she confessed, her eyes locked on the dress as she avoided meeting Ella's gaze. "She lived in the castle with me as a child."

Ella stood, her eyes searching for Aurora's in the mirror. "You were taken from your parents, too?"

The thought of lying to Ella crossed Aurora's mind, but her striking resemblance to Rapunzel kept her from being able to do so. Out of all the girls in the castle, Rapunzel had been Aurora's best friend. There had never been any secrets between them.

"King Midas is my father," Aurora admitted.

Ella's eyes widened, and she instinctively took a step back, as if the truth carried a weight that threatened to crush her.

Aurora frowned, her heart heavy with regret. "He took all those girls so that I wasn't alone in the castle. So that I had friends to play with. I hadn't realized where they'd come from until I was older. I tried getting him to set them free, but…" She sighed. "My father is a very complicated man."

As the truth sunk in, Ella's eyes filled with tears. "So, my sister wasn't alone?"

Aurora shook her head. "No, she wasn't alone. But sometimes I wondered if she would've rather been."

Ella's brows furrowed. "Why do you say that?"

"There were many young girls in the castle, but Rapunzel never mingled with them. She used to say she didn't need a sister, that she already had one—the best one." Aurora met Ella's eyes in the mirror. "There wasn't a day that she didn't talk about you. She missed you very much."

A tear slid down Ella's cheek. "If you knew who I was in the Dreamworld, why didn't you say anything?"

Aurora's gaze dropped to the shoes at the foot of the mirror. "Your sister made me promise never to tell you where she was."

Ella's curiosity persisted. "Why not?"

Aurora's heart tightened as she recalled the painful memory. "Your sister saw you in the garden from the top of the tower. She saw when the guards caught you trespassing. She screamed at them to let you go. I had to hold her back so she didn't throw herself out the window after you. I had never seen her so distraught. And then…"

Ella's eyes widened, realization dawning. "She heard of our father's death, didn't she?"

Aurora nodded, her heart heavy. "She blamed herself for what happened. And for that reason, she didn't want you to know she was still alive. She didn't want you to keep risking your life to save her. Letting you think that she died was her way of protecting you, of giving you permission to move on with your life."

Ella turned away from Aurora and began to pick up scattered fabrics from the floor. "If that were true, she would have found me after she freed herself from the tower."

Aurora thought back to when she'd woken up in her father's castle with Tristan. She looked for Rapunzel before she left. She was nowhere to be found.

"I don't know what happened to her after I left," Aurora admitted. "But I can assure you that you are the person she loves the most in this world."

Ella wiped her tears away, her voice trembling as she spoke. "I have on good authority that my sister is alive and well. She showed herself to Killian when she thought he was going to die. Perhaps she was hoping he would take her secret to his grave. She underestimated him. His strength. His love for me."

Aurora knew Rapunzel well enough to know that she rarely underestimated anyone, but that wasn't the time to analyze her sister's intentions. She sensed that Ella needed reassurance more than facts in that moment.

"Whatever the reason that has her away, it doesn't matter anymore." Ella tossed the pile of fabrics aside and sat next to her sleeping baby. The weight of the years of longing and pain seemed to hang in the air. "If my sister doesn't want to be part of our life, of our children's lives, then that will be her choice. I have carried the weight of her absence for far too long. I owe it to myself to move on. I owe it to my kids."

Aurora nodded. "I'm sure she would want that for you, too."

Ella was quiet for a long time, the silence interrupted only by the soft breathing of her baby. "I'm feeling a little tired. I think I'm going to try to sleep a little before the baby wakes up."

"Of course." Aurora turned her back to Ella. "Would you help me out of the dress?"

"Actually, you can keep the dress on. It looks

beautiful on you. And there's also something I want you to have."

Aurora watched as Ella retrieved a piece of parchment from a drawer and handed it to her. As her fingers brushed against the paper, she found herself tracing Tristan's name. It was an invitation to Tristan's coronation, a formal acknowledgment of his ascent to the throne.

She looked at Ella, surprised. "How did you know?"

Ella offered a soft smile. "I worked in the palace for many years. I've seen the King of the Shores introduce many women to Prince Tristan. But not once did I see Tristan's eyes light up the way they did when he talked about you."

Aurora's heart lifted as she remembered their conversations, the moments they had shared. It was a bittersweet reminder of the connection they had forged, even amidst the challenges and secrets that had surrounded them.

"What did he say?" she asked, her curiosity overwhelming her better judgment.

"Not much," Ella admitted with a small shrug. "He seemed very intrigued with the sundrop flower and the Dreamworld. But then he asked about you, and I saw a glint in his eyes. It was the same glint I saw in yours when you talked about him a moment ago."

Looking at his name on the parchment, she felt her heart tighten in her chest. The thought of not seeing him again, of letting him go, made her ache deep within her soul.

"I could never make it on time," Aurora murmured, her gaze fixed on the invitation.

Ella's voice was gentle. "You see that white horse out there? That's Azul. He's a special horse, capable of not only incredible speed, but flying. If you want to go, he could get you there on time."

Aurora's heart fluttered at the mere possibility of seeing Tristan one last time, of explaining her actions, of seeking forgiveness. The thought of his presence, even if just for a fleeting moment, was both exhilarating and terrifying. She felt as though her heart were caught in a whirlwind, her emotions tumbling in a storm of conflicting desires.

But reality settled in, a heavy weight on her chest. She had broken his heart, shattered his trust. The pain in his eyes when he walked away was etched into her memory. She couldn't bear to see that pain again, to witness the love and hope drain from his gaze.

"No," Aurora finally whispered. "As much as I

want to see him, I can't. Not after what I've put him through."

Aurora crumbled the invitation in her hand. "Remember the paper I gave you before you left the Dreamworld?" she asked Ella. "I asked you to keep it safe for me?"

"Ah, yes." Ella went to retrieve it from another drawer, then handed it to Aurora. "What is it?" she asked.

Aurora stared at the blank page for a moment, lost in the memories it held. "It's a list I found in the Dreamworld of my family tree," she explained. "I figured if I ever made it out, I would never again return to that tower. So, I needed to know what other places I could go. I found an illusion of my mother once who gave me a list of her family. Thank you for keeping it safe for me."

Ella leaned in, her curiosity getting the better of her. She peered at the paper that was still in Aurora's hand. "But it's blank," she noted.

Aurora smiled knowingly. She walked over to a candle burning on the table and held the paper over the flame. As if by magic, letters began to appear on the paper, glowing a deep shade of red before settling into their original inky black. "There it is."

Ella's eyes widened in amazement. "I've never seen anything like it."

Aurora chuckled softly. "As much as I hate the Dreamworld, it also has its own fascinating wonders."

Ella leaned against the table, regarding Aurora thoughtfully. "So, where will you go now?"

Aurora looked at the crumbled invitation in one hand, then at the family list in the other. Her heart ached with conflicting desires, torn between what she wanted and what she believed was right. "If I go to Tristan, I'll keep him from moving on, and that wouldn't be fair to him."

Still, the thought of leaving without saying goodbye to Tristan nearly shattered her entire being.

A heavy silence hung in the air as Ella absorbed Aurora's words, her eyes full of empathy. "So, what will it be?" Ella pressed gently.

A pleased smile curved Aurora's lips. "I'll bring Azul back along with your dress."

*A*urora's heart raced as she dismounted from Azul. The wind had been relentless, leaving her golden hair a tousled mess. She glanced around the palace courtyard, her brown eyes catching the glint of sunlight against polished armor and elaborately ornamented carriages.

As she stepped into the grand foyer of the palace, her heeled shoes echoing on the marble floor, Aurora's gaze was drawn to the coronation hall. A throng of elegantly dressed guests filled the space, their hushed conversations creating an undercurrent of anticipation. Her heart quickened as she weaved through the crowd, determined to catch a glimpse of the moment Prince Tristan would ascend to the throne.

"The prince is never late," a man's voice murmured nearby.

"I've heard no one can find him in the palace," another voice responded.

With a deep breath, Aurora's steps quickened. Her father, King Midas, stood at the front of the hall. But an inexplicable unease settled over her, sending a shiver down her spine. She veered behind one of the grand pillars, seeking to hide from his sight.

Spotting a small door tucked away in a corner, Aurora darted toward it. The narrow corridor stretched before her. But before she could take more than a few steps, a strong hand seized her arm, pulling her into a room with endless shelves filled with books.

Aurora spun around, alarmed. But then recognized Killian. "You scared me," she breathed in relief.

Killian's rugged face softened, his stormy eyes studying her. "Is Tristan with you?"

Aurora shook her head, puzzled by the question. "No, why would he be?"

The furrow deepened between Killian's brows, a shadow of concern clouding his gaze. "He's gone," he uttered, the weight of those two words sinking heavily in the air.

Aurora's heart stuttered. "What do you mean 'gone'? It's his coronation day."

"It's not just his coronation. It was also a public alliance with your father."

A chill swept over Aurora, her eyes falling to the ground. The intricate patterns of the marbled floor seemed to blur as her thoughts whirled.

Killian's head dipped in a respectful bow. "Rest assured, your secret is safe with me, Princess."

Before Aurora could respond, the library door was flung open. A guard rushed with his face pale. "Killian, it's Ryke. Hurry."

The echoing clang of footsteps reverberated as Killian stormed out of the room. Without a second thought, Aurora trailed after him. The sound of a man's voice, sharp and furious, reached her ears even before they entered the coronation hall. The atmosphere was charged, heavy with a hint of dread.

As they crossed the threshold into the hall, Aurora's gaze locked onto a man with jet-black hair who stood defiantly before her father.

"What did you do to the prince?" The man's voice dripped with anger and desperation. "I should have you hanged in the courtyard at once!"

Aurora hid behind one of the pillars, straining to catch every word.

Killian swiftly positioned himself between the two men, his broad frame serving as a barrier. He spoke in a measured tone, attempting to defuse the escalating confrontation. "Ryke, not here. This is not how the leaders of a kingdom behave."

The man, Ryke, seethed as his eyes shifted from King Midas to Killian. "My cousin is missing, and where were you?" His words were punctuated by a low growl. "Weren't you supposed to have been guarding him?"

Killian's expression hardened. "I was put in charge of guarding his army, not the prince."

"Then you're no good here," Ryke snapped with unbridled frustration.

Killian's gaze darkened, his attention shifting to a woman with long, dark hair seated in the front row. "Lexa, take him away before I forget who he's related to."

Lexa rose from her seat at once and reached for Ryke. "Honey, please. Let's take a walk outside."

Ryke ran a hand through his already disheveled hair. "If he's somewhere drinking from that blazing flower again, I swear to the heavens, Lexa, I will kill him with my bare hands."

Aurora's mind raced. Tristan couldn't have consumed the sundrop flower. He had no reason to return to the Dreamworld, not anymore.

"I know, honey." Lexa's voice was soothing as she pulled Ryke away with her. But then she gave Killian a panicked look over her shoulder and mouthed, "Find him."

Killian turned his gaze toward King Midas, his voice a low rumble. "I'm going to ask one last time: where is the prince?"

Midas' chest puffed out in regal defiance, yet beneath his veneer, something flickered in his eyes. "And I am going to repeat one last time: I have no knowledge of his whereabouts."

Killian leaned in, his voice laced with a dangerous edge. "If I discover that you did something to the prince, I will personally detach your head from your body. Is that clear?"

Midas' nostrils flared, his regal façade slipping as frustration seeped through. "The only reason I'm still standing here is because I am a man of my word. But make no mistake, if the prince doesn't show, our alliance is over, and I won't stop until his entire kingdom becomes mine."

Killian stepped back, his gaze sweeping the guards surrounding them. "Send out a search team to find the prince. Now."

Aurora's back pressed against the pillar, her mind racing. Her father's guilt-ridden expression was not lost on her, but as he exchanged words with one of his counselors, his puzzlement seemed genuine. Her gaze flickered toward the scene, piecing together fragments of information.

And then it struck her—a name whispered in the back of her mind. A figure that would instantly benefit from Tristan's disappearance. From Tristan's death.

Rumpelstiltskin.

TRISTAN

$\mathcal{A}$ cloth covered Tristan's head, blinding his sight and plunging him into a disorienting void. His hands were bound tightly behind his back, restraining any attempts at freedom. The rough texture of a wooden chair beneath him sent a jolt of apprehension through his veins. The air was thick with the musty scent of rust and mildew.

Abruptly, a hand seized the cloth that blinded him, unveiling the scene with a swift motion. Torchlight flickered against damp stone walls, casting eerie shadows that danced like specters. The dungeon was hot and humid, constricting his breath.

"Well, well. If it isn't the Prince of the Shores." Rumple's voice echoed in the damp space, his words laced with a sinister amusement. He emerged from the shadows, his figure materializing just outside the iron bars. "We meet yet again."

Tristan's jaw clenched as he met Rumple's gaze, his eyes burning with defiance. "I've always known you would come for my crown," he retorted. "But I never pegged you as a coward."

A dark chuckle reverberated through the cell as Rumple sauntered closer. The torchlight danced upon his face, highlighting the malicious glint in his eyes. "I am not a coward. I am, however, impatient. You see, I'm in desperate need of a kingdom, and I just can't wait any longer."

"So, this is it? You're going to end my life to take my throne?" Tristan's voice rang with a challenge, his spine straightening as he stared down his captor.

Rumple's lips curled into a twisted smile. "Don't be so morose, Tristan." He leaned against the bars. "No one's life needs to end tonight. All you have to do is change the terms of our deal, and you'll be free to go."

"To what, exactly?" Tristan asked skeptically.

Rumple's smirk deepened. "Announce me as your new king at the coronation ball."

For a fleeting second, Tristan almost believed Rumple was joking. "You can't be serious," he scoffed. "You want me to hand over my kingdom without a fight? What kind of king do you think I am?"

Rumple's eyes gleamed with a twisted mirth. "You are not a king. You are nothing but a mere shadow of your father. And it's time for your kingdom to have a real ruler at its reins."

Tristan cocked his head, amused. "If I was truly in my father's shadow, I wouldn't have made an alliance of peace with King Midas," he reasoned. "Now, perhaps you haven't given much thought to this but handing over my throne would dissolve that alliance. Without it, Midas will resume his attacks, and you'll be left without a kingdom. And truth be told, you are no match for him."

Rumple's laughter sliced through the air, a chilling sound that sent shivers down Tristan's spine. "You don't have to be stronger to win, Tristan. You just have to have the right weapon."

Tristan's brow furrowed in confusion. "If you're referring to the scorpion's venom, Midas destroyed the last vial," he said. "There is no other weapon against him."

A malicious grin played on Rumple's lips. "*Tsk tsk.* Now, that's where you're wrong." He wagged a finger in the air. "He does have a daughter, does he not?"

Tristan's blood ran cold, a chill sweeping through

him like a violent tsunami. "Leave Aurora out of this," he demanded.

Rumple's grin widened, his eyes gleaming with delight. "Now, what fun would that be?"

Anger surged within Tristan like a roaring inferno. "If you truly want to get to Midas, go after his gold," Tristan said, desperation fueling his words. "His daughter means nothing to him."

Rumple's gaze darkened, his amusement giving way to a cold, calculating resolve. "Maybe not," he conceded with a shrug. "But she does mean something to *you*."

Tristan's chest tightened, fear and fury churning within him.

"Rumpelstiltskin!" Aurora's voice echoed from somewhere within the mansion. "Show yourself!"

Rumple's eyes lit up with twisted satisfaction. "Ah! Right on time."

Tristan strained against his bonds, his muscles burning with the effort to break free. The rope bit into his skin. "You touch one strand of her hair, and I will end you."

With a snap of his fingers, Rumple conjured a parchment that floated down to rest on Tristan's lap. "Sign our new agreement," he demanded, pushing a quill through the iron bars, "and I'll ensure that nothing happens to her."

Tristan's heart raced as he scanned the parchment, his mind racing to find a way out of the trap that had been set. A sense of urgency flooded his veins, his thoughts consumed by the stakes that hung in the balance.

At that, a tiny fairy with wings like a hummingbird fluttered into the cell. Her eyes met Tristan's for a fleeting moment, and he saw deep sorrow in their depths. It was a fleeting connection, a moment of shared understanding that left Tristan wondering about the leverage Rumple held over her.

Tristan's hands were finally free. The burn of the rope marked his skin. The fairy returned to her cage, and Rumple drummed his fingers against the bars. Tristan grabbed the quill with shaky fingers, glancing at the agreement before him.

"Rumpelstiltskin!" Aurora called out louder than before. Her sweet voice coursed through his entire being, then lodged in his heart like an anvil.

He clutched the quill tightly, his heart torn between duty and love, between the throne and the woman who had ignited his soul. The silence of the dungeon was shattered by the echoing footsteps of a destiny he couldn't escape, a destiny that would be etched in ink on the parchment before him.

"Tick tock, Your Highness," Rumple's voice was light and hopeful, like he knew he'd won. "What's it going to be? Your kingdom, or your princess?"

AURORA

$\mathcal{A}$urora stood in the cluttered expanse of Rumpelstiltskin's living room, an odd mixture of awe and unease swirling within her. The room was a cacophony of artifacts, a hoarder's paradise where cobwebs shrouded relics of the past. The paintings on the walls seemed to gaze at her with faded eyes, and the old cuckoo clock on the far wall seemed frozen in time.

A rustle of fabric announced Rumpelstiltskin's arrival, drawing Aurora's attention to the door. He entered the room with an air of calculated charm, his presence commanding the space. She had heard rumors of his manipulative ways, but witnessing his craftiness firsthand was another matter entirely.

"Rumpelstiltskin," Aurora began, her tone firm.

"The Dreamworld stripped you of your royal manners, I see," Rumple interjected, his lips curling into an enigmatic smile. "What can I do for you, princess?"

Aurora's eyes bore into him. "Where is he? I know you have him."

Rumple grin widened, a glint of amusement dancing in his eyes. "Smart and beautiful. Quite a rare combination to find."

"Let him go," Aurora demanded. "Take me, instead."

Rumple's amusement lingered, his fingers tapping thoughtfully against his chin. "Now, what would I do with you? As Tristan himself said, you would be of no use to me."

Aurora squared her shoulders. "I have my father's blood. I can turn anything into gold. I can enrich you. Make you more powerful than anyone, including my father."

Rumple regarded her with a calculating gaze. "Are you saying you still have your gold?"

"I do," she lied, trying to keep the nerves from creeping into her voice.

"Very well, then." Rumple retrieved a silver chalice and a knife, placing them on the table. "Prove it."

Aurora's mind glitched, searching for a solution to this test. "I want to see him first."

Rumple's grin was sly, his eyes glinting with insight. "Don't peg me for a fool, child. If you still had your gold, your father would've had you back in that tower."

Aurora's resolve stiffened. "Fine. I may not have his gold, but I am in line for his throne."

Rumple circled her. "And what good will that do for me?"

Aurora met his gaze head-on. "My father's kingdom is worth a lot more than Tristan's. With his gold, you will become the most powerful ruler in all the kingdoms."

Rumple toyed with his necklace. "Is that what you think I want?"

Aurora's voice remained steady despite the tension in the room. "What is it that you want?"

"Assuming that's what I want…" Rumple studied her carefully. "Are you saying that if anything were to happen to your father, you would relinquish his kingdom to me?"

Aurora puffed out her chest. "You have my word."

A tense silence stretched between them, both

players locked in a high-stakes game of manipulation. Aurora's resolve held strong.

Rumple's eyes bore into her, a flicker of uncertainty clouding his expression. "And you wouldn't fight me for it?"

"I didn't inherit my father's thirst for power," Aurora assured him. "I am not interested in his throne or his gold."

Rumple's skepticism wavered, his curiosity piqued. "You're either a brilliant liar or a naive young princess."

"All I care about is Tristan's safe return. You give me your word, and I'll give you mine—a promise that the most powerful kingdom will be yours."

Rumple's grin stretched across his face, a smug triumph dancing in his eyes. "Seems like the saying holds true: good things do come for those who wait."

"So, we have a deal?" she asked.

"Hmm, not quite." His words hung in the air. "You see, your father stole something from me, and I want it back."

Curiosity sparked in Aurora. "What was it?"

"It was something of sentimental value to me. And since I will have to wait to claim my so-called powerful kingdom, this item will make waiting a little more bearable."

Aurora's mind swirled, seeking the puzzle pieces to complete the picture he was painting. "How can I get it for you if you don't tell me what it is?"

"It's a wooden spinning wheel," Rumple said. "But with a golden needle made by fairies."

The revelation hit Aurora like a bolt of recognition. She knew exactly what he sought, and her heart weighed heavy with the knowledge of its location. "Consider it done."

Rumple's smirk deepened. "You see, I only consider something done when it's, well… done."

With an enigmatic flourish, he conjured a parchment onto the table. Aurora's gaze was drawn to the blank canvas until a quill appeared, poised above the parchment. As if guided by an unseen hand, the quill began to write, each stroke forming words of the pact they were forging.

"That might take a little while," Rumple said casually, gesturing toward a door across the room. "Shall we go find that spinning wheel?"

Aurora followed Rumpel's lead, descending into the depths of his mansion. Torches lined the narrow hallway, casting flickering shadows that danced along the stone walls.

"Aurora!" Tristan's voice captured her attention, making her heart jump. Squinting into the distance, she caught sight of him behind a cell at the end of the dungeon.

"Tristan!" She ran to his cell and pressed herself against the iron bars, reaching for him.

He cupped her face as he rested his forehead on the cold bars. "Don't do it," his voice trembled. "Whatever it is that he's asking from you, don't do it."

Aurora offered him a soft, gentle smile. "You granted me my freedom. Now, it's my turn to grant yours." With that, she pulled away.

"Aurora, don't!" Tristan's voice grew faint as she walked away. "We can find another way! Aurora!"

She stopped in front of Rumple, who stood waiting for her, watching with a satisfactory glee at hearing Tristan scream Aurora's name.

Ignoring Tristan's pleas, Rumple gestured toward a door, its copper handle gleaming with the reflection of the fire. "Shall we?"

He stepped aside, granting Aurora entry with a wave of his hand. Confusion crossed her features as she regarded him.

"It's a special handle made of elven metal," he explained. "All you have to do is imagine the location where the spinning wheel is, then open the door."

Aurora closed her eyes, her mind conjuring memories of her mother's bedroom, the images vivid as they surfaced. The white sheet covering the wheel near the window, the sun's rays filtering through the curtains.

Drawing a deep breath, Aurora opened her eyes and reached for the door handle. As it yielded to her touch, a sense of anticipation rippled through her. She stepped inside the room that held a past she had locked away.

Dusty wood greeted her senses, mingling with the faint scent of memories. Aurora moved toward the window, her fingers brushing against the familiar fabric of the white sheet. As she unveiled the wheel's spindle, the golden needle sparkled, bathed in the warm embrace of the setting sun.

Rumple approached, his eyes wide with nostalgia. "Ah, yes." His fingers traced the contours of the spindle. "It hasn't changed a bit."

Aurora narrowed her eyes. "What's so special about it?" she asked.

"Your parents never told you?" Rumple scoffed. "Figures. Well, princess, you've got yourself a deal." With a snap of his fingers, the parchment reappeared in his hand, unrolling to reveal the pact they had woven. "Sign on the bottom and your prince is free to go."

"Where's the quill? Aurora asked.

"If the prince means that much to you, then sign it with your blood." Rumple gestured toward the golden needle.

Aurora took a deep breath, then pricked her finger on the tip of the needle. It stung as blood pooled at the tip of her finger. She pressed her finger onto the parchment without a second thought. As her mark settled onto the page, the parchment vanished, and Rumple's gaze was fixed on her.

But for some reason, her vision blurred and she began to see two of Rumple.

"How are you feeling, dear?" he asked.

Nausea rose from within her, making her light-headed. "What did you do to me?"

"Me? Absolutely nothing. The needle, however…" He gestured toward the needle again. It glowed brightly, then vanished into a puff of dust with tiny little fragments of gold floating in front of her. "Did I forget to mention the needle was made of pixie dust?"

Aurora's eyes widened. But before she could say anything, Rumple blew at the air, sending the pixie dust particles into her face.

She coughed, and her vision became hazy.

"Not to worry, dear. This is a much lighter dose. No one will take over your mind," Rumple continued as Aurora staggered away from him. "But you will, however, be compelled to do exactly what I tell you to do."

Aurora tried reaching for the door, but the room was spinning. Rumple stepped in front of her and placed a hand on the door to keep her from leaving.

"You will say goodbye to Tristan, then you will go in search of Prince Hendrick, who will no doubt be eagerly anticipating your arrival. Oh, how special that reunion will be."

"Don't do this," she pleaded.

"Too late, dear. A deal is a deal."

Aurora's vision cleared, bringing Rumple's wicked grin into full focus. His eyes were gray like two full moons, something Aurora had only seen in one other person's eyes. Her father's.

"Your darkness is from the Dreamworld, isn't it?" She didn't need an answer. She knew it was. "I lived in that darkness for a long time, but I cannot imagine having that darkness live within me. I wouldn't wish that on my worst enemy. Not even you."

His eyes flickered in surprise, but only for a moment. Then his smirk was back. "It's always nice doing business with the royals," he said with an unsettling playfulness as he swung the door open. "Until we meet again, princess."

Through the door, it wasn't the dungeons that greeted Aurora on the other side—it was a royal bedroom. A king-sized bed, tousled silk sheets, and the lingering scent of Tristan in the air.

She stepped inside, the door clicking shut behind her, only to open once more. This time, it was Tristan who rushed through, urgency and relief etched across his face.

"Aurora!" His voice carried a hint of panic as he closed the distance between them, engulfing her in a protective embrace. His fingers trembled against her skin, as if ensuring that she was truly there. "What did you do?"

She couldn't quite manage an answer. The world seemed to shrink to just the two of them. All that mattered was that he was there, alive, and safe.

With the barest of hesitation, her fingers found their way into his tousled hair, pulling him closer.

"You saved me," he breathed, then pulled back to meet her eyes.

"You saved me first," she whispered.

They held each other's gaze for a long moment. Then, throwing caution to the wind, their lips met in a fervent collision. Tristan's mouth molded against hers, conveying a depth of emotion that transcended words.

Their bodies moved in unison until they collided onto his bed. The air was charged with electricity. Pushing her skirt out of the way, Aurora straddled his lap, his warmth encompassing her. Every touch from him was both familiar and thrillingly new.

Tristan's lips ventured across her skin, imprinting kisses that left her gasping for breath. Aurora's nails dug into his back, an anchor in the storm of sensation that engulfed her. The friction was mind-scattering, dizzying, all-consuming. And all Aurora could think about was just how much she wanted to remove every layer between them. To feel his skin on hers one last time.

His tongue dipped between her lips, and a jolt of electricity zapped every nerve-ending in her body. She grabbed a fistful of his hair, trying to hold on to the fraction of time they had left. She wasn't ready to let him go. She couldn't bear to part from him. Not yet.

Pleasure surged, leaving them both intoxicated by its potency. Aurora's gasps and moans mingled with his, making a delicious duet of longing and need. Time blurred, and the world faded to nothingness. And for that brief moment, Aurora knew in her bones that this was yet another goodbye between them.

A wave of sorrow surged through her, an ache in her chest that threatened to consume her. Reality crashed back, and soft sobs began to escape her lips.

Tristan's kiss, which had been fervent against hers, softened like the delicate touch of a feather.

"I have to go," she cried.

He cupped her wet cheeks and rested his forehead against hers. "Don't go," he whispered breathlessly. "Stay with me."

Aurora wanted to stay. Wanted to never leave his side, but a force beyond her control kept her from forming the words. She thought about telling Tristan what Rumple had done, about the compulsion of the pixie dust, but she couldn't bear the thought of Tristan putting his life at risk by chasing Rumple down and demanding that he release her. She feared he would hand over his kingdom on her behalf, and she simply could not let him do that.

"I can't..." Aurora's heart bled with every sob that escaped her trembling lips. "I made a promise that I must keep. To Hendrick."

Tristan's eyes shot open. It was as though the prince's name jolted Tristan back to reality. To a reality that would shatter both of their hearts.

"I understand," he finally said, caressing her cheek. "If I were him, I would be counting every moment of every day for all eternity until the day I got to see you again."

"I need you to know that regardless of the reasons I had in the beginning… you were never a pawn to me," she confessed. "My love for you was true."

His response was gentle. "I know."

She reached for his hand, their fingers intertwining. "It still is," she whispered.

Tristan met her gaze, his thumb caressing the back of her hand. "I know."

When neither of them spoke, Tristan rested his forehead on hers and closed his eyes. "All I want is to freeze this moment and stay here forever with you."

"That sounds like a dream," she admitted, "but as we know, dreams end, and reality sets in, forcing us to move on."

She could feel Tristan's shoulders deflate. "Right," he sighed, squeezing her hand as though bracing himself to face the harsh reality they both knew awaited them. "I guess it's time to wake up, then."

Gazing into his eyes, she pressed her lips to his with one last tender kiss.

The door burst open as a group of guards hurried in, their presence scattering the fragile cocoon of their private world. "We found him!" The words spilled out with both urgency and triumph, relief flooding their panic-stricken faces as they promptly bowed to their soon-to-be king. "Your Majesty."

With a composed grace that masked her broken heart, Aurora rose to her feet, smoothing down the folds of her dress. Killian followed the guards into the room, his eyes immediately finding Aurora's as he silently gave her a questioning look. In response, she offered a subtle nod, signaling that everything was all right.

Killian's shoulders visibly relaxed, a sigh of relief escaping him. Then he turned to address the guards. "Send out word to the guests that the coronation will resume. And someone inform the tailor. The prince will require a new attire suitable for the ceremony tonight."

"Sir!" Another guard burst in, his voice trembling as he addressed Tristan. "It's Ryke, sir. Seems like he's refusing to allow King Midas to stay in the palace. Please, come. He must know of your return."

Tristan's eyes locked onto Aurora's for a fleeting moment before he took her hand. "Don't leave," he pleaded. "I'll be right back."

As he turned away, their hands slipped apart, and Aurora felt the weight of his absence settle around her like a heavy shroud. The room emptied, and voices and footsteps faded until silence reclaimed the space.

And there she stood, alone amidst the echoes of what they'd shared. Tears welled up again, but she held them at bay, determined to be strong. The room seemed to expand, its walls stretching to encompass a sea of memories—whispered confessions and stolen kisses.

And just like that, the sweetest release became the cruelest farewell.

TRISTAN

The grand hall of the palace, illuminated by a constellation of flickering candles, was a sight to behold. Banners of deep blue and gold, the colors of Tristan's kingdom, hung with an air of regality, fluttering gently in the cool breeze that swept through the high arched windows. The moonlight filtered through the glass, casting a soft glow that danced on the polished marble floor. The atmosphere was thick with anticipation, the murmurs of the gathered nobles and dignitaries creating a low hum that resonated through the air.

As Tristan stood by his throne, his heart raced in synchronicity with the growing excitement in the room. In mere moments, he would ascend to the throne of his kingdom, and the grandeur of the hall seemed to echo the weight of the responsibility that was about to be placed onto his shoulders.

Among the sea of faces, he searched for Aurora's in the crowd. She wasn't there. She hadn't stayed. He'd returned to his room only to find her gone. The memory must've wiped away his smile because when his eyes landed on his cousin, Ryke's brows were furrowed with concern.

Tristan forced a smile and then glanced at Lexa, standing at Ryke's side. Killian stood with the guards by the double doors, his cautious gaze sweeping the room. King Midas, with his golden crown and opulent robe, sat on the front row with an unreadable expression.

Tristan's crown, a magnificent creation of gold and precious stones, lay atop a velvet cushion, glinting enticingly in the gentle light. Tristan took a deep breath, feeling the weight of his heritage and the hopes of his people pressing against his chest. As he approached the throne, the crowd's murmurs grew hushed, and a sense of gravity settled over the hall.

The ceremony began with the royal herald announcing Tristan's achievements and his rightful claim to the throne. The crown, studded with sapphires and diamonds, was placed onto Tristan's head. The royal scepter was then handed to him, a symbol of power and authority. Holding it, Tristan felt the lineage of kings before him and the promise of the future.

"Today marks a new chapter in the history of our kingdom," Tristan began, his voice carrying easily through the grand hall. "Today marks not just my coronation, but the dawn of a new era for our kingdom. An era of unity, prosperity, and peace."

The applause swelled, and Tristan exchanged a knowing glance with Ryke and Lexa. He could feel their unwavering support radiating from their smiles.

As Tristan took hold of the gleaming scepter, a hush descended once more. The room seemed to hold its breath as he turned toward King Midas.

"King Midas," Tristan called, his voice clear and steady, "please join me."

Midas stepped forward, his expression unreadable. A large ornate bowl, half-filled with crystal-clear water, was placed on a stand in front of the throne. This was no mere formality; this was the binding of two kingdoms, the forging of an alliance that would shape the course of history.

Tristan turned to Midas, a silent understanding passing between them. "In the spirit of unity, we form an alliance with King Midas," Tristan continued, "binding our kingdoms together for mutual prosperity." He then turned to a nearby attendant, who presented a knife to each of them.

Tristan approached the bowl. He made a small incision on his palm, the sting a reminder of the sacrifices leaders must make. Beside him, Midas did the same, and together they held their bloodied hands over the bowl. The droplets mingled, a poignant symbol of their shared alliance.

As the mingling blood shimmered in the water, the crowd erupted into applause. It was a moment of hope, a tangible representation of the bonds they were forging. Yet, even as the clapping echoed through the hall, a sudden tension crackled in the air.

Midas, with a swift move, tried to grab Tristan's arm. Instead, he caught Tristan's bleeding hand. The gasps of horror echoed through the hall.

Midas smirked, a wicked glint in his eye. "Thank you for the alliance," he whispered, his voice dripping with venom, "because now your kingdom will be mine."

A shiver raced up Tristan's arm, and a creeping sensation spread across his skin like liquid gold. Tristan watched in horror as his hand began to turn to gold, the very flesh changing into a shimmering, metallic hue. The gasps in the room intensified, and he felt the weight of the crowd's gaze on him with astonishment and dread.

Midas' grin widened, a cruel triumph dancing in his eyes. He had orchestrated this, and used the alliance as a means to seize control. And in that moment, as the truth crashed over Tristan like a tidal wave, he realized that the battle for his kingdom had only just begun.

AURORA

*A*urora's room was lit by flickering candles that made long shadows dance across the walls. She was busy gathering clothes—dresses, tunics, and soft fabrics—but her thoughts kept drifting to Tristan. It was like her mind was a swirling storm of leaves, each one a memory of him. She could almost feel his touch, warm and comforting against her soft skin.

A bittersweet ache tugged at her heart as she remembered their last kiss, his last words that now seemed to hang in the air like echoes of a song long gone. She had left without waiting for him, unable to bear another goodbye.

The sound of clashing steel and distant shouts from the guards outside her father's castle snapped her to attention. Her heart raced, and her body tensed, her fingers involuntarily tightening around the fabric in her hands. The guards were on high alert, their duty-bound calls to arms penetrating the stillness of the night.

Aurora's decision to sneak into the castle was risky, but it was a risk she had to take. She needed to free the women her father had enslaved. She would also never make it across the Northern Kingdom empty-handed. Part of her also wanted to say a silent goodbye to the only place she had ever known, no matter how much it had felt like a gilded cage—a prison masquerading as a home.

Her eyes swept the room, taking in all the things she'd collected over the years—little treasures that made her feel safe. She touched a delicate porcelain ballerina, a gift from her mother, her fingers tracing its smooth surface. It felt like a piece of another life, one she was now determined to leave behind.

She started collecting the jewelry, the clinking sound filling the room as she carefully placed them in her leather pockets. These precious pieces would help her on her journey, maybe even buy her safe passage. And then there was Ella's dress, which she packed carefully in a separate bag.

With a deep breath, Aurora took one last look at

her room. Her eyes landed on Millie, a gold sentinel in the center of the room.

Aurora drew close and traced the delicate features with the tip of her fingers, a silent farewell to a friend who had witnessed more than her share. The memory of their laughter, their whispered secrets, swirled around her like a gentle breeze.

Then, came the memories of that night…

Ten years ago…

Aurora slipped through her bedroom door, shutting it with a deliberate gentleness. In the center of the room, Rapunzel and Millie sat in a makeshift circle, legs crossed. Between them, a delicate bowl held silvery water, and a sundrop flower floated serenely on its surface. Aurora took her designated spot on the floor, her heart shuddering with anticipation.

"Everyone is sleeping," Aurora began, her voice carrying a hint of nervousness. "So, how do we do this?"

Millie folded her arms, her lingering irritation evident. "I refuse to help you any further until you return what you stole."

Aurora gave Millie a quizzical look. "What are you talking about?"

"Oh, Millie," Rapunzel chimed in, her tone nonchalant. "It's just an object, a trinket passed from one person to another. What's the big deal?"

Millie's eyes narrowed at Rapunzel, her temper flaring.

"It's a family heirloom. You wouldn't understand because you don't have a family."

Rapunzel waved off Millie's insult, her fingers absently picking at her cuticles. "If you want to insult me, Millie, you'll need to find new material. You've exhausted all the orphan jabs in the book. And if you must know, Aurora never stole anything. I did."

Aurora gave Rapunzel a horrified look. "You stole her heirloom?"

Rapunzel waved a hand as though brushing off the gravity of her actions. "I'll give it back as soon as we return. It's no big deal."

Millie glared at Rapunzel. "No big deal? How would you feel if I cut your hair?"

"Enough, both of you," Aurora cut in. "We can't go into another realm arguing like this. It'll lead to disaster." When her friends remained silent, Aurora continued, her tone softer. "I know we've had our differences lately, and we may not always see eye to eye, but none of that changes the fact that we're best friends. We grew up together. And Millie, you may not have been locked up by my father, but you've spent more time here with us than with your own family. You both helped me sneak out to see Hendrick, and because of you two, I fell in love. If my father hadn't interrupted our wedding, neither of us would be here now. I'm not doing this just for me and Hendrick, I'm doing it for all of us."

"And how exactly does any of this benefit me?" Millie's voice dripped with cynicism.

"Don't be so daft, Millie. The Kingdom of Hyla claims your precious fairyland," Rapunzel cut in. "As princess and future queen, imagine what Aurora could do for your people."

Millie looked at Aurora, surprised. "You'd help the fairies?"

Aurora's smile was reassuring. "Of course I would. No fairy should ever live in fear of being taken." Aurora knew that was one of the main reasons fairies didn't leave their home or travel outside of their perimeters. Because of their ability to shrink to the size of a butterfly, they were often taken and sold as trinkets. But Aurora would make sure to put an end to such hunting. "Under the rule of my kingdom, fairies will receive protection, and anyone who takes them will face the same punishment as kidnapping a human."

Millie's voice quivered with emotion. "You'd do that for us?"

"Yes, Millie." Aurora reached out to touch her friend's hand. "But there will be no kingdom if I don't find Hendrick. I need your help. I won't be able to do this without you."

Millie nodded, her guard slowly lowering. "Okay, I'll help you."

Rapunzel sighed. "Finally."

Aurora cast a pleading glance at Rapunzel, silently imploring her not to provoke Millie further.

Rapunzel, surrendering with a shrug, leaned forward. "So, tell us about the Dreamworld. What exactly are we getting ourselves into?"

"The Dreamworld is unpredictable," Millie explained. "It may take you where you want to go, but it won't yield its secrets without a fight."

Aurora nodded. "I can fight. I've been practicing."

"The Dreamworld is different," Millie warned. "It will use your worst fears, exploit your vulnerabilities. You can't let it distract or harm you. If you die in there, you die out here."

Aurora released a nervous breath. "Don't die. Got it."

Rapunzel raised an eyebrow, remembering something. "What about that clock thing you mentioned? The eclipse?"

"Ah, yes!" Millie retrieved a parchment from her bag.

"You brought instructions?" Rapunzel teased.

"No," Millie shot back with a glare at Rapunzel. "These are just my notes when I asked Ensley about the drink."

Rapunzel's eyes widened in surprise. "Wait, you've never done this before?"

"I know what I'm doing," Millie insisted.

Rapunzel eyed Aurora with a hint of worry.

But a comforting hand settled over Aurora's, and she looked down to see Millie's reassuring touch. "I said I know what I'm doing. Now, did you get something that belonged to your father?"

Aurora nodded and extended her hand toward Rapunzel.

Rapunzel retrieved the object from her pocket—a golden, bee-shaped ring.

"Will this work?" Aurora asked, showing the ring to Millie.

Millie recognized the jewel and nodded with a knowing smile. "That is perfect."

For as long as Aurora could remember, that ring had never left her father's finger. It was a cherished possession of senti-mental value. She also knew that time was of the essence. The moment her father noticed it was missing, their window of opportunity would slam shut like a trap.

"So, what do I do with the ring?" Aurora asked.

"Take it with you into the tower," Millie instructed, glancing down at her notes. "Then, when you confront the illu-sions, ask them about your father's powers. Ask how to rid him of them."

Rapunzel hummed skeptically. "And they'll just tell her, like that?"

Millie looked up from the parchment with uncertainty in her eyes. "Let's hope they do."

"And if they don't?" Aurora asked.

"Then you'll have to fight them for the answers," Millie replied. But then her tone turned cheery as though trying to grasp at the minimum positivity. "But once you have that infor-mation, and we can finally get rid of your father's gold, you'll have your prince back. Focus on that."

Millie reached for the bowl in front of them, and together, they took in a deep breath.

"Are you ready?" Millie asked, handing the bowl over to Rapunzel.

Rapunzel eyed the bowl skeptically, but took it. "You're sure this isn't poison?"

Millie rolled her eyes. "Shut up and drink."

Rapunzel hesitantly sipped the silver liquid, her face twisted in distaste as if bitterness coated her tongue. Millie retrieved the bowl from Rapunzel and then handed it to Aurora. The moment hung heavy in the air as she accepted it with trembling hands.

Aurora watched with bated breath as Rapunzel succumbed to a deep sleep, collapsing onto the floor beside her. Trusting Millie, she gulped down the drink, feeling the encroaching blackness pull at her consciousness.

The world shifted and swirled as Aurora gave way to the consuming darkness, only to awaken by the edge of a cliff with Rapunzel towering over her. Millie's voice, her only anchor to reality, resonated in her mind like a distant echo.

"Listen to my voice," Millie's words seeped through Aurora's drifting consciousness. "When you hear the tolling of a bell tower, you have to jolt yourselves awake."

But Aurora never made it into the tower she was supposed to have entered. And when the bell tower rang, despite Millie's incessant pleas for Aurora to wake up, she didn't listen. Millie had warned them about the illusions and how they worked. Aurora had expected those illusions to come at her with all forms of sharp blades, but what unfolded before her was a cruel twist.

Hendrick stood by the edge of the woods, resplendent in his royal wedding attire, his brown skin radiant beneath the silvery moonlight, and his blue eyes beckoning her into the heart of the forest. Memories of their wedding day surged through her, and the temptation to reach out to him was almost irresistible. Rapunzel hurled herself at Aurora, tackling her to the ground in a desperate bid to halt her from going after him. But Aurora was consumed by desperation. She was not going to leave without Hendrick, but she also knew Rapunzel wasn't going to leave without her. So, Aurora had no choice but to push Rapunzel off the cliff, ensuring that she woke up.

Inside Aurora's mind, Millie's voice grew frenzied. That was when she heard the screams. Millie and Rapunzel were in trouble in the real world.

As the bell tolled with a deafening resonance, Aurora's father's voice echoed through the heavens, a bellowing bark that shook her very core. He had caught them. The night sky ignited with bolts of lightning, a celestial battle raging overhead, no doubt mirroring the chaos unfolding in reality.

With frantic desperation, Aurora hurried toward Hendrick. Her heart ached with longing, her steps fueled by a yearning she could hardly contain.

Yet, it was only when the lunar eclipse reached its zenith that she finally crashed into his embrace. For a fleeting moment, the illusion felt real, her senses overwhelmed by the warmth of his touch and the familiar twinkle in his eyes. But as her finger-tips brushed against him, the cruel truth unraveled. Hendrick was nothing more than a mirage, an illusion conjured from the deepest recesses of her own mind.

A vengeful smirk played on the illusion's lips as it dissi-pated into a cloud of ephemeral smoke, leaving Aurora utterly alone, surrounded by the suffocating darkness.

The illusion of Hendrick had crumbled into nothingness, leaving Aurora with an ache in her chest that mirrored the same emptiness she felt on her wedding day. For a fleeting moment, despair threatened to consume her entirely.

Then, like a specter materializing from the shadows, Millie emerged. Her wide eyes frozen in a state of disbelief.

"Millie?" Aurora took a cautious step back, wondering if that might be yet another illusion.

Millie's mouth opened and closed, as if grappling with words that refused to form. Her expression danced between confusion and shock. "I'm not supposed to be here," she stam-mered. "This wasn't the plan."

Aurora's blood ran cold as dread washed over her. If Millie was there without having drunk from the sundrop flower, there was only one plausible explanation, one that sent a shiver down her spine.

"*What… what happened?*" *Aurora's voice quivered with dread, already bracing herself for the answer.*

"*Your father…*" *Millie whispered, her gaze haunted.* "*He turned me into a statue of gold.*"

Back in the present, Aurora turned to Millie's golden statue. "I am so sorry, my friend," she murmured, her voice a hushed confession to the statue that seemed to hold the weight of her regrets. "I failed you again."

In the mirror, Aurora saw her own red, puffy eyes, evidence of the tears shed during her journey back from Tristan's palace. It was better this way, she told herself, to leave without another farewell that would shatter her heart. Even though their last departure had left her heart in pieces.

With a gentle swipe of her hand, Aurora brushed away a lingering tear. She knew that the road ahead would be marked by more tears, more moments of silent anguish. Yet, she couldn't afford to dwell on her pain at that moment. Not when her current mission called for her undivided attention.

Aurora went to stand by the window, waiting for the guards at the entrance to finish roaming the castle grounds. Once they returned to the double doors, she would have a short window of time to use the underground tunnels to exit out back.

Glancing at the cuckoo clock above her fireplace mantle, Aurora wondered what was taking the women so long. She had sent them with a message to meet her in her bedroom at sundown. They should've been there ages ago, and Aurora couldn't be caught roaming the castle. Her father had left a strict order that if she returned, she would be locked up again.

Attempting to distract herself, Aurora settled beside the windowsill, her fingers weaving her golden strands into a single braid, the rhythmic motion soothing as she allowed her thoughts to drift beyond the pane.

Outside, her father's sunflower garden stretched as far as the eyes could see, a field of gold and green. It was the same garden where Ella's father had plucked the sunflower that eventually led to Rapunzel's capture, her freedom stolen in the cruel exchange of one flower for another. The weight of the past settled heavily in Aurora's heart with the pain that had once taken root in those very grounds.

The sunflower garden had become a living reminder of the choices that had forever shaped their lives. Its beauty was tinged with sadness, a reflection of the path that had brought her to this point. It was no wonder that Aurora had chosen to sever her ties to all of it, signing it over to Rumple without a hint of regret.

Yet, even as she turned her gaze from the sunflower garden, another sight drew her in: the bee farm that her father had cultivated. Nearby, a swing swayed in the breeze, memories of childhood laughter intertwined with each creak of the rope. She had been a daddy's little girl once, cherished and adored by a man who had built that swing with love and devotion. But over the years, that man had changed, consumed by his own golden ambitions.

She remembered the day when he left for the Dreamworld, his return marking a shift that had forever altered the course of their lives. The golden powers he had acquired in that realm had twisted him into something unrecognizable, a cruel ruler who had imprisoned his own daughter in a tower. The loving husband, the doting father, all of it had been eclipsed by the insatiable hunger for power.

Aurora's heart ached for the loss of that man, for the distance that now separated them. His descent into darkness had been marked by tragedy—the loss of her brother, the spiraling despair that followed, and finally, the death of her mother. The weight of those burdens had broken something within her father, something irreparable. The selfish ruler he had become seemed to mirror the castle itself—a beautiful façade concealing layers of sorrow and regret.

Locked away in the tower of the castle, Aurora had yearned for the father she once had. The man who had lovingly built that swing, the man who had been her world. But the more she reached out, the further he slipped away.

"Aurora?" a soft voice came from across the room. Aurora spun around to find a group of ten women silently tiptoeing into her room.

"Girls!" Aurora's voice was choked with emotion. Eagerly, she moved to embrace each of them, feeling their essence, their struggles, their relief, as they melded in a string of tight embraces.

The door closed gently behind them.

"We didn't think we would ever see you again," one of the women said.

Aurora's gaze darted around the room, her eyes searching for a face that should have been among them. "And Rapunzel?" she asked.

The women exchanged glances, a silent debate unfolding among them as they contemplated who would bear the burden of delivering the news.

Taking a deep breath, Talia—the eldest among them—spoke. "The night you fell asleep, your father took Rapunzel away. We never saw her again."

Aurora remembered what Ella had said about her sister. That she had appeared to Killian. If Rapunzel truly had escaped, Aurora had no doubt she knew how to fend for herself.

She then swiftly changed gears, her tone firm, a commander ready to lead her troop. "My father's alliance ceremony has been delayed. We must use this time to escape."

Their eyes widened in surprise as Aurora produced a handful of jewelry, dividing it among the women. The jewels sparkled, each one carrying a promise of a new beginning.

"Take these. In case we get separated, we all have a way to get as far north as possible."

"Where will we go?" one of the women asked.

Aurora dug into her satchel again and pulled out a parchment. "This is a map of where we'll be going. I marked the location in case we get separated along the way."

Guiding the women toward her closet, she pushed against the back wall. The stone slid open to reveal a secret opening. "These steps will lead to the tunnels," Aurora explained.

"What about the guards down there?" Talia asked.

"You leave the guards to me," Aurora said,

handing the map to Talia. "Take this. Lead them safely, and I will meet you all by the stables."

Talia accepted the map with a hesitant nod. "Will you not be coming with us?"

"In order to clear your way, I'll need to create a diversion," Aurora explained. "But don't worry. I'll be right behind you. Now, go!"

Reluctantly, Talia nodded, and the women began their descent into the hidden pathways. Once they disappeared into the secret opening, Aurora closed the secret door to ensure the passage wouldn't be found. She then returned to the window to check on the guards.

A glimmer of gold shimmering with the reflection of the moonlight caught Aurora's eyes. She blinked several times, wondering why a kaleidoscope of colors surrounded Midnight's statue.

A gasp escaped her as she watched the golden coat that had bound Midnight for so long begin to break, releasing him. The golden veneer that had him encased was fading fast.

Aurora's heart quickened, her breath catching in her throat as she watched in astonishment. The gold was receding, giving way to Midnight's original form. The shock of it had Aurora hypnotized, her mind grappling to make sense of what was happening.

"You did it!" A melodious voice rang through the room, a voice both familiar and unexpected.

Aurora spun around, her eyes widening in disbelief as she beheld Millie standing at the center of the room. The shock of Millie's presence jolted through Aurora like an electric current.

Millie rushed into Aurora's arms, enveloping her in a tight embrace. Aurora returned the hug with a mixture of confusion and joy, her mind racing to process the impossible reality before her.

"I can't believe you did it!" Millie's voice was filled with awe and excitement.

Confusion gripped Aurora. She hadn't done anything; the vial of venom was destroyed by her father. "I didn't…" she stammered, struggling to believe her eyes. "How did you…?"

Millie pulled back, her eyes searching Aurora's face. "How did I what?"

Aurora's thoughts churned, attempting to make sense of the situation, to bridge the gap between the reality she knew and the reality that was unraveling before her.

"I didn't…" Aurora's words trailed off, her eyes narrowing as she struggled to find the right words. "We didn't…"

Millie's expectant expression mirrored Aurora's confusion. "Where's Tristan? And your father?"

"They're at Tristan's coronation——" The realization hit Aurora like a physical blow, suddenly dispelling the fog of uncertainty that had clouded her thoughts. The blood in her veins turned to ice. The fear that had been lurking beneath the surface now surged to the forefront of her thoughts.

"Something must've gone wrong..." Aurora's voice trembled as she sank onto the windowsill.

"What do you mean?" Millie's concern deepened as she sat next to Aurora.

Aurora stared blindly across the room. "I don't know."

"Then we need to get on a horse and go see him at once," Millie insisted, rising to her feet, her hand gesturing urgently toward the door. "What are you waiting for?"

Aurora looked up at Millie, her eyes filling with tears. "I can't go..." she said with trembling lips. "Rumple has me under compulsion. Unless he releases me, I can't ever return to Tristan."

Burying her face in her hands, Aurora began to sob, utterly gutted. Her tears slid down her face like a burst dam. Her insides contorted with pain as she cried into her palms.

"Does Tristan know?" Millie asked.

"No," Aurora said, wiping the tears from her face. "And he can't know. Otherwise, he will go to Rumple, and I'm afraid of what other trap that conniving monster will set."

Millie frowned. "Then what will you do?"

Aurora sucked in a deep breath before rising to her feet. "I will finish what I came here to do," she said, glancing once more at the guards outside. "Then after I free the women, I will go to Hendrick like I was told to."

"Aurora—"

"Goodbye, Millie." Then, without another word, Aurora fastened her satchel and sprinted out the door.

"Aurora, wait!" Millie called after her, but Aurora didn't have the luxury of time. The women had most likely reached the tunnels by then, and they would no doubt be caught unless Aurora lured the guards in the opposite direction.

Footsteps echoed through the castle as she tore through the corridors, no longer bothering to hide. Guards appeared, ordering her to stop, and Aurora felt its walls closing in on her as she pressed forward.

"Stop right there!" The command rang out, echoing off the stone walls.

Aurora's pulse quickened, her breaths coming faster as she sprinted. She burst through the castle doors, her breath catching in her throat as she emerged into the open air.

But as she was about to descend the stone steps, she was greeted by a line of guards, their stances unyielding, hands poised on the hilts of their swords.

"Hands in the air!" a burly guard commanded.

Aurora's breath hitched as she raised her hands, her gaze locking onto the guards before her.

Summoning every ounce of determination within her, Aurora descended the stone steps with grace and purpose, shedding the cloak's hood with a defiant motion.

"I'm your princess," she declared, her voice ringing with authority. "Let me through at once."

The guards bowed their heads in respectful acknowledgment, yet their stance remained unyielding. Their loyalty to the king was a barrier she couldn't easily surmount.

"Forgive me, Princess," one of the guards spoke, his voice laced with regret as he stepped forward. "But we have strict orders from the king to seize you if you were to ever enter this castle again."

Two guards stepped forward, their movements swift and precise as they reached to seize her. Aurora's heart clenched as she felt their hands on her, their grip firm.

"No!" Aurora's scream tore through the air.

Then, as if in answer to her plea, a surge of blue fire erupted from the sky. The guards cried out in pain as the flames threatened to engulf them, their armor clanging as they fell on top of one another.

Aurora looked up to find Millie riding Azul through the sky, flames spewing from his mouth. The Pegasus' wings spread wide with power and grace.

The guards reached for their swords, confused as they faced a threat they could not comprehend. The flames of Azul's power lashed out, a force of nature that left them scrambling for cover.

Millie's maneuvers were swift and calculated. Another wave of blue fire erupted, threatening to consume the guards as they evaded the flames. The clash of armor resounded like a battle cry.

As the guards' grip on her arms loosened, she wrenched herself free, her pulse racing with a new surge of energy. She whistled loudly, the sound cutting through the chaos like a clarion call.

Midnight galloped into view, his white coat shimmering in the moonlight. Aurora ran, her feet pounding against the stone steps. With a swift, agile motion, she used a fallen guard as a makeshift step to propel herself onto Midnight's back.

As she mounted her stallion, a final wave of blue fire erupted, catching hold of the grass and spreading like wildfire. The sunflower garden was engulfed in the flames within seconds.

"Go!" Millie called out, her arms waving from above as Azul's wings soared through the sky. "I'll hold them back!"

With a nod, Aurora urged Midnight forward, his hooves pounding against the ground as they galloped to the north. The echoes of the chaos behind her slowly faded, replaced by the steady rhythm of Midnight's gait.

She headed toward the stables. If they were fleeing through the rough terrain of the mountains, then all of the women were going to need their own horse.

TRISTAN

The grand hall buzzed with shocked whispers, the air thick with tension as the onlookers processed the shocking turn of events. All eyes were fixed on the front of the hall where a confrontation of monumental proportions was unfolding.

Tristan's fingers tingled with the crawling sensation of the gold's advance, a force that threatened to consume him entirely. King Midas' wide grin conveyed that he had planned this betrayal all along.

"People of the Shores!" King Midas' voice boomed through the hall, resonating like a tolling bell. His arms spread wide, embracing the rapt attention of his audience. "Behold your new king!"

Gasps erupted like a sudden gust of wind, and

Tristan's senses picked up the shivers that ran through the air. The crowd's collective inhale was fraught with astonishment, their eyes locked onto Midas, who seemed to bask in his own machinations.

Killian charged forward, fists clenched in righteous fury, but Tristan's commanding gesture halted him in his tracks. He stopped midway down the aisle, nostrils flaring.

"Do not be rash in your proclamation, Midas," Tristan uttered through gritted teeth, his willpower steeling him against the metallic invasion.

Midas leaned in close, his grin twisting into a sinister mask. "I had anticipated this moment," he hissed with chilling satisfaction, his breath an icy stab against Tristan's ear. "To witness your downfall and taste the sweetest revenge."

A mirthless chuckle escaped Tristan's lips, even as the relentless march of gold crossed his shoulder. "You've always reveled in your cruelty," he retorted. "But you underestimate the forces that stand against you."

"Normally, I would wait until you're completely gone," Midas whispered. "But I wanted my words to be the last thing you heard. Goodbye, Prince of the Shor—" Midas' voice faltered, his eyes widening in disbelief. A sudden cough erupted from his throat.

Tristan stood resolute, his gaze locked onto Midas. His eyes showed no surprise, no trace of fear, as he watched Midas struggle against an invisible force that clawed at his throat.

"What is happening…?" Midas choked, his expression shifting from arrogance to sheer bewilderment. Panic clawed at the edges of his eyes as his attempts to regain control of his breath faltered.

Tristan's gaze remained steady, his expression unfazed. The crowd watched in shock as the gold on Tristan's arm began to recede. Midas' triumphant expression twisted in confusion, his eyes darting between his own hands and the retreating gold. The once-defeated prince now stood defiant, like a phoenix rising from the ashes.

"What…?" Midas' voice cracked, his incredulous whisper slicing through the charged silence like a shard of shattered glass.

A ghost of a smile tugged at Tristan's lips. "Did I forget to mention?" he said, his tone laced with an almost casual nonchalance. "I was once stung by a scorpion. That means my blood has scorpion venom in it."

Midas' eyes widened, pupils dilating in dawning horror as the truth unraveled before him. The realization that their blood was now irrevocably intertwined seized his features, a realization that struck with the force of a fatal blow. His face contorted in pain as the venom coursed through him.

Midas' once-confident posture crumbled, his knees buckling beneath him as his body contorted in agony. His fingers clawed at his throat, as if seeking release from the vise that tightened with every heart-beat. His gasps for air were the desperate pleas of a king now dethroned by his own ambitions.

The grand hall that had witnessed his rise now bore witness to his fall.

Once the gold vanished from Tristan's skin, he wiped the blood from his hand, then with a swift gesture, he signaled the guards forward. "Take him away," his voice rang out, clear and authoritative. The words bore the weight of justice long overdue. "He not only assaulted the king but also shattered the terms of our alliance."

Killian stepped forward, his eyes gleaming with a vindictive satisfaction. Without hesitation, he seized Midas by the arm, his grip firm as he hauled the weakened king away.

"Thank *you* for the alliance," Tristan added, wiping the blood from his hand. "Now, our kingdoms are one."

*T*he moonlight bathed the castle in a soft, silvery glow, casting elongated shadows on the cobblestone pathways. Tristan stood by the window of his study, watching as the ship carrying Ryke and Lexa disappeared into the horizon. The gentle lapping of the waves against the ship's hull was a distant whisper, but the weight of the day's events was a loud, echoing drumbeat in his heart.

The room behind him was filled with the low murmurs of his advisors, their voices blending into a cacophony of opinions and judgments. The scent of old parchment and the musty aroma of the wooden furniture filled the air, a stark contrast to the fresh sea breeze that occasionally wafted in.

One advisor's voice rose above the rest, a stern pronouncement. "King Midas' actions are in clear violation. Your father would have executed him swiftly."

Tristan turned, his gaze steady. "I am not my father," he declared, his voice firm. "Midas will not face execution. He shall return to his kingdom and rule without his powers."

"But, sir..." Another advisor hesitated. "Why extend mercy, sir?"

No one could fathom the depths of his motives. As vile as Midas was, he was Aurora's father. His fate should lie solely in her hands.

"My decision is final," Tristan replied. "Let him be. Stripped of his powers, he poses no threat to us."

The room's heavy wooden door creaked open, and Wendy stepped inside. "King Midas is asking for you, Your Highness," she signed.

Tristan inhaled. "Thank you, Wendy."

The room grew quiet as the advisors, one by one, slipped away, their murmurs dissipating, leaving the room in a hush.

Tristan took a moment to compose himself before making his way up the staircase to the room where Midas was taken. The door was left open, revealing him hunched over on the edge of the bed.

Tristan cleared his throat, a subtle cue that caught Midas' attention. He sat a bit taller as Tristan approached. In the stillness of the moment, neither of them uttered a word.

"Congratulations," Midas finally said, his tone low and deflated. "You defeated me."

"You left me no choice," Tristan replied.

"How did you know?" he asked, giving Tristan a

side glance. "How did you know I was going to betray you?"

"I didn't," Tristan confessed, "but I was prepared for it."

"You couldn't have predicted the venom in your blood would counteract my gold," Midas said. "You were brave in the risk you took. I underestimated you. My daughter, on the other hand, was right to believe in you."

Tristan's chest tightened at the mention of Aurora, and he forced his voice to remain steady despite the emotions swirling within him. "I never wished for any animosity between us."

Midas let out a mirthless chuckle. "You took the only thing of value I ever had, and now you have the nerve to say you don't wish to become my enemy?"

"Your daughter is worth so much more than gold. How could you have chosen your own power over her happiness?"

Midas' eyes narrowed at Tristan. "Everything I've ever done was to protect my daughter. She may not have approved of my methods, but it was the only way to keep her alive."

"Living as a prisoner is no way to live."

Midas waved a dismissive hand in Tristan's direction. "I don't have to explain myself to you. Just send me to the gallows and let's get this over with. All I ask is that my daughter not be present at my execution."

A heavy silence draped over them, the weight of his words hanging in the air.

"You will not be executed," Tristan replied.

Midas turned to look up at him, surprised.

"We are allies, and our kingdoms are one," Tristan continued. "My guards will escort you back to your castle. I am also willing to honor our alliance and offer you my protection to prevent your enemies from taking your throne."

Midas' eyes glimmered with a hint of gratitude, but the dim of sadness still lingered. "I was wrong about you," he whispered, his voice carrying the weight of a shattered man. "You will become a legendary king one day."

Tristan responded with a grateful nod. "That means a lot coming from someone as powerful as you."

Midas turned away, his face a portrait of shame and grief. "I am no one," he murmured, his voice a mere echo of the man he once was. "My gold was all I had."

"You have your daughter," Tristan assured him. "I am positive that if you reach out to her, she'll forgive you. She has a wonderful heart."

The corner of Midas' lips tugged slightly. "That she does. She took after her mother. But I cannot in good conscience ask for her forgiveness," he murmured, his shoulders weighed down by the burden of his self-perceived failure. "I am not sorry for the things I've done. For the power I acquired. And I shall not rest until I have regained my gold."

In a swift motion, Midas reached for the sundrop drink resting on Tristan's nightstand. The liquid disappeared in a single gulp.

Tristan snatched the bowl from his hand, but it was too late. Midas' eyes rolled back, and he crumpled onto the bed, his body limp and defeated.

Tristan stood frozen in place, shocked. The world seemed to fade into a hush, with only the distant sound of the sea flowing through the open window.

TRISTAN

Onths later, the once-devastated land was now buzzing with activity. Homes were being rebuilt, children played in the streets, and the air was filled with the sounds of laughter and hope. Tristan, in simple attire, was among the villagers, lifting beams and helping to reconstruct a village ravaged during the war.

The horizon was momentarily obscured by a rising cloud of dust, signaling the approach of a vehicle. The rhythmic sound of hooves pounding the ground grew louder, harmonizing with the creaking of wooden wheels. As the dust began to settle, the silhouette of a chariot emerged, its intricate designs and craftsmanship evident even from a distance. The chariot's wheels, reinforced with iron, carved deep tracks into the soft earth.

The chariot bore the emblem of the Chanted Kingdom—a white owl in full flight, a symbol of peace and friendship.

As the chariot came to a graceful halt, the door swung open and Queen Snow stepped out. Her raven-black hair slid down her shoulders, providing a stark contrast to her porcelain skin. Her blue eyes, reminiscent of clear winter skies, scanned the surroundings, taking in the reconstruction. Beside her, Emmett descended, his broad frame and stern expression a clear indication of his role as her protector. His armor, though dulled from travel, still gleamed in the waning sunlight, and his hand never strayed far from the hilt of his sword.

Following closely behind the chariot was a large, wooden truck, its sides decorated with carvings of mountains and forests. The truck's heavy wheels groaned under its weight, and as it too came to a stop, the back door was flung open. A group of dwarfs jumped out with the strength and determination of an army. Their beards, ranging from fiery red to deep brown, were braided and adorned with trinkets, signifying their individual achievements. Tools of various shapes and sizes hung from their belts, clinking together and creating a melody of readiness. They looked around, their keen eyes assessing the work that hadn't yet been done.

The arrival of such esteemed guests and helpers brought a renewed energy to the village, as the locals greeted them with cheers and gratitude.

"Snow. Emmett," Tristan greeted them, embracing them both. "Your help is much appreciated."

Snow smiled, her eyes twinkling. "We heard of your efforts here and wanted to lend a hand. And of course, bring some provisions."

As Tristan helped unload the food, he entered one of the nearly reconstructed homes to store it. The room was dim, but in the corner, a familiar figure sat on one of the vegetable crates, his impish grin unmistakable.

"Rumple," Tristan said cautiously.

Rumple held up a parchment—a contract—signed with blood. "Your Sleeping Beauty tricked me," he said with an annoyed grunt. "She offered me a golden kingdom, yet there is nothing left but rust."

Tristan's lips curled in a sly smile, though he fought to suppress his amusement. "That wasn't her doing, but it sure is fitting," he remarked, a hint of mockery in his tone. "You, sitting on the throne of a worthless kingdom. Exactly where you belong."

Rumple's irritation simmered beneath the surface, but he waved off Tristan's words with an air of superiority. "Nonetheless. Midas is trapped in the Dreamworld, and a deal is a deal."

Tristan's expression hardened. He had a distinct feeling that this conversation was heading in a direction he wouldn't like. "Why are you here? I have no deal with you."

Leaning forward, Rumple's eyes gleamed with malicious intent. "Oh, but you do, my king," he purred, relishing the power his words held. "We are now allies, which means you will provide my kingdom with the necessary provisions to survive."

Tristan's chest swelled with defiance. "I will do no such thing."

Rumple's response was a mocking smile. He gestured to the ominous contract he held, a wicked glint in his eyes. "Now, now. Don't be so hasty in your decision," he cooed. "After all, our kingdoms are one. Now, to show you my appreciation, I am willing to release your beloved of her compulsion."

Tristan's brows furrowed in confusion. "What compulsion?"

Suddenly, the blood stain on the parchment

turned inky black. "You didn't think your princess left you of her own accord, did you?" He chuckled darkly. "Tsk tsk, Tristan. Shame on you."

Before Tristan could respond, a knock echoed through the room. He turned toward the sound, his senses on high alert. Standing at the threshold was a tall man with dark skin, his presence casting a shadow over the room. In his arms, he cradled a box of provisions.

Once he stepped onto the light filtering through the window, his face came into clear view. *Prince Hendrick.*

Tristan turned back to Rumple, wondering if that was his doing, but Rumple was gone.

Hendrick cleared his throat. "I come on behalf of my father, the King of Hyla. He wishes to offer his support and extend his gratitude for your actions."

Tristan shook his head, still processing. "My actions?"

Hendrick placed the box on the floor with a sheepish smile. "You brought me back," he said as if it should've been obvious. "Going against Midas was a bold move, and you will forever be praised for your courage."

Tristan wasn't entirely sure how to respond. Yes, he had defeated Midas, but he didn't do it alone. He couldn't have done it without Aurora's help. Had she not told him about Tristan?

His heart twisted in his chest at the thought that she might've moved on so quickly. And forgot him so effortlessly.

"It needed to be done," Tristan said simply, unable to stop himself from looking past Hendrick toward the door. Had Aurora come with him?

"Have you traveled alone?" Tristan asked.

Hendrick followed Tristan's gaze toward the door, confused as to who he might've been looking for. "I've brought a few servants to help me unload the carriage with the timber my father is donating for the rebuild."

Tristan nodded. "Right. Thank you very much for your support. I am most grateful."

Hendrick raised a hand. "Trust me, we are the grateful ones. I know I shouldn't speak for Aurora, but... I know she is just as grateful as I am for what you've done."

At hearing her name, Tristan's heart thudded against his ribcage. "How is she faring?" he asked.

Hendrick sighed, his gaze distant. "The last time I laid eyes on her, she was as radiant as ever. I believe she went north to live with distant family."

"Wait..." Tristan's heart thundered. "You're not together?"

Hendrick shook his head. "No. I mean, I proposed another wedding the moment I saw her since her father annulled the last one, but... seems that in the time we've been apart, her feelings for me had changed. And I don't blame her. We fell in love too young, too fast."

Tristan rubbed a hand over his face. "But she fought so hard to find you."

"I know. But it seems that loving someone and *being in love* with them are two different things," Hendrick explained. "She made it very clear which one she felt for me, and it wasn't the latter."

The room seemed to grow quieter, the very air thickening with Hendrick's words. Each syllable echoed in Tristan's mind, a haunting reminder of the choices he'd made, and the path he hadn't taken. The silence was heavy, pressing down on him, making it hard for him to breathe.

"Anyway, sorry for rambling to you about my personal life," Hendrick said with a chuckle. "Please, accept our kingdom's support in anything you need. Anything at all. Don't hesitate to ask."

"Aurora..." Her name slipped out of Tristan in one rushed breath. "Where can I find her?"

Hendrick's brows shot up as though he'd been

expecting anything but that question. "Uh. Briar Rose Farms, most likely."

Hendrick's words were like a door that had been previously shut but was now pushed ajar, allowing a bright light of hope to seep through.

The image of Aurora, with her golden hair and the love they had shared, flashed before Tristan's eyes. His smile grew wide. "Thank you," he said, giving Hendrick an attaboy slap on the arm. "Your visit has been most helpful."

Without waiting for a response, Tristan rushed outside, the bright sun beaming down on him. He took a deep breath, attempting to steady his whirlwind of emotions. The weight of responsibility, the pain of past mistakes, and the hope for a brighter future melded together, forging a new determination in him.

He would find Aurora and mend the broken threads he had severed.

He would find Aurora, no matter the cost.

AURORA

*A*urora's hands embraced the cool, dew-kissed earth as she welcomed the first light of dawn. A gentle breeze rustled the leaves. The morning sun, still tender and new, cast a warm, golden glow over her uncle's sprawling farm.

With each graceful motion, Aurora's body awakened to the new day. Beads of dew formed on her skin, and her clothing felt fresh and revitalizing against her body. The sun's gentle rays illuminated the endless rows of vibrant crops, their lush green leaves dancing joyfully in the breeze.

Her uncle's farm stretched out as far as the eye could see. It had been her mother's home once upon a time, and now it sheltered Aurora, giving her a sense of belonging in a world that had grown increasingly unfamiliar. The farm was her refuge, a place where she sought comfort, finding a connection to her mother's memory in the earth beneath her fingertips.

As Aurora nurtured the garden, her mind drifted to her mother's stories of flowers and herbs, of the seeds they had sown together, and the countless bountiful harvests she had celebrated during her childhood. In the serene morning light, she felt her mother's presence more than ever. Even as her heart ached with the void left by her absence.

A sudden gust of wind brought a sharp scent of cedarwood, breaking through the monotony of Aurora's thoughts. She turned, dirt-streaked and sweat-drenched, to see Tristan approaching.

In that tranquil haven, where time seemed to hang suspended, Tristan emerged from the haze, a figure both commanding and impassioned. His tall, dark silhouette cut through the mist, casting a long, enigmatic shadow on the emerald clearing beneath his feet. His royal attire billowed gracefully with each determined stride, the fabric whispering secrets that befitted a king.

She squinted against the brightening sun, unable

to believe her eyes. Perhaps it was yet another mirage. It wouldn't have been the first time she had imagined him walking across the field toward her. But unlike previous fantasies, this one never faded. It just kept getting closer and closer, and Aurora's heart began to beat faster.

The wind blew, throwing his blond hair in all directions. It was longer than she'd remembered. The scent of ginger and cedar encircled her.

In silence, Tristan closed the distance between them, each step echoing with the weight of their past. He wasn't just making his way across the meadow, he was weaving through the labyrinth of their hearts. With each step, the chasm that had divided them for so long grew narrower, and the magnetic pull stronger.

He carried an air of elegance, even in the midst of the rustic landscape. When he finally reached her, she'd been expecting him to speak, but he said nothing at all. His eyes, as soft and warm as the morning sky, locked onto hers with an intensity that sent a wave of tingles through her body. It was as if he could see beyond the dirt and sweat, straight into the depths of her soul.

His breathing was slow and steady, but she knew

that if she reached out to touch his chest, she would feel his heart thump like a drum against the palm of her hand.

"You didn't stay with Hendrick," Tristan finally spoke, his eyes never leaving hers.

"I couldn't," she breathed, unaware of just how the mere sight of him had left her breathless. "My heart belonged to someone else."

"Did you not come back to me because of Rumple's compulsion?" he asked.

Aurora's eyes widened in surprise. "How did you…?"

"He's released you," Tristan said.

Aurora placed a hand over her chest. "I wanted to tell you," she confessed, "but I was afraid of what would happen to you if you confronted Rumple. He's too ruthless."

Tristan grabbed her hands and pressed them to his chest. His heartbeat was strong against her touch. "You should know by now that I will fight heaven and hell for you."

"I know. That's why I didn't tell you," she said. "If anything were to happen to you, I couldn't live with myself."

"Aurora—"

"You don't understand." She pulled her hands away and turned toward the sun casting its golden glow across the rolling hills. "I survived a decade in a world of nightmares, and yet… walking away from you just about killed me."

"My love…" He cupped her face and peered into her eyes. "If you need more time, I'll give that to you. But know that to me, no matter how much time passes, you are the one. You are my true love. There is no other."

Aurora closed her eyes, reveling in the warmth of his touch against her cheeks. "I never needed time," she whispered, her eyelids fluttering open again. "I've always known it was you. It will always be you. For all eternity."

Surrounded by lush, green meadows and the gentle hum of nature, Tristan's eyes sparkled with happiness and contentment.

"Aurora…" Hearing her name on his lips made her want to leap into his arms. But she suppressed her urge so as to hear what he had to say. "I've brought this especially for you."

Taking one of her hands, he lowered himself to his knees. With his other hand, he held up a ring.

Aurora gasped as an emerald stone glistened in the sun. "Tristan, that is beautiful," she breathed.

"It belonged to my mother," he said, the corner of his lips curving upward. "She made me promise that the recipient of this ring should already have my heart. That has been you from the moment you pushed me off that ship the first time we met. You don't just have my heart, Aurora. You *are* my heart."

"Oh, Tristan…" Joyful tears slid down her cheeks.

"I've asked you once before, and now I'm asking you again," he said, holding her gaze. "Aurora, will you do me the honor of being my wife?"

She flashed him a beaming smile. Her once-independent spirit had found its perfect match in Tristan, and their love had somehow grown stronger with each day they'd spent apart.

"Yes, Tristan!" She beamed. "I would love to be your wife!"

Her body was buzzing with excitement. She waited until he slipped the ring onto her finger before leaping into his arms. He caught her in midair and buried his face in her hair. It smelled like wildflowers.

As the sun rose from the horizon, casting a palette of purples and pinks across the sky, they shared a tender kiss. It was a kiss that spoke of passion, of understanding, and of the promise of a future together filled with love and happiness.

"This feels like a dream," she whispered against his lips.

"No, my love." He smiled against her mouth, then tightened his embrace around her, so firm, so sure, as though he knew this time he would never again let her go. "This… is real."

EPILOGUE

RAPUNZEL

*R*apunzel had always been adept at finding her way into the most guarded sanctums, and this time was no exception. The towering gates swung open before her, seemingly unguarded. She stepped into Queen Snow's castle. The hallways were lined with elaborate ice sculptures, capturing the memories of Aria's rule.

Rapunzel found her way to Emmett's study without a guard escort, as her audacity often demanded. The study was a realm of knowledge, a sanctuary for contemplation and decision-making. But on that day, it would be a battleground for wills.

Emmett looked up from his paperwork, surprise etching across his features as he beheld Rapunzel's presence. "How did you get in?" he asked, his voice a blend of curiosity and annoyance.

Rapunzel replied with a wry smile, "My showing up unannounced has never bothered you before."

"I am married now," Emmett said, his gaze returning to the documents before him.

"Oh, I know that," Rapunzel said dismissively. "That's why I waited for your wife to go on her travels before coming to see you. I heard she went to visit Tristan and Aurora's new baby—"

"Quit the chitchat. I hold no secrets from my wife."

Exploring the study, Rapunzel's eyes wandered over the paintings adorning the walls. Among them was a portrait of Emmett, his queen, and their newborn child.

"Even so," she mused, "my showing up would no doubt stir up all sorts of trouble, especially with your marriage being a little rocky and all."

"My marriage is fine," Emmett insisted, but his words rang hollow as Rapunzel sensed a flicker of doubt.

"Fine isn't great," she said, sitting on his desk. "Besides, she's a new queen, and with a newborn baby… I can only assume there hasn't been much attention given to you."

"You can exit where you entered," Emmett retorted bitterly.

"Look around, Emmett." Rapunzel gestured at the room, and his eyes widened as he beheld that the study had transformed into a nursery. Cribs crowded the space, baby paintings covered the walls, and scattered toys littered the floor.

"What is this?" he said, rising to his feet.

"It's a mindscape, darling," Rapunzel explained, her voice dripping with honeyed mockery. "And all that you see… are your insecurities."

Emmett slammed his fist on the table. "Get out of my head," he demanded.

Rapunzel inspected her perfectly manicured nails, seemingly unperturbed. "Not until I get what I came for."

"You are not welcome here," Emmett growled.

"Oh, please." She waved him off. "Tell me something I don't already know."

"What do you want?" he hissed.

"Some food would be nice." She touched her stomach. "I am famished."

He slapped his desk again. "Quit wasting my time, Rapunzel."

"As I recall, I used to be worth your while."

"I don't have time for this." Emmett stormed

across the room, but when he attempted to leave through the double doors, he found himself inexplicably back in the same room.

"Release me at once!" he demanded, his patience wearing thin.

Rapunzel smiled slyly. "Give me your sword, and you're free to go."

Emmett's hand instinctively reached for the hilt of his Elven metal sword, hanging on his sheath. "My sword?"

"Yes, that exact one. I need it," she said.

Emmett laughed incredulously. "And what could you possibly need with my sword?"

Rapunzel shrugged nonchalantly. "I have my reasons."

"Then maybe the better question is…" He sauntered back into the room, his gaze locked onto her. "What makes you think I will give it to you?"

"Would you prefer I tell your wife about your little unfinished business with Rumple?" she threatened, reaching for a vial of blue liquid on his desk.

Emmett's eyes widened, and beads of sweat formed on his forehead. "I have no idea what you're referring to."

"Oh, but you do," she assured him, swirling the

vial in her hand. "At your brother's wedding, Rumple told you to put this cure into your brother's drink. And if you failed to do so, he would come to collect his debt."

Emmett's composure wavered, but he refused to yield. "How did you get that?"

Rapunzel set the vial down, her smile chilling. "We're inside your head, Emmett. Everything in this room holds your most precious secrets, and I have access to all of it."

"Since when do you do Rumple's dirty work?" he asked, his gaze darting around the room as if searching for more secrets that might have been exposed.

"I don't work for anyone," she said. "I'm here as a favor to you. Better me than him, wouldn't you agree?"

Emmett's frustration was evident in his expression, but he managed to keep his voice steady. "How considerate of you."

"Believe it or not, I hold no ill will toward you," Rapunzel confessed. "So long as you hand over your sword."

Emmett's jaw clenched. "I will do no such thing. If Rumple wants to collect his debt, he'll have to come and get it himself. As for you… leave my castle and never step into my kingdom again."

"Hand over the sword, Emmett," she demanded with a more commanding voice. She was done playing nice. "Don't make me come after your family."

Emmett's breath caught, and he steeled himself. He marched across the room and grabbed her by the arms, pinning her against his desk. His eyes blazed with fury.

"Threaten my family again, and I will end you," he hissed.

A twisted smile played on her lips. "Nice and rough. Just like old times."

"I mean it," he said firmly, his grip tightening.

"So protective," she mused. "I've always known you would become twice the man your father ever was."

"What do you know about my father?" Emmett's voice came as a dangerous growl.

"I know he gave you that sword," Rapunzel said. "I also know the reason he gave it to you was out of pity. He knew he was going to give the throne to your brother, and he didn't want you to feel bad. What a trade, huh? Shows how little he thought of you."

Her words struck a chord, and she knew it. "My

father gave me this sword as a reward for all the battles I won."

She pushed herself toward him, making his grip tighten. "Then look me in the eyes and tell me it didn't feel like a slap in the face."

His brows furrowed, but his grip began to soften. "How could you possibly know how it made me feel?"

"Oh, Emmett." She rolled her eyes. "I have been inside your head more times than I could count. I know everything. And I must say, it's pathetic that you've attached such sentimentality to that sword when the man who gave it to you has done nothing but cause you pain and make you feel less than your own twin. Give me the sword and be rid of the one thing in your life that keeps reminding you that you're not good enough."

"I *am* good enough…" Emmett declared, his voice rising with conviction. "For my wife and child. That is all that matters."

"You mean the wife whom you serve?" Rapunzel taunted.

"My wife deserves where she stands," he hissed.

"But do you?" she challenged.

"I am honored to serve my queen. Now, get out of my head!" he barked, his patience at its breaking point.

"As you wish."

With a wave of her hand, the surroundings shifted, and they were no longer inside Emmett's study. They stood outside, the biting cold gnawing at their senses, and instead of having her pinned against his desk, Emmett had her pressed against a gnarled tree.

Emmett, reeling from the abrupt shift, cast a bewildered gaze around. "Where are we...?"

Rapunzel's voice cut through the icy air. "You see, while we were having our little conversation in your head, I was here, luring you out."

His brows furrowed in confusion. "Why?"

"So I can do *that*." Rapunzel pointed a slender finger toward his castle, and when Emmett turned, his eyes bulged at the sight. Towering flames devoured the grandeur of his castle, roaring with unrestrained fury. The crimson inferno licked at the sky, casting long shadows that danced in the night.

"What... what did you do?" Emmett's voice quivered.

"I tried asking nicely," Rapunzel replied, her voice as cold as the night air. "But you refused."

Emmett's hand instinctively went to the hilt of his sword, his fingers curling around the worn leather grip. And with a swift move, he brought the weapon to bear, pressing the gleaming blade against Rapunzel's throat. His gaze bore into hers, the flames of the castle reflecting in his eyes.

She didn't flinch. "Tsk tsk. Haven't you been taught that the safest way to hand over a sword is by the hilt?"

Emmett's grip tightened, the sharp edge of the blade grazing her skin. His anger surged, and he growled through gritted teeth, "Give me one good reason I shouldn't just end you right here, right now."

"That's not the example you want to set for your child, is it?" With a deliberate movement, she pushed the blade down and away from her throat. She extended her hand toward him, palm upturned. "By the hilt, please?"

Emmett's defiance wavered, and his fingers went slack. The sword dropped from his grip, landing on the snow-covered ground with a resounding thud.

"Don't ever show your face here again," he spat bitterly.

Without another word, he turned on his heel and began to walk away, his silhouette fading into the night. Rapunzel watched him go, her eyes reflecting the flickering flames that continued to consume his castle. The weight of her actions pressed down on her, a heavy burden she had chosen to bear.

She bent down and retrieved the sword, the Elven metal gleaming in the dim light. As she held it in her hand, a whisper escaped her lips, almost lost in the crackling of the inferno in the distance—"You'll thank me one day."

What is Rapunzel up to?

— Read her story in the FINAL instalment of Fairy Tales Reimagined, book 8: Tower of Gold —

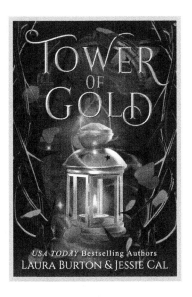

Want to share fan theories and join the Fairy Tales Reimagined community? Come and join us on Facebook for funny memes, games, giveaways and be the first to see cover reveals.

@fairytalesreimagined

Printed in Great Britain
by Amazon

38259119R00223